Readers Love BRU BAKER

Stealing His Heart
"[H]ighly recommended."

—Library Journal

Downward Facing Dreamboat
If you're looking for a sweet story to just lift your day, this is it."

—Love Bytes Reviews

Camp H.O.W.L.
I am absolutely obsessed with reading series in order… (a)nd I have to say, I am excited about getting to the next two installments."

—MM Good Book Reviews

King of the Kitchen
"Highly recommended reading if you're looking for a mix of serious and fun – just don't attempt reading this novel on an empty stomach!

—Rainbow Book Reviews

By BRU BAKER

All in a Day's Work
Bad, Dad, and Dangerous Anthology
Branded
The Buyout
Campfire Confessions
Diving In
Downward Facing Dreamboat
Holidays Are Where Your Heart Is
Homemade from the Heart
King of the Kitchen
Late Bloomer
The Magic of Weihnachten
More Than Okay
One Night in Dallas
With Lex Chase: Some Assembly Required
Talk Turkey
Traditions from the Heart

DREAMSPUN BEYOND
CAMP H.O.W.L.
Camp H.O.W.L.
Under a Blue Moon
Hiding In Plain Sight
CONNOLL PACK
Stealing His Heart

DREAMSPUN DESIRES
Tall, Dark, and Deported

DROPPING ANCHOR
Island House
Finding Home
Playing House

Published by DREAMSPINNER PRESS
www.dreamspinnerpress.com

BRU BAKER

ONE NIGHT IN DALLAS

DREAMSPINNER
PRESS

Published by
DREAMSPINNER PRESS

5032 Capital Circle SW, Suite 2, PMB# 279, Tallahassee, FL 32305-7886 USA
www.dreamspinnerpress.com

This is a work of fiction. Names, characters, places, and incidents either are the product of author imagination or are used fictitiously, and any resemblance to actual persons, living or dead, business establishments, events, or locales is entirely coincidental.

One Night in Dallas
© 2022 Bru Baker

Cover Art
© 2022 Reece Notley
reece@vitaenoir.com
Cover content is for illustrative purposes only and any person depicted on the cover is a model.

Trade Paperback ISBN: 978-1-64108-456-7
Digital ISBN: 978-1-64108-455-0
Trade Paperback published October 2022
v. 1.0

Printed in the United States of America

It's been a long two years, and this book is dedicated to everyone who helped me come out the other end. Much love to you all.

Chapter ONE

"FOLKS, THIS is the captain. We thank you for your patience as our crew sorts out the mechanical issue we've got going on. I've just been informed a part has to be flown in from another airport. The flight attendants are going to begin the process to get you all deplaned, and the gate agent will have more information about your new flight time as soon as we get an update from the crew."

Paul let his head thunk against the window, then reared back when he thought about what he'd done. He always made a point of touching as little as possible on a plane. He wasn't a clean freak or a germaphobe by any means, but he'd read too many things on the internet about how dirty planes were on the inside. A flight attendant tell-all was one clickbait headline he could never resist.

Passengers all around him were grumbling about the inconvenience. Some were outright yelling—he figured those people had probably been traveling since before dawn like him. How hard could it be to put people in metal tubes and shuttle them from Chicago to Tahoe? He was spoiled since flying out of Chicago often meant he could snag a nonstop flight. No such luck this time. There had been zero options for a nonstop.

A combination of storms over the Midwest and mechanical failures had turned his six-and-a-half-hour travel time into an all-day odyssey that was now stranding him in Dallas for the time being.

Paul stretched but made no move to stand up. He was in the last row of the plane. Not his favorite, but he'd been lucky to score the seat after storms had forced his Phoenix-bound flight to land in Kansas City. He'd been able to rebook himself on a flight from Kansas City to Dallas, which had been delayed twice because of the weather and once because they couldn't get the plane door to shut.

Normally he'd be pickier about seats even on a rebooked flight, but he had to do everything he could to get into Tahoe tonight. So here he was, chilling next to the flight-attendant galley and the chemical stink of the bathroom, waiting for the crowd of passengers elbowing their way down the aisle to ease so he could exit.

His phone buzzed in his pocket, and he stood up to dig it out, frowning when he saw Bran's name lit up on the screen.

"Hey, man. They're making us get off the plane. Mechanical problems," he said instead of bothering with a greeting.

"I saw. I have an alert set up on my phone for your flight number. It's delayed an hour."

That was more information than the captain had given them.

"Don't wait for me for dinner. God only knows what time I'll make it to Reno."

Bran laughed. "We're golden as long as you're here in your tux by four tomorrow. Ellie will slaughter you if you mess up her visual aesthetic by leaving us down a best man."

Paul knew that was very likely a direct quote. Ellie was a pretty calm person, but she was taking this wedding *very* seriously. A destination wedding across the country was enough to turn even the chillest person into a bridezilla. He watched the passengers a few seats ahead of him ease into the aisle. He stood up without thinking, wincing as he smacked into the bulkhead. It knocked his glasses askew, and he ignored the snicker from his seatmate as he righted them.

"With the luck I've had today, maybe I should rent a car and drive in. At least then I'd definitely be there by the wedding."

"Dude. You're in Texas. That's not close."

Wasn't it? Paul hated road trips and always preferred to fly. It seemed like Tahoe should be drivable from here.

He sandwiched the phone between his shoulder and cheek as he made his way out into the emptying aisle. He hadn't brought a carry-on other than his book bag, and he was pretty sure he was going to regret it. At least their tuxes were at a shop in Tahoe City. He wouldn't survive Ellie's wrath if he walked down the aisle in jeans and a dirty T-shirt.

"Everyone else get in okay?"

He'd been in charge of the utter nightmare that was coordinating the entire bridal party's reservations. Paul wouldn't be willing to go through that much work for his *own* wedding—he endured endless chains of emails and phone calls with the resort on Bran's behalf because Bran was the closest thing to family he had. He loved him like a brother.

Paul was scheduled to be the last of the bridal party to arrive. Everyone else had come in the day before, but Paul was finishing up a patch release for an important client, so he'd had to change his flight and arrive the afternoon before the wedding. It should have given him plenty of time since the limo wasn't arriving at the resort to pick them up for Bran's bachelor party until nine, but it was seven now, and there was no way he was going to make it.

"Avery missed his flight out of Heathrow. He caught a later one, but I think it added a longer layover somewhere. He said he'd make it before the limo, though."

Paul rolled his eyes as he stepped off the jetway, earning himself a dirty look from a woman who must have thought he'd been aiming the annoyed gesture at her.

"Of course Avery missed his flight," he muttered. There wasn't a spare seat at the gate, another downside to being the last one to get off the plane. Paul shouldered his way through the crowd and walked to the bank of monitors two gates down. "You were right. Delayed an hour. But at this point I'll believe it when I see it."

"Hey, now. Lay off Avery. He has a lot on his plate with the move."

According to Bran and the rest of his family, Avery was a "free spirit." Paul thought that was generous. Avery was a man-child who couldn't adult his way out of a paper bag. Not that Bran ever resented him for any of it. He thought his brother walked on water.

"Of course he's got a lot on his plate. He decided to move back to the States with a month's notice. No sane person does that, Bran."

Avery's decision to return to the United States was every bit as spur-of-the-moment as his sudden move out to London had been more than a decade ago. At least this time he'd warned people he was relocating. Avery's sudden departure back then was a sore spot that still ached when Paul pressed on it, no matter how much he didn't want to admit it. Not that Bran held a grudge about it like he did.

"I don't blame him for wanting to save the airfare," Bran said. "And he wasn't teaching any summer classes. It's not like he left the department in a lurch. Lighten up. He's coming home. This is a good thing."

Paul pursed his lips. He didn't want to rain on Bran's parade, so it was better not to say anything at all.

Bran sighed. "You two aren't going to fight at the wedding, are you?"

They weren't. At least, Paul wasn't going to. He couldn't speak for Avery. Paul had never understood what went on in that man's head. It was a lesson he'd learned the hard way.

"Of course not. We both love you and Ellie, and we're there to support you. We probably won't even talk."

Not that Avery really knew Ellie. Bran's long silence proved Paul had scored that hit as intended.

Avery hadn't come back from Europe in the entire time Bran and Ellie had been dating. Paul knew how she took her coffee, what types of movies made her cry, and which board games were her favorite. Which was why he was Bran's best man instead of his brother. Cold comfort since Paul would have to face Avery again for the first time since college, but still.

Paul heard shouting in the background of the call, and he glanced at his watch. It was too early for the limo to the bachelor party, but all of the rental cabins had wet bars that were fully stocked. The groomsmen were likely pregaming it.

"Look, I've got to go," Bran said. "The guys are getting antsy, and I don't want to lose our deposit."

Paul grinned. Their friends weren't *that* rowdy, but compared to Bran they were downright animals.

If left to his own devices, Bran wouldn't have had a bachelor party at all. His idea of a wild night was a football game on the television and one, maybe two beers. The limo was going to take them to a sports bar in Tahoe City, but nothing too scandalous, and certainly nothing that would leave anyone in rough shape for tomorrow's wedding.

"Sure, sure. Go. Have fun. I'll catch up as soon as I get in."

If he got in. The delay had changed from one hour to two while he'd been on the phone with Bran, but he didn't want to be a downer and bring it up.

"Have a safe flight, man. See you when I see you."

Paul tucked his phone back into his pocket and hitched his bookbag up on his shoulder. Maybe he could find a bar to have a beer while he passed the time.

Chapter TWO

AVERY'S LAYOVER in Dallas was thirty-two minutes, and he had to change terminals. Thank God he'd cleared customs in New York. He hated flying, which was one reason he hadn't been back in the States in years. The other being the cost of transatlantic tickets on an associate professor's salary. A London flat without a roommate was a big expense, and he was still paying off his college loans.

Plus he was a coward. He could admit that to himself after being up for over thirty hours of anxiety-ridden travel. The shipping company had been late coming to take the crates from his flat, so he'd been late turning in the keys to his landlord. That had shunted him into rush hour, which had meant full trains and commuters who were not at all impressed by his two rolling suitcases, a rolling carry-on, and his bulky satchel. By the time he'd arrived at Heathrow, he'd been tempted to pitch the suitcases, wardrobe be damned. A smarter man would have sent them with the shipping company. Lord knew he wouldn't need his tweed jackets and brogues in Tahoe.

He had tunnel vision as he sprinted through the packed corridor to make his tight connection, but he registered his flight number being announced on the PA. He slowed, cocking his head as he listened. They were repeating the announcement in Spanish, but he understood enough of it—his flight was delayed, and the gate was changing to one in the terminal he'd just left.

Bugger.

Avery turned back toward the train he'd taken to the terminal. It was ten gates away, but there was no reason to run since his new boarding time wasn't for more than an hour. That was good. It gave him time to get something to eat and freshen up before he got into Tahoe and joined Bran and the guys at his stag night.

He ran a hand through his hair, fingers snarling in a tangle. The real reason he was so flustered by the delays and worried about how he looked wasn't something he wanted to think about. Sure, he didn't want to miss his brother's wedding. But that wasn't until tomorrow afternoon. He had all the time in the world to get there. Even if his flight ended up canceled tonight, he'd have no problem getting to Tahoe well before the late-afternoon ceremony.

No, the reason he was so worried wasn't disappointing the groom, it was how the best man would react. He'd stalked Paul's social media like a preteen girl for years, and Bran was always more than happy to give Avery updates about him. But Avery hadn't spoken to Paul or seen him in person since he'd left for Europe.

Or, more accurately, since he'd snuck away like the coward he was without saying goodbye or even telling Paul he was leaving.

His last visual memory of Paul was of him sleeping as Avery eased out the door of the bedroom they'd shared. He still had the heartbreaking voicemail Paul left him three days later. Avery thought a clean break was the best thing for them, and he'd been wrong. He'd realized how stupid he'd been as he listened to Paul's voicemails, full of angry tears and recriminations. Avery had never hated himself as much as he had the afternoon he stood in the tiny bedroom of his flatshare in Canary Wharf playing Paul's message again and again just to hear his voice. He'd forwarded it over three number changes and half a dozen new phones. Listening to it was his favorite form of self-flagellation. It also served to remind him that he'd committed to this choice, and there wasn't a road back.

He hadn't told anyone about his application to London School of Economics. He'd already been accepted to continue at Northwestern, but he'd wanted something different, something more. He'd applied to some prestigious West Coast schools as well, but London had been a longshot because he'd applied late and needed a boatload of scholarships to make it work. But the thought of all the opportunities he'd have in Europe had made his heart race, and he'd secretly applied to LSE and several other UK universities when he realized he wanted to specialize in international economics for his PhD.

He'd lived in Chicago his entire life, and even though he loved his family, he'd wanted more. To travel, to get access to research opportunities abroad, to expand his horizons and challenge his worldview—none of that was possible in Chicago.

So he'd applied, and even after a space had opened up at LSE, he hadn't said anything because he'd needed his scholarship and visa to go through. When they did, he'd been struck by the enormity of what he was doing. His bravado had wavered, and he kept that to himself too. Partly because he didn't want anyone to try to talk him out of it, because they probably would have succeeded.

He'd told his parents the night before he left. They'd been shocked but proud. But he hadn't told Paul. Or Bran. The two people most impacted by him moving and the two people he'd most regret leaving behind.

He'd lied to himself, trying to paint his relationship with Paul as a casual one where it wouldn't hurt either of them to move on. It terrified him when that hadn't eased the ache in his chest at the thought of leaving. It meant Paul was more important to him than he wanted to admit, and that was dangerous.

So he'd reasoned he could control that outcome by making a clean break and ensuring there was nothing to come back to in Chicago. His brother would forgive him, he knew that. But Paul—Paul wouldn't. Not if he left with no doubt about his intentions. A long-distance relationship would split his focus, and he couldn't afford that. His career was too important, and sacrifices had to be made.

So he'd walked out without a word. Slamming that door with Paul had felt like the right choice in the moment, and even though it hadn't stopped Avery's feelings for him, at least it had done exactly what he'd hoped—it had made Paul hate him and kept Paul from trying to pursue him after he'd left.

Avery stepped onto the train and leaned against the window, watching the lights fly by as the train took him back to the other terminal. Seeing Paul was going to be hard, and convincing him to give him a second chance was going to be even harder. But there was something about Paul that had gotten under Avery's skin and never let go. He hoped Paul felt the same way and could get past how Avery had treated him.

Avery let himself wallow for a few more seconds before he pulled out his phone and shot a text off to his brother.

Flight delayed in Dallas. No worries, I'll still make it in time for the end of your stag night.

Bran never worried that Avery would let him down, which was ironic because Avery often did. But his brother wasn't one to hold broken promises against him. No one in their family did, which had been fine at twenty, but he was looking down the barrel of thirty-five now, and they continued to forgive him for being a self-centered ass. He'd missed his sister Jess's wedding five years ago, countless holidays, birthdays, his parents' huge fortieth wedding anniversary. And now Jess was pregnant.

He was resolved not to miss any more milestones. He'd turned in his notice at King's College, where he taught economics, and even his department chair hadn't been surprised. Not that he should have been. Avery had a reputation as a chronic job hopper. He'd been at the school longer than any of his other lecturer positions, heading into his fourth year. Before that, his record had been two and a half years as an adjunct at his alma mater, the London School of Economics. He wanted to put down roots, but there was always a new project, a new opportunity, a new stepping stone in his career.

He was tired of being someone no one could count on. His friends in academia referred to it as itchy feet. His parents called it wanderlust. But really it was a lifelong allergy to commitment and a healthy dose of FOMO. Avery was always afraid the world would pass him by if he stayed still too long.

And it had, but not in the way he meant. His baby brother was getting married. His sister was about to make him an uncle. Their parents had sold the house he grew up in and moved into a retiree community. And Avery had spent so much time making sure he didn't miss anything in his academic career that he'd missed his family moving on without him.

But not anymore. He was going to find a job teaching here in the States, and once he did he was going to woo the shit out of Paul and convince him to give their relationship another chance.

His phone pinged.

Dallas? I thought you were flying into Denver.

Avery checked to make sure he still had some time before his stop and then texted back.

Gate agent in New York got me on a flight to Dallas because the one to Denver was cancelled because of weather.

The train jolted as it stopped, and he shot a hand out to grab the pole, nearly losing his grip on his phone.

Cancelled? Okay, Madonna.

Avery cracked a grin at Bran's familiar jibe. He'd spent the last twelve years in Europe, most of it in England. His family loved to tease him about his adopted accent and British spelling. He'd have to work on that now that he was back in America.

Fine. Canceled. Better?

Bran texted back immediately.

Much. What terminal?

Avery hopped off the train and started for the stairs.

B. Why?

Bran didn't text back right away, so Avery followed the crowd down the stairs. Flights headed east had been grounded, so the airport was full of cranky travelers. Not that he blamed them. No one wanted to be stuck in an airport.

He looked at his watch. The delay might be a blessing in disguise. Now he had time to eat so he wasn't showing up at Bran's stag party and drinking on an empty stomach.

His phone pinged again, and he stopped in front of a sports bar to look at it.

You should stop at Cantina Laredo to get something to eat. Get a drink and relax.

Avery raised an eyebrow at his brother's message but shrugged. Mexican food wasn't exactly easy to come by in the UK, and good Mexican even less so. Dallas was a pretty decent place for his first Mexican meal in the US. It sounded loads better than airport fast food.

He pulled up a map on his phone and made his way through the terminal. The Mexican place was close to his new gate assignment, which was a nice stroke of luck.

It didn't look like anything fancy when he walked up, but there was an empty hostess stand. His stomach rumbled as he registered the smells wafting through the restaurant while he waited. He'd been tied up in knots trying to get to Tahoe on time, and most of his time on the plane had been spent sleeping. Avery couldn't remember the last time he'd eaten.

A smiling woman, the hostess he assumed, approached with a menu in her hands.

"Are you Avery, by any chance?"

He blinked a few times before he registered what she'd said.

"Yes," he said, narrowing his eyes as he looked at her.

"Good! Your brother called ahead. You can follow me on back, sweetie."

Avery glanced around the restaurant. It was fairly busy, but there were seats at the bar, and a few tables were open. Why would Bran have called ahead? Who knew airport restaurants even *took* reservations?

She stopped at a table that already had someone's jacket and bag in a seat. Confusion set in when she put the menu she'd been carrying down opposite them. She must have him confused with someone else named Avery.

"I don't—"

Then he heard it—Paul's voice. He was pacing near the server stand, his phone pressed to his ear and his other hand buried in his hair.

"You can't be serious," Paul said, his voice low and tight.

The excitement that had built in Avery's stomach at seeing him plummeted. Bran had set this up, and clearly Paul didn't want it.

"I know I'm going to have to see him eventually," Paul went on, his back still to the table. "But that doesn't mean I want to have dinner with him. Jesus."

Avery considered slipping away, but Paul turned at that moment. Their gazes locked, and Avery hoped he hadn't imagined the spark of lust that flitted over Paul's face before his guard went back up.

"He's here. We'll talk about this later." Paul hung up and stuck the phone in his pocket, his long-legged strides eating up the short distance between them.

He looked good. Avery had seen pictures of him on Bran's Facebook, but they didn't do him justice. His shoulders had broadened, and he'd put on some muscle. Paul didn't look like the college kid Avery had left behind. He'd been gorgeous then, but he was stunning now. And he was also absolutely fuming.

"I didn't know he was setting us up." Those weren't the first words Avery had planned to say to Paul, but they were what he blurted out when Paul took his seat. Avery silently cursed himself and started over. "Sorry. It's—you look good, Paul. It's good to see you."

Paul's sour look eased a bit. "It's been a long time, Avery."

That wasn't the rousing welcome Avery had fantasized about, but it was a start. Paul was holding himself stiffly and looking at the menu. That had to mean Avery still had an effect on him. Even if it was anger, it was an emotion. Avery could work with that.

"Did you get caught up in that storm? I thought you'd already be in Tahoe by now."

Paul's gaze remained fixed on the menu. "Delays and now a mechanical failure." He paused, his head finally coming up. "We're probably on the same flight to Reno."

"There can't be that many this time of night," Avery agreed. "Mine's delayed. Gets in at ten."

Paul frowned and sighed. "That's the one."

"We'll still be able to make the stag party, if that's what you're worried about. I'm sure they'll be out much later than that."

"I'm not holding my breath. The plane was having mechanical problems. I doubt we're getting out of here on time, even with the delay."

He'd gone back to studying his menu, so Avery followed suit. He needed to treat this like a blind date. Bran had done him a huge favor, and he couldn't afford to waste it.

"Things usually work out in the end," Avery said, wincing when Paul shot him an incredulous look.

"For you? They sure do. Maybe I should be glad about sharing that flight with you, Avery. You always land on your feet."

That was a direct hit… and proof that Paul's looks weren't the only thing that had matured. He hadn't been this assertive back then.

Being with Paul had always been easy. That had been the scariest part. They *fit*. By the end of the year they'd been together, it had been hard for Avery to imagine Paul not being by his side. That was terrifying, so he'd taken the coward's way out and fled without any notice when the opportunity to get his PhD at the London School of Economics presented itself.

This Paul was cynical, and Avery missed the optimistic kid Paul had been. He hated that he'd had a part in ruining that.

Avery had changed too, but convincing Paul of that was going to be a hard sell. He knew that going in, though. Paul thought he was flighty and selfish, and he wasn't wrong. But Avery wanted to settle down now. He wanted to be a better person, and he wanted Paul to be a part of that. Avery needed to make things right with him. He'd let everyone he loved down when he'd abruptly left, but Paul was his biggest regret.

They both jumped a little when the waitress walked up, pad in hand. Avery had been so caught up in his thoughts that he hadn't processed anything he'd read, and he scrambled to scan it when Paul started to order.

Avery tried to focus on the menu, but the words were swimming. He hadn't been prepared to see Paul, and that had given him an adrenaline boost. But it was wearing off, and weariness was catching up with him.

"You still eat meat?" Paul asked after he'd ordered. Avery nodded. "He'll have the chicken tacos. No cilantro. And we'll both have a Tecate."

The waitress left, and Paul turned back to Avery. "That was okay, right? I guess your tastes might have changed."

"No, coriander—sorry, cilantro—still tastes like someone grated a bar of soap over my food. Thanks. I'm not firing on all cylinders. I've been traveling for more than twenty-four hours. Tacos sound great."

Paul made a sympathetic face, which was the most welcoming expression he'd shown since he turned around and saw Avery standing by his table. Progress.

"You know, I thought you were full of shit about that for years? And then I read an article about it, and people explained it exactly the way you do. It's some genetic thing."

"Vindicated at last," Avery teased.

Paul cracked a tiny smile. "About that, at least. There's still plenty you're full of shit about."

They used to tease each other like this all the time, but this didn't feel like flirting. More like Paul warning him to keep his distance.

Time to change the subject. "So, have your best man's speech planned out?"

Paul wrinkled his nose. "You're not mad that—"

Avery cut him off. "God no. You've been his best friend for years, Paul. That's all you. I'm happy I get to stand up there with them at all."

"I'm sure you'd be his best man if you'd been around more," Paul said, and Avery had to fight to keep his face neutral at the dig.

"Even if I had been, you'd be the better choice. You had spreadsheets."

"How else was I supposed to keep track of everyone's flights and food allergies and roommate requests? The bridal party is twelve people, plus Bran and Ellie."

Avery held up a hand. "I'm not saying I question your methods, man. Better you than me. Besides, I'm crap at giving speeches."

Paul snorted. "You're a college professor. Your literal job is giving speeches."

The waitress arrived with tortilla chips and their beers, and Avery grabbed his like a lifeline and took a long swig.

"I doubt Bran wants a lecture about the global economy at his reception," Avery said. "You've always been good at telling stories and getting mushy."

Paul's face tightened, and Avery took another drink, wishing he could take his words back. He wouldn't get very far if he kept bringing up the past.

"I hope we can get there tonight," Paul said after a pause. He held his beer up and clinked it against Avery's. "To Bran and Ellie."

"To Bran and Ellie," Avery murmured. He put his beer down without taking another drink. His head was already swimming, and he didn't want to drink more on an empty stomach. Especially not around Paul. He had him off balance enough as it was. Avery didn't need help making a fool of himself.

"Are you still planning to stay for the week?" Paul asked, stirring Avery out of his thoughts.

"Of course. I wouldn't miss it for the world."

"I wasn't sure, with the move and all."

Avery shrugged. "I have plenty of time to start my job search after the wedding. It's going to take a bit for my stuff to get here anyway, so there's no rush. It was a leap of faith for Bran and Ellie to agree to let me crash with them without an end date."

"Bran knows better than most people that you never stick around too long."

The barb wasn't as sharp as it could have been, since Paul couldn't deliver it while looking Avery in the eye. It still stung, though.

Avery had been thinking about this conversation for years, and it had been on his mind constantly since he made the decision to move back to the States. He wouldn't have a better time than right now to have it, even if he'd rather be well rested for it. It probably wouldn't matter anyway. Pulling off a Band-Aid always hurt, even if you were prepared for it.

"Look, we need to have this out, okay? Because I'm going to be in Bran's life, and I want to be in your life too, if you'll let me. I was an asshole to you, and you don't owe me anything, but I hope you'll at least think about forgiving me. I know I hurt you when I left. I hurt Bran too. I should have been honest with you about being on the waitlist at LSE, and I should have talked to you about it when I found out I got in."

Paul swallowed hard but kept his expression blank. That bothered Avery. Paul had always had such an open face.

"Why didn't you?" Paul asked.

He'd always been one to cut to the quick. Logical to a fault.

"Because leaving you hurt more than I wanted to admit. So I told myself we'd had a casual relationship, that leaving was what I needed to do, and I didn't owe you any explanations. It was a dick move. I regretted it as soon as I got to London, but by then there wasn't a way to take it back. I do regret it. Not from a career perspective, because it was the right thing to do there. But I hate that I left you like that. I really am sorry."

The last voicemail Paul left him made it clear his plan had worked and their relationship was over. He hadn't realized how much hearing Paul snarl at him would hurt, or how much he'd mourn their relationship once it wasn't salvageable. Not that Avery blamed him. He'd grown up a lot since then, and part of growing up was owning your mistakes. He couldn't explain his behavior away. It had been awful. Leaving Paul like that remained the worst thing he'd ever done.

Trying to rekindle their relationship after twelve years of silence might be the second worst. It was selfish and, depending on how Paul felt, might even be cruel. And Avery hated himself a little that he still wanted to try. Did that mean he still loved Paul or that he was a narcissist? Avery wasn't sure. His family was always quick to forgive him and explain away his flaws. Paul wouldn't be.

Paul gave him a stiff nod. Avery was relieved when the waitress appeared with their food. It would give Paul a chance to process and take the pressure off a bit. Paul was the smartest guy he'd ever met, but he was also someone who preferred to think things over before responding. Avery didn't want to rush this. Especially since Paul's knee-jerk reaction was likely to be negative.

"Smells delicious," Avery said, leaning over his plate and savoring the fragrant steam. "Unsurprisingly, Europe is not a hot spot of good Mexican cuisine."

Paul cracked a smile at that. "No, I suppose it wouldn't be."

Avery grinned as he dug into his food.

"Though I don't know how authentic Mexican tacos with flour tortillas are," Paul added, picking up his own fork.

"It's one of the foods I missed the most from home," Avery admitted between bites.

Paul took a sip of his beer. "I would have thought by now you'd be calling Europe 'home.'"

"I never intended to stay there as long as I did." Avery reached across the table to grab a lime off the plate the waitress had left them, their fingers tangling when Paul did the same. His heart jumped when Paul didn't immediately pull away. "The initial plan was to get my PhD and get some teaching time, but every time I started thinking about coming home, another opportunity I couldn't pass up came along."

Paul grimaced and pulled his hand back. "And we both know you can't pass up a good opportunity. In sight, must be right. That could be your personal motto."

Fuck.

"First of all, that's Steak 'n Shake's motto. Another thing I missed. And secondly, you weren't just an opportunity," Avery said. "It wasn't like that, and I'm sorry I made you feel like it was. If I could go back and change anything in my life, it would be how I left that summer."

Paul burst out laughing. "God, you *are* like Steak 'n Shake. Bad for you, but too damn delicious to resist. And addictive as hell after the first bite."

Avery couldn't help but smile. "So you still think I'm delicious?"

"And still empty calories I'll regret the next day," Paul said, but his smile didn't dim. "It's good to see you again. I didn't think it would be, but it is."

The knot of unease that had lodged in Avery's chest when he saw Paul loosened a bit. Paul might not have forgiven him yet, but maybe he could. Maybe he'd been harboring feelings for Avery all this time, just like Avery had for him.

"I've been looking forward to seeing you again ever since Bran announced he was getting married."

"We weren't sure if you'd come. I mean, you missed Jess's wedding."

He'd gotten an earful from his sister and the rest of his family about it too. But it had been unavoidable.

"It was during exams. I couldn't get away. I hate that I missed it. But she's a big part of the reason I'm moving back. I don't want to miss out on my niece's life. It's time for me to be here with my family and put down some roots."

Paul toasted him with his beer. "I'm happy for you, then. I didn't know if you were serious about coming back or not, but it sounds like your mind's made up."

Avery laughed. "Too late to change my mind. My stuff's packed into a shipping container and is making its way very slowly across the Atlantic."

Paul's smile deepened, and he looked genuinely happy to hear Avery's plans. It made Avery's chest ache.

"I guess it really is happening, then. Welcome home."

Chapter THREE

THEY WERE lingering over their second beer after the meal when Paul got a text alert that their flight had been canceled. Avery pulled out his own phone before Paul could say anything, frowning at the screen.

"No more flights out tonight," he said as he scrolled through the airline's app. "That was the last one. We'll have to rebook for tomorrow."

An announcement over the PA directed passengers on canceled flights to another gate where the airline would rebook people and set them up with hotels for the night.

"We're better off rebooking in the app," Paul said. "Otherwise we might not get on an early flight out tomorrow."

"I don't fancy sleeping on the airport floor, though, so we're going to have to go get in line anyway."

Paul snorted out a laugh. "That bastardized accent of yours is a riot. You don't *fancy* sleeping on the floor?"

Color darkened Avery's cheeks, and he shot Paul a lopsided grin. "I never said coming back wasn't going to be a learning curve."

Paul couldn't believe Avery was actually blushing. The Avery he knew didn't blush. He flirted, but not so coyly. The Avery he'd dated in college was more sledgehammer than feather.

Despite himself, Paul was charmed by him. That wasn't a good sign. He needed to put some distance between them, fast.

"I'm going to reschedule in the app," he repeated. "And I still think you should too. But we can stand in line to see about a hotel. Why don't you head over to the gate and I'll get the bill? That way maybe we can beat some of the crowd."

It would also get Avery's sparkling eyes and roguish grin out of his line of sight before he caved any more than he already had. It was a win-win situation.

"Why don't you let me get the bill? You can go over. That was a full flight, and it's going to be a monster queue. I think the gate agent said she booked me in the last seat on it."

With any luck, they'd be able to get on an early flight to Reno tomorrow, especially since Tahoe City was about an hour's drive from the airport. Paul didn't want to think about what would happen if he and Avery missed the wedding. Ellie would strangle both of them, whether or not it was their fault. He felt bad enough about missing Bran's bachelor party. Missing the wedding wasn't an option.

He was going to see Bran marry the love of his life come hell or high water—or canceled flight. And he was apparently going to do it with his college crush-turned-first-heartbreak next to him. It was going to be a long night. Maybe they'd get lucky and the airline would book them in different hotels. Paul could use the break.

Paul left three twenties on the table and sprinted away before Avery could protest. He'd enjoyed spending time with Avery, much to his surprise, but that didn't mean he wanted to be indebted to him.

He didn't bother with propriety, flat-out running down the terminal. Avery hadn't been kidding when he'd predicted a long line. Paul could hear the angry roar of the crowd even half a dozen gates away. Theirs couldn't have been the only flight grounded, because the line snaked around a few times and spilled onto the concourse, reaching down several gates. Everyone looked on edge. He didn't relish the thought of spending the next few hours standing there listening to everyone else grumble.

At least he'd eaten. There was that. Maybe after he got this sorted out, there would still be time to grab another beer before heading to the hotel. His app let him reschedule his flight no problem. He had a middle seat on a flight leaving at 5:45 a.m., which he wouldn't complain about. As long as he was on the plane, he didn't care if he sat on the wing. Any seat would get him there, so he'd just have to deal with the discomfort of being elbowed on both sides for the duration of the flight to Reno.

When he'd booked his flight to Reno, Paul had splurged and upgraded himself to first class. He'd considered it a way to start and end the trip on a high note, but mostly it had been a way to convince his brain that he was going to have a relaxed and fun time despite spending the week with Avery.

After sharing a dinner with him, Paul could see that wouldn't have worked anyway. And he'd still have his luxury experience on the way home, when arguably he'd need it a lot more. He was going to need unfettered access to free booze after spending a week at a romantic ski resort with Avery.

Paul shuffled up a few steps as the line moved. It was slow, but it was moving. There were six harried gate agents dealing with screaming customers up front, and another three stocking bins and coolers with free sandwiches, chips, and drinks. As much as he hated that the flight had been canceled, at least the airline was doing the right thing and giving people free food and a place to stay for the night. He didn't even want to imagine being forced to sleep in one of the torn vinyl chairs in the terminal.

Avery joined him after about twenty minutes, seeming not to hear the squawk from the lady behind them over him cutting in line.

"He's with me," Paul said and then instantly regretted it. It sounded so right, and it had been far too easy to say. He didn't have anything with Avery. Avery hadn't even really been with him when they'd lived together the summer before he disappeared. Paul had been convenient and a nice distraction for him. A way for him to bide his time before dashing off to the next adventure.

Avery grinned and slung an arm around Paul. "Yes I am, sweetums."

Paul grimaced and shrugged his arm off. "The line is insane."

"I haven't seen a queue like this in ages," Avery agreed.

Paul glanced at him to see if he realized he'd done it again, but Avery was scanning the formidable queue of people. He had no idea he was still speaking like the London transplant he was. No matter how much he protested it, Avery was a Londoner now. How long would he be happy back here in the States? He'd always loved to travel and have new adventures. Paul couldn't envision him settling down.

Paul shook off that line of thought. He needed to stop indulging in being angry with Avery. That emotion was dangerously close to love, which is what Paul thought he'd felt for him back then. They'd both been kids, no matter how grown up he'd thought he was in his early twenties. He'd been naive to think his first real love would be the one that stuck. Or loved him back.

It was a lesson everyone learned at some point, and Paul had learned it a little later than most. It had been a harder lesson, too, given that they'd been living together all summer. But it had been a valuable life experience, and he'd put it behind him and moved on.

Mostly.

Love was blind, and he certainly had been where Avery was concerned. The hearts in his eyes had blocked out all of Avery's many faults, and it was time that Paul took some responsibility for that and stopped blaming Avery for doing something that was very in character. This was a chance for a fresh start, and he owed it to Bran to not let his grudge against Bran's brother ruin the wedding.

"Did you get a flight out tomorrow?" Paul asked, eyeing the crowd with a worried look. There was no way Avery would get to Reno tomorrow if he hadn't already done it. They were a good two hours from the front, maybe more at the rate things were moving.

"I did. I'm on a flight at 8:30 a.m."

So not the same one. That was one of Paul's wishes granted. He didn't want to travel with Avery. It was too domestic. Too close to the fantasies he'd had when he thought the two of them would have a long-distance relationship while Avery was at one of the West Coast grad schools he'd applied to, which had been the plan before LSE called. He'd drive himself insane thinking about the what-ifs.

Small talk seemed silly after the history they shared, though. The intimacy of their conversation over dinner had exceeded Paul's comfort level, but chatting away with Avery in this line felt—strange. Like he should know more about Avery than he did. Actually, he did know more about Avery than Avery probably realized. Bran had kept Paul updated on Avery's life, even when Paul hadn't wanted him to.

Knowing what Avery had been up to over the last twelve years had been hard at times, especially when the news involved new people Avery was seeing or new jobs Avery took as he climbed the academic ladder. It always felt like a reminder that Paul had only been another rung, something stepped over when Avery had a chance to work up higher.

But it hadn't been. Maybe it had all been working toward this moment when Paul would run into Avery in a crowded airport and find they could be friends.

"Have you been listening to a thing I've said?"

Paul blinked guiltily and shook his head.

Avery laughed. "I recognized the glazed look in your eyes. I see it a lot in my freshman Introduction to International Economics classes. At least yours didn't have the terror too."

"Your students are scared of you? I'd figure you'd be Mr. Popularity on campus. The professor whose door was always open and who was everyone's best friend."

The class that girls—and some guys—flocked to because the professor was off-the-charts hot. But Paul wasn't going to share that thought. Avery's ego didn't need any help. It was inflated enough on its own.

"Oh God, no. I have a reputation as a total hardass. I'm a difficult grader, and I don't rely on my TAs to teach. Every class is taught by me and every assignment is graded by me."

That was unusual. Paul couldn't remember any freshman class that hadn't been at least partially led by a TA when he was a student. And that was probably doubly true at the prestigious universities in Avery's pedigree.

"How many classes did you teach a semester?"

Avery wrinkled his nose. It was adorable. "Too many. But the kids deserved to be taught and graded by me. It was my class, after all. I mean, I wasn't a total micromanager. I let the TAs run study sessions, and they oversaw group work. But a college education is an incredibly expensive thing. My students deserved to have my attention."

Paul bet it was pretty awesome to have Professor Laniston's attention on you. He wondered if Avery taught in trim little tweed suits. The kind with leather on the elbows and slightly frayed collars like the one he was wearing right now.

He coughed and shifted uncomfortably. Thinking about hot Professor Avery wouldn't help him get through this night.

"That's nice. I mean, it sounds like a hard way to get tenure. But nice."

Avery laughed again, but this time it sounded sharper. Bitter. "Well, that's true. But I was never going to get tenure in Europe."

Ah. The real reason he came home emerged. Paul tried not to smirk with the satisfaction of this revelation. He'd known the "I want to settle down" bit was a flimsy excuse. Avery would still be in Europe if his academic ladder had allowed it. Yet again, Avery's decisions were driven by his raw ambition.

Paul couldn't fault him for it. Unless he'd left someone alone in an empty apartment in London with a broken heart like he had in Chicago.

"I really don't know much about it, only that it's pretty cutthroat. My cousin teaches at Rutgers and always has a lot to say on the matter whenever she gets too far into the wine at Christmas."

June was an adjunct, and she didn't have her PhD. She was never going to get tenure. But someone like Avery, who had a PhD and a pedigree that included teaching at some of the top schools in Europe? Surely he'd get snapped up by some eager economics department here in the States. Especially with his good looks and pseudo-English accent.

"Where are you looking?" Paul asked. "For a spot, I mean."

Avery shrugged and rubbed a hand over his neck. "I've been checking to see who's advertising openings, but it's fairly pointless to apply without an introduction. It's all in who you know and who has read your journal articles. It's rubbish, really. An old-boy's network. I've had some of my former professors put out feelers for me. They're asking around at institutions where they have some pull to see if any economics department could use a new international economics professor."

Paul was used to the tech industry, where if you were talented enough, a good company would make room for you to get you on board. Most of the companies he knew were expanding so quickly that there were plenty of seats at the table if a person was a good technical fit. It had to be frustrating to work in a field that made it next to impossible for people to get their foot in the door without someone on the inside to open it for them. For Avery's sake he hoped his old-boy's network was strong and he was able to find a placement.

"What's the plan if no one has an opening for you?"

"I haven't thought that far ahead. Starbucks barista? Shoe model? I don't know."

Of course he didn't know. That was classic Avery. He didn't need to know. Things had a way of working out for him.

"Don't snort like that," Avery said. "I have plenty of money saved to live comfortably while I take some time to figure out what's next. I'm not in dire straits or anything. I want to make sure that I'm taking a job that's a good fit and not settling because it's the next available thing. I'd actually like to stop all this hopping. Settle in somewhere."

"Get tenure," Paul said.

"Exactly. Get tenure. Become established in a department. Stop writing for my life and start actually *having* a life. Get some grad students to do most of my research. Sit back and start enjoying teaching again."

That sounded like a pretty reasonable goal, actually. Paul hadn't thought about that side of tenure.

"And you really have no idea where you'd like to go? I mean, surely you have some ideal climate or something."

"Pie in the sky, I'd love to be in Chicago. But if I can't, then I don't care. Big city or small, hot or cold. I want some place I can put down roots. I want to be stateside so I can come see my niblings for the holidays."

"Niblings? Is that some British slang I don't know?"

Avery laughed. "It's a gender-neutral term for the children of your siblings. I don't know how many kids Jess will have or when Bran and Ellie will start their own family, so nibling seemed the safest word to use. There was a group of school children in Somerset who launched a bid to get it included in the *Oxford English Dictionary* recently. That's how I found out about it."

"Were they successful?"

Avery's brows furrowed as he thought. "I don't know. Doubtful."

God, why was he so adorable? Paul could imagine him sitting in his apartment with his argyle-socked feet up on a stool reading about school children and their campaign to get a new word included in the dictionary.

Four people in line a few feet in front of them gave up and left the line, dragging their luggage noisily behind them, snapping Paul out of his ridiculous fantasy. An hour in Avery's presence and he was back to the moon-faced daydreams he'd had about their future in college. Ridiculous.

He and Avery shuffled forward again as the gap closed, and this time Paul made a point of taking an extra step away to put more room between them.

"And you won't miss living abroad? You won't miss traveling?"

"I'm not joining a monastery or anything," Avery said with a wink. "I'll still be able to travel. Once I've been somewhere for a few years and gotten tenure, I won't have to teach summer sessions. I'll be able to scratch my travel itch then."

Paul hadn't traveled that extensively. He'd started his job in Chicago as soon as he'd graduated, at the same firm he'd interned for each summer. It wasn't like Paul *never* traveled. He went out fairly frequently to work with clients around the country, and he tried to get to the beach or Vegas at least once a year. He and Bran always went on a boy's trip with their friends too. But Paul had never joined Bran when Bran went to see Avery, for obvious reasons. He'd never even been overseas.

Suddenly he felt small and silly. His life couldn't compare to Avery's. He was boring and predictable. He had a mortgage. A favorite mug. A pair of pajamas that was falling apart but he couldn't bring himself to throw away because they were comfortable. A preferred route through the grocery store. God. He was an old man.

"That sounds like a perfect fit for you, then." His voice sounded strangled even to his own ears, so it didn't surprise him when Avery gave him a funny look.

He cleared his throat. "I hope you land somewhere you can get on the tenure track."

Avery gave him a cautious smile. "Thanks. I'm not going to worry about it until after the wedding. I'm here to help Bran and spend time with him and Ellie. The job search will still be there in a week when I'm back in Chicago."

The line had advanced enough to see the front now, even though they were nowhere near getting there themselves. Half the gate agents looked like they were about to cry. Paul's attention snapped to a thin, harried man who threw his hands against the desk and leaned in, towering over the woman at the computer.

"You have to be fucking kidding me! Lady, I've been in this damn line for almost two hours and you tell me you're out of goddamn hotel rooms?"

Paul's stomach sank. The app had said the airline would have vouchers. How could they be out?

He couldn't hear what the woman said back, but it was not something that satisfied the angry man. "I want a damn hotel room!"

The balding man at the next computer stepped over and put a hand up. "Sir! There is no reason to yell at her. I'm sorry, but the local hotels only give us so many vouchers. There were an unusually high number of canceled flights today, and the hotels are fully booked by passengers who were delayed by the weather. The airline's policy is to give passengers who were delayed because of mechanical failure hotel vouchers, but unfortunately with the great demand for hotel rooms here in Dallas tonight, we don't have any more vouchers available."

"Well make more available!" the man shouted. Paul could only see half his face, but it was bright red.

"I'm sorry, sir, we can't make more available. We don't have more. Now—"

The man kicked the desk hard enough to rattle the computer monitor. "I want a fucking hotel room."

Paul and Avery shared a look. No passengers were intervening. If anything, they looked like they were about to start a riot.

"I'm going to have to ask you to step away from the desk, sir, or I will be forced to call security."

The man kicked the desk again. The woman jumped. She looked terrified, her face bone white above the jaunty neckerchief that all the airline employees wore. Paul took a step forward, unsure of what he was going to do but positive he couldn't stand by and watch that man hurt someone.

Avery put a hand on his bicep and looked over his shoulder. "Airport security is here."

Two security guards strode to the front of the line and started a quiet conversation with the man. He was agitated and still yelling, but at least his focus was off the poor woman.

"I won't step out of line. I was in the damn line for hours, and now they're telling me they don't have a room for me!"

A security guard stepped in closer and raised his voice in response. "If you don't step out of the line, sir, you'll be under arrest."

"You're, like, a fucking mall cop. What are you going to do to me, Paul Blart? Run me over with your Segway?"

The second security guard stepped in and put a restraining hand on the man's shoulder. "Actually, sir, we are off-duty Dallas PD officers."

That seemed to calm the man down. He grumbled again a few times but left the line with them to stand off to the side. They were quiet enough now that Paul couldn't hear their conversation, but a few other disgruntled people in the line had taken up his refrain and were now yelling about hotel rooms.

The bald man held his hands up as the volume rose.

"Ladies and gentlemen," he called out, raising his voice to be heard. "We are out of hotel room vouchers. If you need help rebooking your canceled flight, our agents will be happy to help you. You may also call the airline's customer assistance number, and those agents can help you as well."

The crowd surged forward, half of them shouting and the other half scrambling to get out of the way of the angry mob. An old woman, ninety if she was a day, threw one of the sandwiches the airline had supplied. It hit the bald man square in the chest.

The Dallas PD officers left the man who'd started everything and hurried to the front of the crowd. One of them was radioing for backup, and Paul didn't want to be anywhere near the terminal when it arrived.

Grandmothers throwing deli sandwiches was his limit.

"Let's get out of here," he murmured to Avery, who was watching the scene with a look of absolute shock.

Avery followed him as Paul walked away from the crowd. The tension coiled in Paul's muscles dissipated the farther they got from the melee.

"I can't believe that happened," Avery said, looking back over his shoulder.

Paul couldn't help himself; he looked too. More officers had arrived, and these were in uniform. They'd called in backup. The old lady who'd thrown the sandwich was in handcuffs. Unreal.

"Yeah, you're not in Europe anymore. Welcome back to the Home of the Brave."

"I'm going to call around and see if I can get a hotel room," Avery said. "The airport has its own hotel, I think. That would make it easier to get to our flights in the morning."

They kept walking as Avery made calls, meandering through the thinning crowd as they made their way farther into the terminal. He struck out on every call. Just like the gate agent had said, the hotels near the airport were full. Even for travelers who weren't booking with a voucher.

"We could get a cab to this one," Avery said, holding his phone out to show Paul a hotel listing. "But it's already eleven o'clock, and we'd have to head back almost as soon as we got there."

Fuck. It was *eleven*? The party! Avery seemed to have the same revelation when Paul did from the way his face fell.

Paul whipped out his phone and shot off a text to Bran, letting him know they wouldn't be able to make it tonight. He apologized profusely, but he doubted Bran was in any state to actually read a text right now. He and the other guys had been out for hours. If it was going to plan, they were all drunker than hell.

He texted Ellie too, for good measure. She shot one back seconds later, so the bachelorette party must have been pretty tame.

Be safe. Do you have somewhere to stay tonight?

She was such a nice person. Bran couldn't have found a better match. Paul loved hanging out with her, and she was always so careful not to make him feel like a third wheel.

Rooms are all full. Staying at the airport overnight to make an early flight. See you bright and early tomorrow.

She sent back a heart emoji that made Paul laugh. Avery glanced at his screen.

"Should I be worried that my soon-to-be sister-in-law is sending you heart emojis?"

Paul bit his lip. "Do you think you should be worried?"

Hell. Flirting with Avery was second nature. Why couldn't he stop himself?

"As far as I remember, I'm the only one of us who swings both ways. So no, probably not."

Paul blew out a breath. "Still not batting for that team," he said. "She knows I hate emojis. That's why she always sends me kissy faces and hearts and all kinds of crap. It's like deciphering goddamn hieroglyphics."

Avery laughed. "Hieroglyphics. I love it. I can't tell you the number of times I've been emailed a string of text speak or emojis by a student."

"Our future as a species looks grim."

"You have *no* idea. I'm glad I study economics and not anthropology. That department has been full of absolute lushes at every university I've taught at, and I can see why. They can chart the functions of the behaviors and extrapolate the consequences. Me, I get to bin anything I can't read and give the kid a zero."

Hearing words like extrapolate roll off Avery's tongue in casual conversation was a total turn-on, and Paul couldn't quantify why. He always went for smart men, but there was smart and then there was *Avery*. His professorial persona really did it for Paul, apparently. Luckily he had that affected British accent. It should have been sexy as hell, but knowing Avery's real accent, or at least the one he had before leaving for Europe, it just made Paul laugh.

"Bin it," Paul repeated with a snort. "You really are Madonna, like Bran says. So posh."

Avery shoved at him playfully. "Sod off, I can't help it."

That made Paul laugh even harder.

"I didn't think you'd come back so...."

"Continental? Sophisticated? Worldly?" Avery prompted.

Paul shot him an amused look. "Sure."

"No, what were you actually going to say? I want to know what you think of me. Truly."

That was a can of worms Paul wasn't about to open. His feelings for Avery were too complicated to talk about stranded in an airport after a long day of travel.

"Different," Paul settled on. "You're the same guy I used to know, but different."

Avery's lips tweaked into an off-kilter smile. "I could say the same about you. There's something about you, Paul. You weren't the take-charge type in college, but you wear it well now."

The unexpected praise made heat bloom in Paul's chest. He'd spent a lot of time—too much time—thinking about what impression he wanted to make on Avery at the wedding. He'd wanted to be handsome and unattainable. To look perfectly happy with his life and like he wasn't missing anything. But all that had gone out the window when he'd seen Avery in the restaurant. It was good to know he hadn't made a complete ass out of himself. And it was gratifying that Avery had seen deeper than the surface in the short time they'd been together tonight.

And a little unnerving.

"You've been gone a long time," he said. "I grew up."

Avery took his hand, and Paul didn't pull away even though every nerve in his body was on alert.

"So did I. Later than you. Really, not until recently. Or maybe not even quite yet. I'm a work in progress, but I'm getting there."

Paul didn't know what to say to that. Avery had already apologized for leaving him in Chicago, but somehow what he'd just said felt more like an apology than the actual one had.

"We're all works in progress," Paul said, going for levity.

Avery rubbed his eyes. "God, I'm getting maudlin. I have to find a place to crash."

So did Paul, but he didn't relish the thought of sleeping hunched over his bookbag in an uncomfortable and dirty airport chair.

"Maybe we *should* grab a taxi to a hotel. A little bit of good sleep is better than a lot of bad sleep, right?"

Paul pulled out his phone to Google hotels, but Avery stopped him with a hand to his arm.

"Wait, look at this."

Avery showed him his screen. "I was looking up good places to sleep in the airport and this came up. They're little rooms you can rent to sleep in."

That sounded perfect. A place to charge his phone and sleep would be heaven. And most importantly, put a door between him and Avery.

"We should book online so they don't fill up," Paul said, nodding over his shoulder back toward the hoard of disgruntled people they'd left at the gate. "We can't be the only ones who've discovered this."

"It's in Terminal D. I'm booking mine right now."

Paul pulled up the site on his phone and could have wept with relief when he saw there was still a room available. It was worth $200 to have a place to crash and spend some time alone with his thoughts.

"Thank all that is holy," he muttered as he made the reservation.

Chapter FOUR

THE SILENCE of the airport tram rang in Avery's ears after the roar of the terminal they'd left behind. The nap pods they'd booked were in the international terminal, which was fine because Avery couldn't put the chaos of Terminal A behind him fast enough.

He looked at his watch, wincing when he saw it was nearly midnight. "Shit, I should call Bran."

Paul reached out and stopped him before he could pull his phone out of his pocket.

"I texted him after we rebooked our flights. Ellie said everything is fine there."

Of course Paul would have already texted Bran about their plans. He was the responsible one, after all. Avery slumped back into his seat and watched the tram slow as it came into the station.

"I think this is us," he said, even though Paul was one step ahead of him, already up and inching toward the doors.

Avery rose quickly and immediately regretted his haste. His head spun the second he stood up, his exhaustion getting the best of him. The hand Paul shot out to steady him was the only thing that kept him from pitching forward onto the platform when the tram doors opened.

"Let's stay upright until we get to the pods, eh?" Paul's voice was light, but Avery could see actual concern in his eyes.

Once Avery managed to get prone, he didn't plan to get up again for hours. "Doing my best," he joked.

Paul sighed and grabbed Avery's roller bag, then after a moment's hesitation, hooked his arm through Avery's and tugged him toward the stairs. Avery certainly wasn't going to complain. He'd forgotten how good it felt to have Paul taking care of him. Avery's independent streak was a mile wide, but it had a Paul-shaped hole in it.

The nap pod storefront wasn't far. The lobby barely had room for the two of them to stand shoulder to shoulder, which was an ominous sign of how small the "pods" would be. Avery had assumed that pod was a euphemism, but now? Not so much.

"We both have reservations," Paul told the receptionist, who'd barely glanced up from his Nintendo Switch when they'd walked in.

"We're full," he said, pointing to a sign on the desk.

"And we both have reservations," Paul said, his tone more snappish this time.

The receptionist sighed and put his game aside. He typed for a moment and then shrugged.

"I see the reservations you made, but it doesn't change the fact that we're full. I don't know why the system let you, but we don't have any spaces available. Sometimes when we get a rush it happens. Maybe two people making a reservation for the same spot or something at the same time."

Paul rubbed his temples, and the motion flashed Avery back to watching *The Matrix* with him in their ratty old apartment. It was Paul's go-to move when someone misunderstood how computers work.

"A database wouldn't—"

Avery cut him off with a hand on his shoulder. He doubted this poor kid in front of them had anything to do with an international company's computer systems.

"There's another branch of the hotel in another terminal here, right? Can you see if they have any spaces? Maybe our reservations were for there?"

The guy frowned. "They were definitely here. But like I said, the system does this sometimes. I don't have a room for you."

Avery swallowed a frustrated sigh. "I understand that. But are you able to check the other location?"

"You can book it on your phone," the receptionist offered.

Paul's head dropped, and Avery rushed to respond before he could point out the obvious flaw in that plan.

"I'm afraid the same thing might happen," Avery said, willing himself to keep his voice calm. It was like talking to one of his particularly naive freshmen. Getting short with the receptionist wouldn't help anything. They weren't working with the brightest bulb to start with, and any confusion would dim it further. "So if you could, might you be able to look at their system and see if they have any free pods?"

"Oh, right," the kid said, bobbing his head in understanding. "'Cause, like, it could say they did and they didn't, like it did for us. Yeah, I can look. Hold on."

Thank whatever deity was looking down on them right now, getting entertainment out of the hot mess that was Avery's life.

"Terminal A isn't full," the guy said after a long moment.

Avery waited for him to offer to move their reservations, then allowed himself a single deep breath to bolster his spirits when the receptionist didn't.

"Can you switch our reservations over there?"

"Good idea. We're super busy tonight, so it would probably be full when you got over there," the receptionist said cheerfully. He typed for a few moments, and before he finished Avery's phone buzzed in his hand with an email notification about his changed reservation.

"I put the check-in time as now, but they'll hold it for you for half an hour before they cancel your reservation."

It was the most helpful information the receptionist had offered without prodding, so Avery grabbed one of the twenties Paul had left on the table for dinner and handed it to him. He'd paid the restaurant bill by card and had intended to give Paul's money back to him, but that could wait.

"Could you maybe call over and make sure they don't give it away before we can get there?" he asked, and the receptionist grinned as he pocketed the money.

"Will do!"

The thought of going back to the tram and taking another ride was about as appealing as continuing his conversation with the receptionist, but Avery slid the hand that was still restraining Paul by the shoulder down until he entwined their arms like Paul had on the tram platform. He pulled Paul out of the lobby, and Paul obediently followed, still rolling Avery's suitcase behind him.

"I have reservations about a hotel with software that has a flaw that bad," Paul muttered as they walked.

Avery looked over his shoulder, relieved to see the receptionist staring after them but speaking into the desk phone. This might be the first thing that had gone his way all day. Aside from Bran setting them up for dinner, of course. Running into Paul had been panic-inducing, but things were going well, all considered.

They didn't speak on the tram ride over, but this time Avery was too tired to be bothered by the silence. He didn't care if his pod was the size of a coffin—he desperately wanted to lie down.

"Welcome, I'm Annie. How can I help you tonight?"

This receptionist was about a hundred times perkier than the last one. Hopefully that meant she was also competent at her job.

"Hello, Annie. We have reservations. The, uh, gentleman at the other location called ahead for us?"

Paul snorted, having correctly interpreted his tone. It was about as rude as a Brit got. The politer his tone, the angrier he was, generally speaking. It was passive aggressive, but loads better than grannies throwing sandwiches.

Her lips twitched. "Jonas? He's a sweetie, but there's not a lot going on there, you know? He said you asked him to call, and I'm glad you did, because our system is overbooking and he snagged you the last pod. I had someone walk in literally right as I hung up with him, so you would have had the same thing happen if he hadn't let me know you were on your way over."

"Well, good on Jonas, and hurrah for us," Avery said, the tidal wave of exhaustion threatening to burst through the British stiff-upper-lip training that had taken years to master.

Annie's attempt at a polite smile turned into a full smirk for a moment before she battled it back to her professional facade.

"I need the credit card you used to book and your identification," she said. Paul handed over his credit card and license, and Avery bundled his with his passport. He was confused when Annie handed his credit card back without swiping it, even though she kept his passport to process.

"We can't split the payment between two cards," she said when he gave her a questioning look.

"But we had two separate reservations," Paul said, frowning at her.

Annie's smile dimmed. "Oh no. Jonas said it was for one room."

She put their IDs aside and typed furiously for a moment. "Jonas," she muttered under her breath. "So sorry. When Jonas transferred your reservation to this location, he put you both in one room."

Was it even possible to put two people in a sleep pod? Just like the other location, it was a squeeze to get three of them into the lobby. Avery doubted the pods were much more spacious. Then again, anything was better than sleeping in an uncomfortable airport chair.

"Do you have a double pod?" Paul asked, clearly as skeptical as Avery was.

Annie's cheeks tinged pink. "Er, no. When Jonas called we only had one pod left. But he said that would be fine because you two were obviously, um, close."

Avery smashed his lips together to stop the giggle that was bubbling up. Paul did not seem to find it as amusing.

"We are not," he snapped. "So there's only one pod left?"

Annie fidgeted under the sternness of Paul's gaze, and Avery felt defensive of her. The poor girl had nothing to do with it. It wasn't even really Jonas's fault, idiot though he was.

"Supply and demand," he said, shrugging when Paul switched his glare from Annie to him. "You don't have to be an economics professor to see what's going on. Tons of flights were grounded, and the airlines ran out of hotels. We can't be the only ones to find this place and decide this was the best option. Let's make the best of it, yeah?"

"I can cancel the reservation if you don't want to take it, but it is the only room we have left. I apologize."

Paul's shoulders slumped, and he leaned his weight against the handle of Avery's suitcase. "We'll take it."

Annie hurried through the booking, probably eager to get them out of her lobby. You could cut the tension with a knife, and Avery was glad Paul didn't have one because he wasn't entirely sure where Paul would stick it at the moment. He seemed to be at the end of his tether, which was understandable. Paul's day had been about as frustrating as Avery's, even if it didn't start on a different continent.

"Here are your keys," Annie said, sliding them across the counter along with Avery's passport and Paul's license and credit card. "They get you into your room and into the shared restroom, so please keep them with you. Your pod is down the main hallway and to the left. There are signs."

Avery took the key Paul handed him, confused when Paul also nudged his suitcase over and then took a step back toward the front door.

"I'll see you in Reno," Paul said, motioning Avery toward the door Annie indicated led to the sleep pods.

"You aren't seriously expecting me to let you sleep rough in the airport, are you?" Avery asked, knowing full well he was. It was a very

Paul thing to do. For someone so logical and straightforward most of the time, Paul was prone to big gestures like this. He was a romantic at heart, even if he didn't want to admit it.

Paul looked at his watch. "At this point I'm not getting much sleep no matter what. You may as well use the room and get some rest. I'd be up in four hours anyway to make it to my gate for boarding. This makes more sense. No reason for both of us to be zombies tomorrow."

Avery would rather *neither* of them be zombies. And he wasn't quite ready to be without Paul yet either. His brain had settled into the idea that he and Paul would share a pod, and he wasn't ready to let go of it.

"Don't be ridiculous. We're both exhausted, and we have a busy day tomorrow. The fact that you have an early flight is only more reason for us to share. At least this way you won't pass out from exhaustion and miss your boarding call. Remember that exam you almost missed because you pulled an all-nighter studying and fell asleep right before you were supposed to leave for it?"

It was a risk, bringing up something from their shared history. Paul had been touchy about anything that referenced their relationship, but that had happened before they'd been dating. Back when Paul had viewed Avery as his best friend's older brother, even though Paul had been on Avery's romantic radar for years before that.

Paul wavered and then sighed, stepping away from the door. Poor Annie was watching the scene with wide eyes, and Avery felt another urge to giggle. She'd get a good story out of this to tell her friends later, at least. He couldn't tell if she was raptly interested or mortified and wishing she was somewhere else.

"Fine," Paul said, grabbing Avery's suitcase as he strode toward the inner door. "But I'm blaming you if I miss my flight."

Paul was staying. The exhaustion that had felt so insurmountable ten minutes ago melted away like a heavy blanket slipping to the floor.

"You won't miss your flight, you drama queen. Who woke you up and drove you to your class for that exam, eh? Me."

He'd also gotten a hefty ticket for not having the correct permit to drive on campus, but Paul didn't know that.

Avery grinned and followed him, pulling another twenty out of his pocket to hand to Annie as they passed.

"Thank you," he mouthed.

She smiled sweetly and waited until Paul was through the door before whispering, "There are amenities packs in a vending machine near the restroom. Toothbrushes, face wash. Condoms."

Avery burst out laughing. Rapt interest it was, then. He made a show of crossing his fingers and walked after Paul.

The lobby had been brightly lit and cheerful, a stark contrast to the dim hallway they found themselves in when the door shut behind him. It looked like a dream corridor, stretching on in a huge expanse with doors every foot or so on both sides. Good grief, these things really *were* pods.

Paul's expression was grim, but he set off down the hallway, following Annie's directions. Avery filed along behind him since the corridor wasn't wide enough for two. It was almost like being on a submarine. Between the lack of windows and the low lighting, Avery felt strangely disoriented.

"Shouldn't be too far down," Paul said when the hallway ended and similar corridors branched off to the left and right.

Exactly how big *was* this place?

Paul found the room first and opened it with his card. He sucked in a sharp breath and stepped back so Avery could look into the pod.

It was tiny. Smaller than the guest bathroom in the house he'd grown up in. There was a countertop affixed to the wall as a makeshift desk, with a rolling desk chair tucked under it and a large television that took up most of the wall space over it. Two sconces on the wall provided the same dim light level as the hallway, and there was what could best be described as a love seat against the other wall. If you sat on it you could rest your feet on the desk. He could easily touch both walls at once if he tried, and the room was only a few feet longer than he was tall. They hadn't put an actual bed in it because it wouldn't fit.

Paul was studying a laminated card on the desk. "There are pillows and a blanket in a cubby underneath it," he offered.

The couch was vinyl. It looked like the one his mom slept on for two nights when his appendix almost ruptured in sixth grade and he had to stay in the hospital.

The giggles that had been threatening for a while took over, and Avery stepped inside and slumped against the wall, his shoulders shaking. It was too absurd. It was too much. He'd been on an emotional roller coaster all day, and now he and Paul were going to sleep together in a closet with a bed that a toddler would find cramped.

Surprisingly, Paul joined him. The door clicked shut behind him, and the two of them stood face-to-face, both laughing as silently as they could so they didn't disturb any of the other guests shoved like sardines into the rooms next to theirs.

After a minute or two, Paul wiped his hands over his face and sat on the tiny sofa. He kicked off his shoes and lay down, barely fitting his entire frame on it. Avery was a good inch taller, so there would be no hope for him, even if the thing had been wide enough for two.

It set both of them off into fresh gales of laughter.

"I knew it was pay by the hour, but I didn't realize it was pay by the inch," Paul said, stretching his hands above his head so both his hands and feet were pressing against the walls.

A wave of lust hit Avery so hard it made his mouth water. Paul's laughter hiccuped as he took a sharp breath, either realizing how provocatively he was posed or seeing the naked want in Avery's face. Avery swallowed hard and broke eye contact with Paul, feeling oddly vulnerable at the thought of Paul knowing what he was feeling.

Paul sat up and crossed his arms over his body awkwardly. "I didn't...."

Avery didn't want apologies. None of this was Paul's fault. "Don't worry about it. It's been a long day. And whether it's by the hour or the inch, this place is worth every penny. We'd be sleeping upright anyway out in the terminal. This way at least we don't have to worry about our bags or ending up in the background on some stranger's TikTok."

The defensiveness bled out of Paul's face, and he uncrossed his arms, leaning back against the sofa.

"We might fit if we went head to toe."

Avery spent a moment reviewing the physics of that proposition in his mind before sinking down next to Paul and shaking his head.

"Honestly, I'm not sure how even one person could sleep comfortably on this thing, let alone two. They took a lot of poetic license calling this a bed."

Paul tilted his head. "But did they?"

"Take poetic license?"

"Call it a bed," Paul said, his brow furrowed.

It was the same expression he used to have when he was stuck on a bit of code and trying to puzzle it out while they were out on a date or watching television. He bet Paul was picturing the reservation website, combing over his memory of it to see if any part of the pod description had included the word *bed*.

"Kind of like how restaurants that call it krab with a *k* don't have to actually serve crab meat?" Avery laughed and rubbed at his eyes, his exhaustion returning now that he wasn't on his feet anymore and the fight-or-flight excitement of getting their room had passed. "It's a possibility."

Avery leaned back, letting the back of the couch take the weight off his neck, which had been aching for hours. It was unpleasantly cool and slick, but it didn't matter. Anything was better than being upright.

He massaged his temples, trying to ease the tension headache that had settled behind his eyes, jumping in surprise when he felt a tentative touch on his shoulder. He opened his eyes to see Paul leaning in close, his eyes locked on Avery's.

"You're all out of alignment from sitting on planes all day and lugging that bag around. Not to mention your satchel always felt like it had a ton of bricks in it, and that probably has only gotten worse."

Avery wasn't sure how to read this, so he tamped down his hopeful excitement and scooted forward, settling in so he was facing the wall and Paul was behind him.

"It's not so bad anymore. Most of the books and journals are online now."

Generally speaking at least. Today his satchel was bursting at the seams with all the odds and ends that were too important to ship but wouldn't fit in his suitcases. He'd literally been carrying his most important possessions around on his back all day long, and his shoulders were screaming because of it.

Paul's touches were tentative at first, but once Avery relaxed into the massage, Paul's confidence seemed to grow. Avery was nearly purring under his strong fingers. He couldn't help himself. Paul was ruthlessly seeking all the knots in his shoulders, and it hurt. This was not a seductive massage with light teasing pressure and sensual touches. It was all-out war on Avery's tense muscles.

"Working out some pent-up aggression?"

It was a joke, but not really. As much as Avery wanted to trust that things would work out with Paul, he was very aware Paul had every right to hate him. He'd hoped that the old chestnut *time heals all wounds* would apply, but the moment he'd seen Paul, it had been like the last decade-plus hadn't happened. He could only hope that hadn't been true for Paul. For Avery, the last decade had been self-loathing and pining— for Paul it had been completely justified anger and hurt. Or maybe Paul hadn't thought of him at all.

Paul eased off a bit on the pressure, kneading the muscle with broader strokes. "Maybe. But mostly I don't like seeing you in pain. You've always kept all your tension in your shoulders."

Paul used to give him massages often. Usually as a prelude to sex. As the knots eased and Avery relaxed, his body had a Pavlovian response to the contact. This was a terrible idea.

Avery scooted forward, and Paul didn't fight him. He let his hands fall away, giving Avery a silently questioning look when Avery turned around to face him.

"I didn't set out to hurt you by leaving," Avery said, grateful when Paul didn't immediately look away as he changed the topic.

"I know."

"And I don't want to hurt you now, which is why this maybe wasn't the best idea."

Instead of shutting down like he'd expected him to, Paul grinned and nudged Avery's thigh with his own.

"I know you don't want to hurt me now, which is why this *is* the best idea. I've spent so much time trying to get you out of my system, and I've failed. I'm not going to pretend that I'm not attracted to you. Why don't we relieve the tension so we aren't on edge for the wedding?"

Avery couldn't believe what he was hearing. He'd heard of people suffering from hallucinations from exhaustion—that must be what was happening here. Because he definitely hadn't just heard Paul tell him he thought they should have sex.

Paul must have taken his silence as an affirmation, because he reached out and ran his thumb along Avery's jaw. The fond look on his face made something clench deep inside Avery's chest. This was a terrible idea.

"So we forget that you've spent the last decade-plus hating me, have sex, and move on?"

Paul's smile was predatory in a way that made Avery's pulse jump. "We agree that we're different people now who are not compatible but still have strong sexual chemistry. We have a one-night stand to cut that tension, and then yeah, we move on as friends."

"I don't think attraction is something you can get out of your system like that."

"Look, sex was always good between us. And I for one don't want to spend the next week wondering if it still would be. We've got this idealized memory of what we were like together, and the best way to dispel that and get past it is to have sex."

Was it really that easy for Paul?

"And if I say it's not a good idea and that I don't want a one-night stand?"

Paul shrugged. "Then we don't have one. But this is what I want. I don't want to be distracted by the what-ifs when we're supposed to be focused on Bran and Ellie. This isn't rekindling our relationship. It's two grown, consenting adults having a little fun and getting some much-deserved stress relief."

"So I should pretend I met you in that Mexican restaurant? That we don't have a history together? That I don't know how you like to be touched during sex, or what spot to kiss to have you squirming?"

Paul's breath caught, and Avery thought maybe he'd talked some sense into him, but instead, Paul surged forward and kissed him. The thought of role-playing strangers who'd just met in an airport must have been a turn-on for him.

"One night in Dallas. No strings, no baggage. In the morning we go our separate ways, and when I see you at Bran and Ellie's wedding, we can be old acquaintances seeing each other again after a long time apart. Deal?"

Avery knew it was a bad idea. He knew it was a downright *terrible* idea. But he had Paul warm and willing at his fingertips, and he couldn't bring himself to turn that down. It was likely he'd be shooting himself in the foot with his long-term goal of being back in Paul's life, but he didn't have enough self-control to say no. Impulse control had never been a strong suit of Avery's, and Paul knew exactly how to press his buttons.

"One night in Dallas," Avery murmured, nodding.

Chapter FIVE

PAUL RARELY acted without thinking. He was a by-the-book kind of guy. He was the kind of person friends and coworkers described as reliable. Predictable. Logical. Smart. Thoughtful.

This?

This was pure insanity, and even though he knew he'd be regretting this night for the next decade, he couldn't help himself. Besides, it would be refreshing to have something new to obsess and fixate on regarding Avery. Paul's ghosted boyfriend routine was a bore—even to himself.

Now he was the one setting the parameters. *He* would be the one to walk away in the morning and not look back. The symbolism of it appealed to him, though the driving force behind this crazy idea was the fact that Avery was even hotter than he had been when they'd been in college, and Paul wanted him.

He hadn't been lying when he'd said a one-night stand would get rid of the palpable lust between them and help them both be more present at Bran's wedding. Right now being close to Avery was intoxicating. That wasn't how Paul wanted to spend the next week. A night of no-strings-attached sex would cut the sexual tension. It would also haunt Paul's fantasies for years to come, but that was a problem for another day.

He hadn't planned to sleep with Avery. But between the room mix-up and his admittedly good-hearted but harebrained idea to give Avery a platonic massage, Paul's brain had gone offline. He was thinking with his feelings now, and his dick. And both wanted the same thing they'd wanted for years—Avery.

The tiny vinyl couch made him feel like a teenager groping around in the back seat of a car. At least there weren't windows to fog up or a gearshift to bruise his ribs. He and Avery were still upright, but mostly because Paul still hadn't figured out how to get them prone.

A shiver ripped through him when Avery nuzzled at the exact spot that never failed to send an electric current of want up his spine. Paul had talked a good game about pretending they were strangers, but Avery had been right. The sexual chemistry they had didn't happen overnight. No one-night stand would know all Paul's favorite spots or that he liked it when his partner scratched their nails lightly down his back and up his scalp. They couldn't erase their past any more than Paul could erase the damage this night was going to do in the future. Even knowing that, he didn't care.

This was the closure he'd never gotten with Avery. Would they have had sex that night if Avery had told him he was leaving for LSE instead of just disappearing? Probably not. But they'd never know. It had snaked its way into Paul's fantasies for years, and he was going to act on it tonight. They couldn't rewrite history, but he could at least end things on his own terms.

He tried to ease Avery down onto the sofa, but Avery resisted, pushing back against Paul and stopping him.

"We're not doing this on that manky vinyl. God knows how many arses have been on it. Let's find the sheets."

Paul had to hold back an incredulous giggle. Avery was right—Paul didn't want their bare skin touching the vinyl. God knew if it was ever cleaned. Paul's money was on no. But the Avery he knew would never have stopped sex because he was worried about germs. Maybe he really had grown up.

Paul slid to his knees, opened the cabinet under the desk, and pulled out pillows and a thin blanket, but no sheets.

"I guess you're supposed to sleep on it without any linens," he said, squinting at the blue vinyl. It wouldn't be pleasant to be naked on by any stretch of the imagination, even if you could get over the uncleanliness of it.

Avery laughed and rubbed at his face, his excitement waning enough to let his exhaustion show through again.

"Right," Avery said, grabbing one of the pillows and lying down, then tucking it under his head. He patted the sofa in invitation. "Clothes remain on, then."

Paul wanted more than a heavy make-out session, but they could work around it. He clearly wasn't going to be able to live out all his fantasies, but they could get creative. Avery looked about ready to drop, anyway. He needed sleep more than he needed complicated sexcapades.

"No strings," he reminded Avery before straddling him. He leaned down and kissed him before Avery could answer. Paul was the one who needed the reminder, not Avery. He had already proved he excelled at cutting ties.

Avery practically melted underneath him, and Paul let go and for once allowed himself to simply be in the moment. All of the anger, the hurt, the things he wished he could have said to Avery over the years—he pushed everything aside and poured himself into the kiss.

When Avery brought his arms up to wrap around Paul's back and pull him in even closer, Paul didn't fight it. He let Avery take control of the kiss, rolling them until they were on their sides, face-to-face on the precariously small sofa. Paul didn't know if the butterflies in his stomach were from Avery or the feeling that he could slip off at any time. Maybe both.

Avery's hands opening his fly made the swooping feeling intensify, so Paul decided Avery was definitely the cause. He helped Avery unzip his pants, his arousal spiking when Avery's palm brushed over the front of his boxers as he eased the fabric open. Paul wasn't going to last long at this rate.

He fumbled with Avery's pants, unsure of what he wanted exactly but knowing he needed to feel him under his hands. When he finally made contact, Avery shivered and bucked, almost making Paul tumble off the slippery vinyl.

Paul grabbed on to his shoulders to steady himself, and they both dissolved into giggles.

"New plan," Avery mumbled against his lips before hoisting himself up and kneeling over Paul.

Paul scooted onto his back, and Avery lowered himself on top of him, knees on either side of Paul's hips. The sofa was barely wide enough to accommodate the position, but it was better than being side by side.

Avery leaned down, hovering above Paul's face like he was unsure of his welcome. Paul ran his hands up Avery's back and kneaded between his shoulder blades, encouraging him to bridge the gap between them.

He did, his lips settling over Paul's with a sigh. The position made it easy to frot against him, and Paul did, gratified when Avery moaned softly and started moving his own hips.

This was hardly what Paul'd had in mind when he'd suggested a one-night stand, but it was still thrilling. He'd never been big on kissing with anyone but Avery, viewing it as a necessary stepping stone to sex but not the main event. Now, though, with Avery kissing him like he needed Paul more than air, it was nearly enough to send Paul over the edge.

When Avery brought his hands up to fist in Paul's hair, that was it. Paul drove his hips up and groaned into Avery's mouth, his release sneaking up on him. That seemed to be enough to push Avery over as well, the two of them grinding together like teenagers, their breathing ragged and loud in the small space.

Avery buried his head in the hollow of Paul's neck after he'd ridden through his own orgasm, his breath hot against Paul's clammy skin.

"That was embarrassing," he said, laughing. "Good, but embarrassing."

"I'd be mortified if this was a real one-night stand, but since it's not our actual first time, it's okay."

He knew Avery wasn't judging him for coming from their heavy make-out session. It wasn't enough, not by a long shot, but it would have to do. He and Avery still had chemistry; that much was evident.

"We didn't think this through," Avery said as he sat up.

Paul thought he was talking about the one-night stand, but before he could say anything, he realized Avery was looking at the mess they'd made.

"I have an extra pair of boxers in my bag," Paul said, drawing an incredulous look from Avery.

"Why would you travel with extra underwear?"

"Why wouldn't you?" Paul countered.

Avery climbed off him and pulled tissues out of the box on the desk, tossing some to Paul and turning to clean himself up.

"Fair point," Avery conceded.

He zipped his pants back up with a slight grimace and came back to the couch. Paul scooted to the outer edge and let him climb back in. He folded up his sweatshirt and let Avery use it as a pillow. Paul spooned up against his back, and within minutes Avery was out.

Paul watched Avery sleep, aware it was stalkerish, but unable to help himself. He had given himself permission to have one night with Avery, and he didn't want to waste any of it. He'd prefer to spend the entire night having sex, but this was okay too. Avery was clearly exhausted, and this way Paul had a chance to really *look* at him. When he was awake, Avery was the king of deflection. Paul used to think it was because he was modest, but now he realized it was more of a coping mechanism. Avery had a larger-than-life personality, but he didn't like being the center of attention. Odd for a guy whose chosen profession put him in the limelight in front of dozens if not hundreds of students at a time. But Paul had never seen him teach. He didn't know if Professor Laniston acted differently from the Avery he knew.

He must, since Avery had said he had a reputation for being a hardass. That was definitely *not* the Avery Paul knew. Then again, Paul wasn't the same guy he'd been in college either. People changed. Usually for the better.

Avery's eyelids fluttered, and he shifted, but he settled when Paul tucked the blanket around him. Paul watched him as he nestled deeper into the sweatshirt Paul had used to give him a better pillow than the floppy one the hotel had provided. The wrinkles around the edges of his eyes eased, but the worry lines that had started to dig into his forehead remained. Those were the biggest changes.

Paul wasn't proud of how he'd handled himself after Avery had left. In his lower moments, Paul had daydreamed about transferring to finish his undergraduate degree in London, to surprise Avery and pick things up again. It wouldn't have worked, and Paul wouldn't have been happy even if it had. But it had been a bad few months there while he channeled his hurt and betrayal and accepted it was on Avery, not him.

It would be easy to fall back into that, which was why this one-night stand had been a spectacularly terrible idea. And why if he had any sense, Paul would get up and spend what little was left of the night back in the terminal instead of lying here indulging himself in the what-ifs.

Paul gingerly extricated himself, careful not to jostle Avery as he slid off the sofa. He stripped off his ruined boxers and balled them up at the bottom of his bag so the poor person cleaning the room didn't have to deal with them. He pulled on fresh ones and put his pants back on, making sure he was presentable before grabbing his shoes to put on in the hallway, where there was more room and less chance of waking Avery up. He was out the door with his jacket and book bag before he could second-guess himself, leaving his key card on the desk to make sure he couldn't return. Paul had great self-control, but that went out the window where Avery was concerned.

He got his shoes on and made his way through the winding maze of hallways to the cheery little lobby. It was blindingly bright in contrast to the low light of the corridor. Like surfacing from a submarine at high noon.

Annie was still at the desk, her smile as bright as the lights.

"Did you have a good rest?"

Paul resisted the urge to straighten his clothes or do something else that would look equally suspicious. Though he was sure she knew what they'd been up to—she worked in a place that rented rooms by the hour. Sure, most guests were using them to sleep or freshen up. But most people weren't sharing a cubbyhole-sized room with someone as hot as Avery Laniston.

"Yes, thanks," he said when it was clear she was waiting for an answer. "My friend is still sleeping. We have the room for a few more hours. Can you do a wake-up call for him at seven? He had a long day getting here, and I'm afraid he might sleep through his alarm."

Paul wasn't sure Avery had even *set* an alarm. He hadn't seen him do it, and he'd drifted off to sleep right after they'd messed around. Tomorrow—or rather, today, given that it was several hours after midnight—was going to be stressful enough without Avery missing his flight.

Annie made a note in the system and nodded. "I'll still be the one on shift, so no worries. I'll knock on his door."

Paul's ride over to his terminal was eerily silent with no one else on the tram. He saw more signs of life when he made his way to his gate. He still had two hours before boarding, but the waiting area was already half full. A lot of people seemed to have chosen to camp out in the terminal instead of leaving the airport to find a hotel. Plenty of people were awake and talking, but no one seemed to be causing any trouble. He wondered if the old lady who'd thrown a deli sandwich had actually been arrested.

Paul was worried he'd fall asleep if he sat down, so he settled his bag on his shoulder and kept walking. Pacing around the gate would disturb people, but walking through the main thoroughfare in the terminal would keep him out of everyone's way and also keep him moving. He pulled his phone out of his pocket and shot off a text to Bran to let him know he was up and waiting for his flight and would see him in a few hours.

It surprised him when his phone vibrated almost immediately.

I'll pick you up when you land. We can grab breakfast before we go pick up the tuxes.

Paul knew he was going to be a virtual zombie for the wedding and reception, but he wasn't the star of the show. Bran should already be in bed. And he certainly didn't need to get up early and drive forty-five minutes to the airport to pick Paul up.

I have a rental booked. I'll pick you up at the resort, and we can do breakfast in town. He didn't want to be the reason Bran nodded off at the altar. *Ellie will kill you if you fall asleep during your vows. Better get to bed.*

Paul stopped in front of a bank of vending machines. He needed something cold and caffeinated. If he could make it to boarding, he'd be able to sleep on the plane. It was almost a four-hour flight, so he'd be somewhat functional once he landed in Reno. That meant no sleep now, though.

I'm in bed. Your text woke me up. You and Avery seem to have no idea what time zone you're in. Going back to sleep.

Avery was awake and texting? Paul looked around, a flash of panic waking him up more than the Dr Pepper in his hand could hope to. He needed space from Avery right now so he could figure out how to be calmly aloof.

Avery was nowhere in sight. If he was awake, he must still be in the pod.

A pang of regret coursed through Paul. It had been rude to sneak out. Petty, even. He'd done the same thing Avery had done to him, albeit on a much smaller scale. Still, it hadn't been the adult thing to do.

He thought about texting Avery to apologize, but he didn't want to break the seal on that form of communication. As best man he had everyone's full contact details, so he could grab Avery's phone number off the spreadsheet if he wanted.

Paul hesitated and then put his phone back in his pocket. He'd see Avery in person later, and that would be awkward enough. If Avery wanted an apology he'd give him one, but Paul would be happiest pretending their one night in Dallas hadn't happened at all.

Chapter SIX

AVERY LEANED against the shuttle-bus window, zoning out as the landscape whizzed by. His flight to Reno had been uneventful, except for discovering that his checked luggage hadn't made the trip.

It hardly mattered. He'd be slipping into a rented tux in a few hours, and the airline promised to have his bags delivered to the resort in Tahoe by tomorrow at the latest. In the grand scheme of things, it was a blip.

Not like waking up and realizing Paul had left. It had been disorienting, waking up alone in the room. He'd have wondered if the whole thing had been an exhaustion dream, except he'd been using Paul's sweatshirt as a pillow. Avery had it tied to his satchel to bring back to him.

He regretted texting his brother and spilling everything that had happened. Bran didn't need to worry about Avery's messy personal life right now. But he'd been surprisingly supportive, considering the absolute riot act he'd read to Avery the last time he and Paul had been together. Well, broken up. Bran had gotten a huge kick out of his older brother dating his best friend. It had been the aftermath that had caused problems.

Are you sure this is what you want?

The text his brother had sent him had seemed innocent enough on the surface, but Avery could read between the lines and see the motive behind it.

Paul was important to Bran, and Avery had assured him things were different this time. He intended to stay in the States, and he was serious about pursuing Paul. Agreeing to a one-night stand had been a stupid way to start that, but what was done was done. It would hardly be the biggest obstacle he'd have to overcome in convincing Paul to give dating a second chance.

Paul is stubborn, and you're going to have to work for it. But if you're sure, I've got your back. Be ready to bring your A game this week.

That had been all Bran had said about it, and Avery hadn't dared follow up with him in the light of day. For starters, Bran was most definitely with Paul, and that would be awkward. And more importantly, it was Bran's wedding day. The only drama he should be dealing with was wedding drama.

There had already been plenty of that too. The tux rental shop hadn't done the alterations like they were supposed to, and no one's tuxes fit. Avery doubted his would either. They'd all sent their measurements in, but destination weddings were tricky. The group chat for the groomsmen had kept Avery up to date in real time about how badly things were going. A power outage at the caterer had ruined the seventy-five mini cheesecakes Ellie ordered for the reception, and apparently the rental company supplying the chairs and tables had gotten the wedding colors wrong and all the linens were fuchsia.

The sooner he could get to the resort the better. The wedding wasn't for another four hours, but he felt helpless watching it all play out via text. There wasn't much he could do, but he'd still rather be there for Bran in person rather than through frowny faces and crying emojis.

And selfishly, he'd feel better once he'd seen Paul. Avery knew he had a reputation—probably deserved—for being self-absorbed, but he was also self-aware enough to know he didn't have any right to press Paul into talking to him. Especially during the wedding, when all their attention should be on Bran. And Ellie, of course.

Whom he hadn't even *met*.

God, some big brother he was.

Not that he could have gotten here sooner. He'd left after his last office-hours session of the semester had ended, fulfilling his contract with the university. Final grades were due in a few days, but he'd worry about that tomorrow. There would be plenty of time for that after he met his soon-to-be sister-in-law, hugged his pregnant sister, and watched his brother walk down the aisle.

And begged Paul to give him a second chance. That was last on the list chronologically, but most important in his mind.

He was still kicking himself for falling asleep and wasting what little time they'd had together last night. He'd considered going to find him but decided not to. It was clear Paul needed some space and time to think, and Avery was going to give him that. Or try to.

His phone vibrated. He'd turned off notifications on the group chat a while ago, so this had to be a text. He held his breath, hoping it was Paul.

It wasn't.

Paul says you're taller than him. True or False?

What a weird thing for his brother to ask. But also... did that mean Paul was talking about him? That had to be a good sign.

Yes. An inch or so.

He waited a few minutes, his curiosity getting the best of him when Bran didn't respond.

Why?

It took a few more minutes before Bran replied. The billboards for Lake Tahoe were becoming more frequent, and the last sign said they were only about forty miles out. With any luck he'd be at the resort in less than an hour.

Because your tux needs to be altered, and we're running out of time. Ellie bought some kind of fabric tape, and we're doing it ourselves. Paul has your pants on right now since he's the closest in height to you.

A second later a photo came through. Paul was standing on an end table in a rustic-looking cabin wearing a pair of tuxedo pants with one leg hanging off the table while two other men worked on his hem.

Avery wasn't sure how he felt about the photo. Heat flared in his belly at the thought of Paul wearing his pants, but the other men kneeling in front of him produced an equally hot bolt of jealousy. Ridiculous—both because he had no claim over Paul and because those had to be two of the other groomsmen, and Avery knew from the group chat that all of them were straight.

He zoomed in on Paul's face. He looked exhausted, but he was laughing. It was hard to look at Paul and not smile himself. Avery's impatience grew until he was almost twitchy with it. He wanted to be there, seeing that smile in person and helping his brother.

Taping my pants? I hope the jacket fits. What's the plan there? Staples?

Bran sent an emoji of a brain exploding. *That is actually a brilliant idea. The tape didn't work as well on the jacket sleeves because they're lined. I'm totally calling the front desk for a stapler.*

Avery's laugh was startlingly loud in the silent shuttle cabin. Several people shot him annoyed looks.

I'll pick one up when I check in.

Bran's response was immediate.

No need to check in. I already did that for you. Come to cabin 8. I have your key card, and Kevin is already done with getting his tux taped, so he said he'll run your stuff over to your cabin.

All the groomsmen were sharing cabins, and Avery's roommate for the week was one of Bran's coworkers. He'd exchanged a few pleasantries with him via the chat over the last few months, but all he knew about the guy was he had an allergy to eider that meant they couldn't have any down comforters or pillows in their cabin. Kevin seemed like a nice enough guy, even if he wasn't the groomsman Avery wanted to be bunking with. He hadn't been the slightest bit surprised to see himself not placed with Paul, though, especially since Paul had been the one to make all the room arrangements.

The group chat stayed silent for the rest of the drive, so Avery assumed they were busy with the stapler. His impatience grew as the shuttle made its way through three other Tahoe City resorts before trundling up to the hulking monstrosity the wedding was at.

Avery waited until the shuttle drove off and then took a deep breath of the fresh mountain air. It was the kind of gorgeous day you only get a few times a year in London. For all he knew, bright blue skies, crisp air, and a mild breeze were the norm for Lake Tahoe in the late spring, but it was a novelty for him, and he intended to enjoy it. He'd never been here before. Bran had taken up skiing after Avery moved away. This was a special place for him and Ellie, and Avery was glad to get to know that piece of them.

The main building was huge, looking more like a small Alpine town than a ski resort. There were multiple attached buildings dotted with fairy-tale-like turrets and windows. There was snow on the ground but only a faint dusting on the rooftops. He could imagine how picturesque it would look with frost coating the windows and mounds of snow dripping from dips and valleys in the roof. Standing here it was easier to imagine he was in the Alps than the Sierra Nevada range.

A set of wide stairs led up to what he assumed was the lodge's reception area, but Avery bypassed it, waving away the bellman who came to help him with his nonexistent luggage. The sign at the edge of the circular drive in front had an arrow pointing to the cabins, and he set off that way to find Bran's.

The path was wide and paved, which made sense a minute later when a golf cart zipped by him. Avery stepped out of the way, stumbling into the snowbank as he danced away from the motorized cart that came way too close for comfort.

The path wound around the cluster of main buildings, and in the distance he could see the tops of what he assumed were the lodge's cabins. They were barely visible through the tall evergreen trees that dotted the landscape, sparse around the lodge itself but thicker down the path.

He could see why Bran and Ellie loved it here. The shorter trees that stood in the shade of their elders still had snow cradled in their boughs. It looked like something out of a movie, complete with curls of smoke coming out of some of the cabin chimneys.

A golf cart horn startled him out of his reverie, and Avery dutifully stepped into the snowbank once more to let this one pass him as well. He was surprised when instead of flying by him, it stopped and idled by his side. He couldn't stop a wide smile from splitting his face when he realized Paul was the one driving it.

"There isn't any parking down by the cabins, so we have to keep the cars at the lodge," he said by way of greeting as Avery climbed into the cart with him. "Ellie sent me out to pick up the flowers to dress up the cheesecakes we got earlier."

"It's been one disaster after another, I gather."

As soon as Avery was safely in the golf cart, Paul took off. Avery had to shoot out a hand to brace himself on the dashboard.

"Graceful," Paul said with a snort. "Yeah, if I wasn't so sure that Bran and Ellie were made for each other I'd think all the things that have gone wrong so far were a sign they should call it off."

Paul glanced over at him, and Avery got the distinct impression that *he* was one of the things Paul was talking about. He bristled a bit at that, but this wasn't the time.

"The tuxedos, the cake, our flights—what else?"

"Your luggage, for one. Bran told me," Paul said, cutting another look over at Avery. "I grabbed some basic toiletries and a change of clothes for you while I was out. Figured you'd want some creature comforts."

It hadn't even occurred to Avery to think about what he'd do about toiletries and clothes until his bags arrived. He'd purchased a disposable toothbrush this morning from the vending machine outside the bathrooms at the pod hotel. It had been gritty and unpleasant, but better than going another day without brushing his teeth. He ran his tongue over them self-consciously, wondering if Paul getting him toiletries was in part a critique of his breath last night. Then again, Paul hadn't had a toothbrush either. So he was overthinking things.

"I appreciate it. You didn't have to do that."

Paul looked over again, but this time his expression was softer. "You don't have a rental car, and I was in town anyway. It was the least I could do."

That was far from true, but Avery wasn't going to press him on it. He'd like to think that Paul's thoughtfulness was a result of this new leaf they were turning over with their relationship, but Avery knew him too well to believe that. Paul would have picked things up for him even if he still hated him. It was the kind of guy Paul was.

Kind, thoughtful, and apparently hell on wheels when those wheels were on a golf cart. Avery braced himself again as Paul took a sharp bend in the path at full speed. The golf cart rocked up onto two wheels briefly, the entire frame shuddering when it sank back down.

"It would be a shame to make it all the way here from London and then die in a fiery golf cart crash hours before the wedding," Avery said, not letting go of the rail once they were back on four wheels. "You're a menace."

Paul laughed. He'd reached behind them to brace the crate of flowers and shopping bags as they'd made the turn, and he rubbed Avery's knee as he brought his arm back into the cab.

It did more to soothe Avery's pounding heart than he'd care to admit.

"Gotta take fun where you can," Paul said, his smile dimming a fraction when he glanced over at Avery.

And here was the one-night stand awkwardness that Avery had been so worried about. He knew Paul wanted him to jump in and assure him they were both adults who could put last night aside and pretend it hadn't happened, but Avery didn't want to pretend. To him it was confirmation that they still had great chemistry.

While he couldn't brush off last night, he also knew he couldn't afford to scare Paul away. So nonchalance it was, even though that was the opposite of how Avery felt.

"Save the fun for the dance floor tonight," Avery suggested, watching as Paul's shoulders sank a fraction and his grip on the steering wheel relaxed.

"Speaking of the dance floor, your great aunt Mildred asked me to save her a dance," Paul said with a smirk. "Bran said her senior community has hip-hop dance lessons, and she told him she'd learned how to twerk."

Aunt Mildred was eighty-seven years old, and he had a feeling Paul was going to be eating his words later. She might not get that low, but there was zero question in Avery's mind that she would absolutely try to twerk on Paul. Probably after pinching his ass.

He couldn't blame her. It was a spectacular ass. One he'd love to twerk on tonight, too, if not for the fact that his entire family would be there. He hadn't seen his parents since they'd visited London over his Christmas holiday, and he knew from the texts he'd gotten from them earlier that he wouldn't see them until the ceremony. Everyone but the bridal party was staying up at the main lodge, and Ellie was at the salon with his mother now, getting ready.

"Your dad got stuck watching a kid, so he's not over at the cabin. Your cousin is down with altitude sickness, and he got roped into toddler duty."

"Dad told me. Aunt Eve couldn't come because she had patients she couldn't reschedule, so Grace came alone with their little guy, Duncan. They live in Evanston, so they all flew in together yesterday. I don't think she's going to make it to the wedding, but Dad said something about a hotel babysitter this evening so he won't have to keep Duncan all evening."

"I think he's eating it up, honestly," Paul said. "He told me it's like training for when Jess has the baby. Your mom already has a bassinet for their condo, so I think they're a little excited to finally be grandparents."

Avery hadn't known Paul was so close to his family. It made sense, but somehow it was still a surprise. He'd met Paul when Bran had brought him over for family dinner nights their freshman year of college. That wouldn't have ended just because Paul and Bran graduated. It was easy to forget that time didn't stop when you left a place. Avery had spent the last twelve years drifting further from his family, and Paul had spent it getting closer to them.

"I'm pretty sure Mom has been preparing for this since we were born. She started talking about grandkids before we were all even out of college."

"I think retirement and downsizing has been hard on her. She's been volunteering a lot."

Avery being away had been hard on her too. She'd gotten more persistent about nagging him to come home ever since she'd retired last year.

Paul pulled up to a small A-frame cabin and parked the golf cart. "You go on in so they can finish with your tux. I have to take the flowers to the caterer and help set up the wedding tent before the maid of honor spontaneously combusts from rage. The hotel set the chairs up facing east, so we need to move the flower arch and all kinds of shit. We've got wedding-party photos in about an hour, so if you're going to shower, hurry."

He handed Avery two bags filled with clothes and toiletries, and Avery climbed out. The wedding was at sunset, and the plan was to get photos done before the ceremony so they didn't lose the light. The reception would be inside the lodge, because it got chilly quickly in the mountains when the sun went down.

Paul pulled away but stopped before he got far and glanced over his shoulder at Avery. "I'm glad you made it."

Avery grinned. *That* was the greeting he'd been hoping for. "Me too."

He didn't linger to watch Paul drive away. Avery had a brother to hug and a tuxedo to MacGyver, and with any luck, there would be time left over for that shower. He definitely needed it.

A man he didn't recognize opened the door to the cabin, but Bran was right behind him. He let out a whoop and rushed toward Avery, then lifted him off his feet in a bear hug.

"Cutting it close as always," Bran teased. He introduced Avery to the guys in the room and told him to put his stuff down on the table. "As much as I'd love to catch up, it's gonna have to wait. Your tux is in the bathroom. Throw it on and we'll see how good Paul's memory is. He said he had a good idea of how long your legs were from standing in line with you last night at the airport. We didn't do anything with the jacket since that's more likely to fit off the rack."

Avery almost choked at the thought of how accurately Paul might gauge his height and why. The mental image of being hip to hip with Paul last night, grinding against each other like horny teenagers, flashed through his head.

Bran snorted. "Yeah, that's the same look he had. Must have been a memorable line. Go change."

Avery ducked out of the room, ignoring Bran's snickers. He'd brought this on himself, telling Bran about what happened last night. Well, a heavily redacted version of what happened. Bran didn't need or want any of the details, and Avery didn't want to give him any. He wondered if Paul had said anything.

The tux hanging on the shower rail didn't look like it had been hastily hacked together by a group of men with fabric tape. The hem was clean and straight. He was extra careful putting on the pants, unsure of how fragile they were with tape holding the hem together. They pooled a little around his ankles, but with shoes they'd be perfect. Paul had judged it accurately, which gave him a thrill. Paul knew exactly how much taller he was and where his waist fell—that had to be a good sign. There's no way that would be something the average one-night stand would notice and remember. Score one for Operation Reconciliation.

He slid into the coat, flexing and extending his arms to check the fit. Seemed fine to him.

There was a sharp rap on the door, which opened before he could say anything. Bran poked his head around.

"Oh, that looks good."

"I think it's fine. Everything seems to fit."

Bran blew out a breath, and Avery got his first good look at his brother. He'd been his usual boisterous self when Avery had walked in, but now he could see the lines around Bran's mouth and the bags under his eyes.

"You doing okay?"

Bran offered him a tired smile. "I've been trying to take care of everything that's gone wrong so Ellie doesn't have to. I wanted her to have a fairy-tale wedding, but I guess I didn't count on the fact that most of those stories are actually pretty dark."

"As long as no bridesmaids cut their toes off to fit into their shoes, I think everything will work out," Avery said, smiling when Bran laughed as he'd intended him to.

"Pretty sure they would if they had to. They've been helping the caterer with the last-minute cheesecakes and God only knows what else."

"Something about flowers and a maid of honor meltdown. Paul gave me a ride on his way to help with that."

Bran ran a hand over his face. "Right. The florist didn't have enough to spare any for the cake table, so Paul said he'd take care of it. Marnie—she's Ellie's sister—is kind of terrifying. Paul was the only groomsman brave enough to volunteer to help her with the tent. Neil swears he saw her eyes glow red when he told her about the tuxes."

That was a very Paul thing to do.

"Do you think he needs help? I was going to grab a shower, but I could go move stuff if you need me to."

Bran shook his head. "Paul will handle it. The hotel staff is down there too. I think he's mostly there to make sure Marnie doesn't end up with a manslaughter charge."

Chapter SEVEN

FOR ALL the dysfunction and disaster that led up to it, the ceremony went off without a hitch. Paul had never been jealous of Bran and Ellie's relationship, but tonight, standing beside them as they promised to love and cherish each other for the rest of their lives, he felt a niggle of envy creep in.

He'd never dated anyone he could see a future with. Not since Avery. And that future had been childish and silly. What twenty-year-old fantasized about SUVs and mortgages and hauling kids to soccer practice?

He had, and then Avery had done him the favor of breaking his heart and showing him how ridiculous it was to pin all those hopes on a college relationship. Getting married and having a family hadn't been something Paul had thought about before Avery, and it wasn't something he'd spent too much time thinking about after him either.

Those thoughts had been Avery-specific, and they died when their relationship did. And thank God for it, because Paul loved his life. Settling down like Bran wasn't something on his radar. Paul liked his bachelor lifestyle. He didn't want to be in a position to need to justify things like his workaholic schedule or the hours each week he spent practicing with his men's softball team. Paul didn't answer to anyone but himself.

They were in the lull between the ceremony and the reception now. Bran and Ellie had snuck off for a few minutes alone before entering the reception hall as man and wife, leaving the bridal party milling around in the lobby until they were ready to go in.

He'd mostly avoided Avery until now. The photographer had spent nearly an hour lining them up and posing them, and they'd been otherwise occupied during the ceremony. But Paul's luck was ending, because Avery was headed straight for the spot Paul had staked out near the bank of floor-to-ceiling windows that overlooked the grounds.

The sun hadn't quite set yet, but it was dark enough that he could watch Avery's approach in the reflection in the windows. He looked stunning in his tux. He'd taken the time to shave before the ceremony, and he'd taken Paul's breath away when he'd first seen him. Yesterday he had a five o'clock shadow, which looked good on him. Freshly shaven, though, his dimples and the slight cleft in his chin were prominent. It was unfair that he looked delicious either way.

Paul kept a short beard because he'd always hated his jawline. It wasn't as sharp as Avery's, and he'd been self-conscious about it since his teens. Clean shaven, he looked about ten years younger than he was. He was approaching an age when that would be a positive rather than a negative, but it had been years since he'd seen himself without it. The last time he'd shaved it had been when the Blackhawks were in the NHL playoffs, and the next time would be far in the future if they kept playing the way they were.

"Have your speech prepared?" Avery asked.

Paul turned around and made a face of mock surprise. "We're supposed to give a speech?"

"Funny." Avery patted his chest. "I have mine right here."

"In your heart?"

Avery laughed and peeled his tuxedo coat back enough to reveal a folded piece of paper in his breast pocket.

"I would have expected a veteran public speaker like you to wing it."

"Nah, I always work from notes. Bran gave me clear talking points to make sure I stay out of trouble."

"No mentioning previous girlfriends, no talking about anything that happened on a spring-break trip, no embarrassing stories, no inside jokes," Paul recited, laughing when Avery nodded ruefully. "I got the same talk."

"Takes all the fun out of giving a speech, but hopefully this means they'll be short."

Paul hoped so too. Otherwise his three-minute best-man speech would stand out as brief. He didn't love public speaking, and he hated being the center of attention. The only part of the best-man gig that had given him pause—aside from learning Avery was on the list of groomsmen he'd be stuck with for a week—was the requisite speech he'd have to give at the reception.

"Got somewhere else to be tonight?"

Avery wiggled his eyebrows suggestively. "You know it. I've got a hot date with a comfy bed and the pajamas you bought me. I am knackered."

Paul could relate.

"I haven't even been in my cabin long enough to know if the beds are comfortable yet, but that sounds like a plan. I've been on the go since I got here this morning."

"I haven't even seen mine. Bran checked me in and gave me my card, and he had Kevin take my stuff over for me earlier. He also asked if I minded going over to help you get things set up for him and Ellie in the cabin later. I already called and asked to have the room cleaned. It was a mess."

Paul hadn't thought to call housekeeping, so he was glad to hear Avery was on top of it, even though he was less than thrilled to be paired with him. They'd gotten ready in Bran's cabin, and last Paul had seen it, it had beer bottles and take-out containers on most of the flat surfaces.

Paul had a bag of rose petals, bath salts, and other things Bran had asked him to use to turn the cabin into a honeymoon suite. He'd assumed Bran asked him because asking Marnie would have been too weird, but if he was having Avery tag along then that reasoning went out the window.

Was this another attempt at matchmaking, like the restaurant setup yesterday?

"The DJ is summoning us," Avery said, pointing to where the rest of the bridal party was lining up. Bran and Ellie turned the corner a second later, looking so joyful and in love that Paul couldn't help but grin back at them.

Marnie fussed over him, fixing his hair and straightening his collar before thrusting an arm through his and manhandling him into line in front of Avery and a woman whose name Paul had already forgotten. He was tempted to swat her hand away when Marnie reached over to tweak his bow tie, but he settled for catching her hand, giving it a squeeze, and pulling her toward the doors when he heard the DJ introduce them.

He loved Ellie, but he was counting the seconds until he didn't have to deal with her overbearing sister anymore.

DINNER FLEW by, and the pit in Paul's stomach grew with every plate he saw the catering staff clear. Time was ticking down to the toasts, and even though he'd had his speech written weeks ago and had practiced it until he was blue in the face, he was still nervous. He didn't want to let Bran down or embarrass him and Ellie in front of their friends and family.

Avery rested a hand on Paul's knee, which he'd been jiggling to work off some of his nervous energy. Bran and Ellie had put them next to each other, because of course they had. By this point, Paul didn't doubt Bran was playing matchmaker. And as annoyed as that made him, he was grateful for it now, because the only way this could be more nerve-wracking would be if he had to do it without Avery's calming presence by his side.

The hand on his knee gave him something else to obsess over briefly, but soon after, the DJ cut the classical music that had played throughout dinner and announced that the bridal party toasts were about to begin.

He'd hoped Marnie might go first, but it was his name that rolled off the DJ's tongue next. Shit. He took the microphone the waiter was holding out to him, hoping his hands weren't so sweaty it would slip out of his grip.

Avery gave his knee a squeeze and released it, and Paul got to his feet, his hands shaking as he pulled his speech out of his pocket. He'd practiced it, but his mind went blank the moment he stood up. He tried to focus on the words, but they were too small and swam in and out of focus.

"Uh, good evening. We're here tonight to celebrate Bran and Ellie, and it's an honor to, uh, be here with them. It's... they're," he took a breath and tried to center himself enough to focus on the words on the paper, but his hand was shaking. This was why he hated public speaking.

"Bran is my closest friend, and uh, Ellie is the love of his life. It's, uh, it's so special to see how happy they are together and uh, how lucky they are to have found each other."

Paul paused, trying again to pick up the thread of the speech he had written, but he dropped the paper.

Avery stood up and took the mic from him with a low chuckle. Paul nearly collapsed in relief, but Avery put an arm around his shoulders to prevent him from sitting down.

"You have to understand, Bran gave us a strict list of things we weren't allowed to say tonight. Have you ever seen a classified document with half its text redacted? Paul's speech looked like that, with most of the page blacked out. Because what Paul didn't tell you is he's been family since he and Bran met in college. Because that's the kind of guy my brother is—when he adopts you, it's for life. Which is how I know he and Ellie are going to have a very long and happy marriage. Bran plays for keeps, and if he decides you're worthy of being in his life, then he fights to keep you there. Even if you move across the ocean and settle on a different continent."

The audience laughed at that, and Bran heckled Avery good-naturedly about his faux British accent.

"Oy, wait your turn," Avery said, pointing menacingly at his brother. "I'm not done saying nice things about you yet."

He took his own speech out of his pocket and gave Paul's shoulder a squeeze, releasing him and letting Paul slide back down into his own seat while he went on with his planned speech.

Paul picked up his water glass and drained it, though it didn't do much to soothe his dry throat. He'd totally choked, and Avery had rescued him like it had been their plan all along. He blew out a quiet breath, surprised when without missing a beat in his speech, Avery let his fingers brush over Paul's shoulder to comfort him.

It was an absent gesture that felt incredibly intimate, and a thrill shot through Paul at the slight contact.

"What I mean to say is, Ellie, welcome to the family. I can't wait to spend more time with you and get to know the woman who has put that smile on my brother's face. To the newlyweds!"

Paul fumbled for his champagne glass, even more embarrassment flooding through him when he realized he'd failed to do that part when he'd disastrously ended his own toast.

Avery clinked his glass against Paul's and sat down, his hand finding Paul's under the table and twining their fingers together for a brief squeeze. He started to release him, but Paul curled his fingers around Avery's, stopping him from letting go.

Avery didn't make eye contact as he watched Marnie stand up to give her speech, but Paul noticed his smile deepen, and he made no move to release Paul's hand again. The tight discomfort in his throat from his humiliating speech eased a bit. Should he be annoyed Avery could walk back into his life and have this effect on him? Probably. But for right now he wasn't going to look a gift horse in the mouth. He was going to take the life raft.

By the time the speeches were over and it was time to cut the cheesecake and start the dancing, Paul had almost convinced himself that his speech *wasn't* as awkward and awful as he thought it was. No one else likely noticed that he'd lost his place and panicked. Marnie had cried. Not a sniffle, but hiccuping sobs she'd tried to talk through, and no one could understand her. At least he hadn't done that.

"Did you have your heart set on dessert, or is this a good time to slip away to fancy up the cabin?"

Avery's lips brushed his ear as he spoke, and Paul pointedly ignored the shiver the unexpectedly intimate contact sent through him.

"After the first dance, maybe."

Avery made a thoughtful sound and sat back. "Good point. Though I would like to be out of here before the garter toss."

"They're not doing one. Ellie says it's sexist."

"Good on Ellie. It's creepy too."

Paul didn't disagree. But a lot of wedding traditions made little sense to him. Ellie's father had given her away at the altar, which seemed more sexist than the garter toss, though much less gross. One of Paul's cousins had hiked her garter practically to her crotch when she'd gotten married, and her husband had taken it off with his teeth. They'd tied his hands behind him with her veil to make it harder. So bizarre.

The DJ called Bran and Ellie out to the floor while the catering staff served the cheesecakes that Paul and Bran had driven all over town this morning buying. He doubted most of the guests could tell they were from grocery store delis and not the fancy bakery they'd intended.

"Can we have all the unmarried guests out on the floor with our bride and groom?"

Paul wrinkled his nose and contemplated staying put. Avery didn't seem inclined to join in either, but when Bran made direct eye contact with them and waved them out, they both sighed and edged their way to the fringe of the crowd.

"The newlyweds are putting their own spin on the bouquet toss, ladies and gentlemen. Bran and Ellie have each selected someone to give their bouquet and corsage to as a symbol of their belief that love finds people when they are ready to open themselves up to it. Are you all ready?"

The women on the floor all cheered, and most of the men looked like they'd rather be anywhere else. Paul was in that camp. This had to be Ellie's idea—Bran was not this sentimental. Though maybe getting married had that effect on people. Paul didn't know, and he had no plans to find out.

Everyone cooed when Ellie gave her bouquet to one of the bridesmaids, and Paul was so caught up in the spectacle of the crying woman tackle-hugging Ellie that he completely missed Bran walking straight to where he and Avery were standing.

His stomach fell at Bran's shit-eating grin, which was the only warning Paul had before Bran was tucking his corsage into his breast pocket. The crowd laughed when Bran plucked a rose out of it and stuck it behind Avery's ear.

Bran pulled Paul into a one-armed hug. "I'm sorry, Ellie made me do it. It'll be over before you know it," he whispered into his ear before releasing him and giving Avery a bear hug and a comically exaggerated kiss on the cheek.

"I had nothing to do with that," Avery said when the music started and Bran hurried back to the center of the dance floor.

"I believe you."

"I'm sorry. I know you don't like to be a spectacle any more than I do."

Paul snorted. He did hate being the center of attention, but it hadn't lasted long. All eyes were on Bran and Ellie now as they took the floor for their first dance as a married couple. He couldn't keep his own eyes off the rose that was still tucked behind Avery's ear. What was Ellie playing at? And why did Bran let her do it? Ellie knew they'd dated, but she didn't know all of Paul and Avery's history. But Bran did. He knew why the two of them wouldn't be good together.

"Would the rest of the bridal party please join the happy couple on the dance floor?"

Shit.

Paul expected to be paired off with Marnie again, since they'd walked down the aisle together and shared an introduction to the reception. But instead of taking the hand he held out to her, she winked and grabbed another bridesmaid.

The bridesmaid Avery had been paired with.

Oh God.

This had to be what Bran meant when he'd said it would be over before he knew it. Everyone else was already out on the dance floor with Bran and Ellie, and it would be conspicuous if he and Avery didn't join them. Goddammit.

Avery offered him a rueful smile and held his hand out. Paul reluctantly stepped closer and let Avery whisk him onto the dance floor to join the other couples. Paul had never really been a dancer, so he let Avery lead, focusing instead of ignoring the eyes on them.

Including Avery's *parents*. This was humiliating. He'd worked so hard to get over Avery, and things had been weird with Bran and Avery's family for years after the breakup. Bob and Joan were great people. They'd made sure Paul knew he was welcome at their house. But it had taken him a long time to feel like they thought of him as Bran's friend and not as the boy Avery had dumped.

He snuck a glance over at Joan, who was watching the dance floor with her hands over her heart. The look she gave him when they made eye contact made it clear it wasn't just Bran and Ellie she was teary over. Great. Back to square one there.

Avery and Paul moved their way around the floor with all the grace of middle schoolers at their first homecoming dance, which was, not coincidentally, the first and last dance Paul had attended. Bran wasn't doing too much better with Ellie. Odds were good Bran wouldn't be dancing again after this, and Paul knew for damn sure *he* wouldn't.

The DJ opened the floor to everyone after the first song ended, and Paul dropped Avery's hand like it was lava. Avery chuckled but didn't fight him on it, following him as he wound through the growing crowd. He bypassed the head table and went straight to the bar. Paul needed a drink and a moment to clear his head, preferably in that order.

He saw Avery get waylaid by his parents, and the tightness that had been growing in his chest eased. Bob and Joan had swarmed Avery during the photoshoot before the ceremony, and they'd likely keep him well occupied now. That meant Paul could enjoy his drink and then slip away to decorate the honeymoon suite. He'd have to come back to the reception after that, but some time away from the bustle of the party—and more importantly, Avery's charm—would do him worlds of good.

He knocked back the shot the bartender gave him and made a beeline for the lobby. Before he made it, though, Avery appeared at his side and slung an arm around his shoulders.

"Decoration time?"

Paul bit back a groan of frustration. "Why don't you stay and catch up with your parents and your sister? They're all flying home tomorrow after the wedding brunch, so you should take the chance now while you have it. I can take care of the room."

"I will have plenty of time with them when we're all back in Chicago. I'm house-sitting for Bran and Ellie while they're in Bali, so I'll be around. Mom made sure to tell me multiple times the condo has a guest room too. So even after they're back, I'm planning to stick around."

Paul wanted to argue, but he knew it would be pointless. Avery was a stubborn bastard, and Paul would only make things worse by fighting. He didn't want Avery to know that he was getting under his skin, which meant he couldn't call attention to how much he wanted to put some space between them.

"It'll be quick. Bran has all the stuff in his suitcase."

Paul had intended to walk to the cabin to stretch out his absence, but with Avery tagging along, he decided snagging a golf cart would be a better choice. Get in, get out, get through the rest of the reception, and then he could excuse himself to his cabin. A couple of hours away from Avery and a good night's sleep would cure what ailed him for sure.

"It better be just hearts and roses and not freaky sex stuff," Avery warned as they climbed into the cart.

Paul didn't know what kind of sex stuff Avery would consider freaky, and he didn't really want to think about that or what sex stuff Bran might have at all. They were best friends, but they didn't talk about their sex lives in anything other than broad, sweeping terms. It was a habit they'd started while Paul was dating Avery, since Bran didn't want any details about that. He could see through Avery's veiled attempt to goad him into talking about sex and was determined to avoid it.

"As far as I know, it's flower petals, bath salts, and stuff like that. The bellman was supposed to get Ellie's suitcases and bring them over, so we'll have to check to make sure they got there."

"Boring hetero vanilla sex stuff, got it," Avery said.

"Of the two of us, you'd be the closest thing to an expert on hetero sex stuff," Paul blurted, cursing himself for not being able to ignore Avery's bait.

"True. Does that make you the resident expert on boring vanilla?"

Damn it, this was exactly why he should have ignored Avery's comment. Avery knew precisely how to tease and where to poke to engage Paul in a debate. Avery loved to talk, and Paul used to love listening to him ramble about the most inane things.

"Though role-playing strangers meeting in an airport and having an illicit tryst isn't that vanilla. I guess your tastes have changed as you've aged," Avery teased.

Paul pulled up to Bran's cabin and yanked the parking brake abruptly enough to make the cart shudder.

"Nope. Still pretty vanilla," he said, unable to let Avery have the last word despite his better judgment.

When Paul opened the front door, Avery leaned in and murmured, "That's always been my favorite flavor anyway."

Paul stood there dumbly, staring after Avery as he swept past him into the cabin. Somehow Avery always threw him off balance, though this time he had no one to blame but himself. He knew better than to respond to Avery when he was in this kind of playful mood.

He found Avery standing in the kitchenette area unwrapping a gift basket the bellman had brought by earlier. Paul had been the one to answer the door when it came, but they'd been in a rush, and Bran hadn't done more than glance at the card and stick it in the small refrigerator.

"I sent them a basket of cheeses and snacks for tonight," Avery said when Paul walked in. "I did it for Jess's wedding too. One of my colleagues said he and his wife didn't get to eat at their reception because they were too busy greeting everyone and celebrating, and by the time they got back to their room, they were starving and room service was closed. Poor guy ended up ordering pizza off Postmates on his wedding night."

Paul hadn't even thought about that. It made sense, and with all the other arrangements he'd made for Bran and Ellie, he should have thought about that one.

"Don't look so shocked," Avery said, pulling a handful of grapes out of the fruit basket the hotel had provided and rinsing them at the sink. "I can be thoughtful."

He could be. He could also be incredibly thoughtless. Avery was a fine balance of many things, and Paul was realizing those things had shifted and the equation was different now than it had been when they'd dated.

"Go do your thing. I'm going to arrange a charcuterie board for them so all they have to do is take it out of the fridge when they get hungry."

Paul left him slicing cheese and salami and dug Bran's suitcase out of the closet. Ellie's had been placed next to it, thankfully. One less thing for Paul to worry about. He held his breath as he opened the plastic bag that Bran had told him had everything he needed to decorate, relieved beyond measure when it had a bag of flower petals, a bottle of bubble bath, a lighter, and candles. He'd let Avery get into his head. No weird sex toys or flavored lube, thank God.

Paul took his time laying the flower petals out on the bed in the shape of a heart. Trite but time-tested. There was a claw-foot tub in the attached bathroom, and he scattered a few more petals on the floor and counter in there before adding candles and placing the bubble bath near the faucet. He moved a stack of towels from the counter to the small table near the tub and laid out the bath mat that was folded neatly over the edge.

Avery was still in the kitchenette when he finished. The cheese board he'd made looked amazing. He'd had no idea Avery could make something that looked so fancy.

"Do you think we could get room service to bring them a bucket of champagne on ice? There isn't anything but beer here."

Both Bran and Ellie hated champagne. Ellie favored sweet wines, and Bran stuck to beer and the occasional mixer, but Paul bet he'd make an exception so he could share a glass of wine with his wife tonight.

"I'll stop by the front desk when we go back over and have them send something," Paul said.

A nice riesling or even a moscato if they had it. Ellie wasn't ashamed to admit her taste in wines leaned toward the basic part of the spectrum, and thanks to her, Paul had learned he liked them too. He'd been firmly in the anti-wine category before her.

"You're sure all your things got over to your cabin earlier?"

No point in making Avery come back here, especially since it was the honeymoon suite. He doubted Bran would appreciate his brother third-wheeling it as he and Ellie started their first evening as husband and wife.

"Kevin took the stuff over. I don't think my suitcases will be here until tomorrow at the earliest, but I really did appreciate you picking things up for me when you went into town today. I hadn't even gotten far enough to think about toiletries and pajamas."

"I bought some track pants too. I'm sure you can bum anything else you need off Bran or Kevin."

The jeans and sweater he'd been wearing yesterday had looked great on him, especially paired with the oh-so-stereotypical tweed blazer he'd had on, but they hadn't looked like something Avery would be comfortable hiking and skiing in. He'd have to rent a ski suit, but he'd still need something to go under it.

He wasn't prepared for Avery to lean in and kiss him. The contact was over almost as quickly as it had begun, but the peck made Paul's lips tingle and his cheeks heat.

"I really appreciate it. Truly, Paul. It's been a long time since I had someone look out for me, and it means a lot."

Paul knew from Bran that Avery had dated over the years but never lived with anyone again after Paul. Not that Paul was any better. He'd shied away whenever his relationships started down a more serious road.

It should have felt weird to buy Avery underwear and other things, but it hadn't. He hadn't given it a second thought. And that was what was scary. Paul hadn't specifically set out to buy those things; he'd absentmindedly grabbed them because Avery was on his mind and he knew he'd need them. It was a completely unwarranted level of intimacy, and Paul needed to get his head back on straight before he made a complete ass of himself.

"Let's head back, shall we? Can't keep the happy couple waiting."

He waited until Avery cleaned up the last of the mess in the kitchen and followed him back out to the golf cart. Paul needed to get through the rest of the reception and he'd be fine. All the activities they had planned for the week were group outings, so it wasn't like he was going to keep being thrust into situations like this with Avery. It would be a totally different dynamic with the rest of the bridal party there, and he'd have Bran to use as a human shield. He owed Paul that after the corsage and first dance thing Ellie had pulled.

He stumbled when he realized Avery was sitting in the driver's seat.

"Did you want to drive?"

Avery did a double take and laughed. "Old habits. Sorry. This is the passenger side for me. I guess I was zoned out and not paying attention."

"You can drive us back if you want, as long as you promise to stay on the correct side of the road," Paul joked.

Avery scowled at him but slid across the bench seat. "That's one of my big worries about moving back. I have to retrain my brain, and it's going to be hard."

Paul made a dismissive sound. "It'll come back to you. It's all muscle memory, and you learned to drive here. If anything, I'd think your natural instincts would be toward our side of things. I bet you'll be surprised how quickly you fall back into old habits."

Avery studied him for a moment before answering. "Already am," he said, and Paul got the distinct feeling he wasn't talking about driving anymore.

Chapter EIGHT

AVERY WANTED to get out of this bloody tux and sleep for two days. The reception had wrapped up an hour ago, but he and Paul had stuck around to gather the wedding presents and help Marnie box all the decorations and various things that needed to be shipped back to Chicago. They could deal with the logistics of that later—his priority was getting the reception hall cleared so he could go to bed.

His parents and sister had disappeared about twenty minutes ago, since they'd been dead on their feet. He was too, but tired seemed to be his new normal, so he could soldier through. Besides, if Paul was staying, he was staying. Both out of solidarity and because he intended to stick as close to Paul as he could over the next week. He wasn't going to waste this golden opportunity. They'd be in the same city afterward, but Chicago was a big place, and Paul had a life there. It would be much easier for him to avoid Avery there than it was here, when they were pushed together every day for meals and outings.

He'd thought the itinerary Paul and Marnie had put together was ridiculous at first, but now he was looking forward to everything on the overpacked list. They were all opportunities to get close to Paul and convince him not to ignore the chemistry they shared.

"Do you think we should trash the flowers? Or bring them back for the cabins?"

Avery looked at the vase in Marnie's hands. There were dozens of them throughout the room.

"Do the vases belong to the florist, or are they ours?"

They wouldn't be worth shipping back to Chicago, unless Ellie wanted them for sentimental reasons. There wasn't anything special about them aside from what they'd been used for.

"I paid a deposit on them that I'll lose if they don't get returned. So ditch the flowers?"

Paul walked up with a stack of boxes in his arms. He'd taken off his tuxedo coat later in the evening, and his shirtsleeves were rolled up, exposing his forearms. How he could look so effortlessly gorgeous while also looking exhausted was a mystery. Avery was torn between wanting to kiss him and wanting to take a nap with him. Both sounded amazing. And unlikely, going by the wide berth Paul had given him as soon as they'd made it back to the reception.

"I'm sure Ellie would like to have them at brunch tomorrow. She can decide what she wants to do with them after that."

Why was Paul being so logical and thoughtful a turn-on? It made Avery want to tackle him right there.

"Good point," Marnie told him. "What should we put them in tonight?"

Paul set the boxes on the nearest table. "I saw some empty buckets in the kitchen. I'll ask if we can borrow a few."

He turned to Avery, making eye contact for the first time in hours. "Could you take the boxes to the front desk? They're letting us keep them in the storage room until we can get them to FedEx to send them home."

"Will do."

"And you can head out after that. I still need to settle up the bar tab."

Avery shot him a questioning look, and Paul shrugged. "It's my wedding gift to them. I took care of the bar, Marnie paid the florist. Your parents paid the catering bill, and I think Ellie's parents paid for the venue rental. That way Bran and Ellie could afford their dream honeymoon."

Avery raised his eyebrows and whistled, and Paul frowned.

"What? Should I have gotten them a blender they'd never use? This was practical."

Practical and several thousand dollars more than a blender. But Avery kept his mouth shut.

"I didn't say anything. It was a very generous gift."

"He's one to talk," Marnie scoffed. "Ellie told me you paid for the photographer, Avery, so don't pretend like you got them a toaster."

He grinned and mimicked Paul's modest shrug. "They already had a toaster."

Paul huffed out a laugh, a smile teasing at the corners of his mouth. "Right. So now that we've all compared gifts like the Magi, can we get a move on? They can't finish closing up the room till we're out, and I'm sure the staff want to go home. Marnie, you gather up the vases so you have them set aside for the florist, and I'll go get those buckets. Avery, when you take the boxes to reception, make sure they give you a receipt for each box. You can give me the tags tomorrow at brunch."

In-charge Paul was very attractive. Avery resisted the urge to give him a military salute and settled for nodding as he took the boxes and added them to the cart near the door. They'd need tape and labels, but they were fine for now. And he'd bet just about anything that Paul already had those tucked away somewhere in his luggage.

He and Marnie made a scarily efficient team. Avery watched them move around the room in sync for a minute before another wave of exhaustion hit and he turned his attention to navigating the cart toward the lobby. A bellman rushed over to help as soon as he reached the main wing of the hotel, and Avery happily gave the job over to him.

It didn't take long for the front desk to tag the boxes and give him the receipts, but the ballroom was empty when he wandered back toward it afterward. He'd hoped he could catch them and share a golf cart back to the cabins, but his luck had finally run out tonight.

Avery drove himself over, parking in the little lot that led to the cluster of cabins the bridal party was in. He hadn't been to his, but it had to be close. Bran had pointed it out earlier when he'd given Avery his key. His was at the end, another neat little A-frame. He hoped it had the same wall of windows looking out into the forest that Bran's did. It would be a nice backdrop to work against. Avery had things to finish up this week since he'd left London in a hurry and hadn't submitted his grades for the semester. He had everything he needed with him. Thank goodness all coursework and exams were digital these days. He actually preferred paper assignments and blue-book exams, but that was the academic traditionalist in him. And he had to admit it was much easier to mark essays you could actually read, instead of having to decipher the panicked chicken scratch of first-year university students.

There weren't any lights on in the cabin, which didn't surprise him. Kevin had left with the rest of the guests an hour ago. He'd likely fallen straight into bed, just like Avery wanted to.

He loosened his bow tie and pressed his key card to the door, opening it as quietly as he could. Bran's cabin had a sitting room, a small kitchen, and a separate bedroom, but this cabin was smaller. He'd been right about the wall of windows, and there was enough moonlight to illuminate the outlines of the furniture in the room so he wasn't stumbling around completely blind.

He still stubbed his toe on an end table and bit back a curse. The room had the same kitchenette as Bran's, but the sitting room area was little more than an alcove. The main features in the room were two queen-sized beds, neither of which was occupied.

There was a suitcase and a garment bag on one bed, so Avery claimed the empty one. He kicked off his shoes and left them by the door, out of the way in case Kevin came home later. He must have picked up one of the bridesmaids. Avery was impressed. He hadn't seemed like that much of a player when they'd met earlier.

Since he was alone, Avery flipped on the light and continued getting undressed. His own garment bag was hanging in the open closet, with his satchel and the bags Paul had given him on the floor underneath it. He hung up the tuxedo before digging in the bags to come up with a toothbrush and a fresh pair of boxers. There was a pair of pajamas in there too, but Avery didn't think Kevin would swoon if he saw him in his underwear. He usually slept naked, but concessions had to be made when one had a roommate.

Besides, it was strangely comforting, knowing Paul had been the one to pick out the boxers, especially after teasing him last night about not traveling with a spare pair. Avery laughed when he noticed they were decorated with a colorful taco print. A nice reminder of their dinner last night. He hoped he wasn't reading too much into it. For all he knew, these were the only ones the store had in his size. But Avery preferred to believe that Paul had stood in front of the display and picked them out because they made him think of Avery and the time they'd spent together. They'd gone out for tacos a lot when they'd been dating. More because the taco truck on campus had a buy one/get one free special on Tuesdays than because they both loved tacos, but it was still a fond memory.

He heard the cabin door open while he was brushing his teeth. There weren't any toiletries out on the bathroom counter, so he assumed Kevin would need to get in there now that he was back. Avery hurried through finishing and gathered up his socks and underwear, giving his new taco boxers one final check in the mirror to make sure he was decent before opening the bathroom door.

"Wasn't sure you'd make it back tonight. Who was the lucky girl?"

Avery ducked into the closet to throw his things in his satchel. He'd just stood up and started to turn around when he heard Paul's voice instead of the one he was expecting.

"Marnie," Paul said, looking shocked to see him. "I mean, that's who I was with. I helped Marnie take the flowers and presents back to her room. She'd been sharing with Ellie, so she had the most space to store them since she's alone tonight."

Avery stumbled and fell backward, his head rapping hard against the mirrored closet door. The glass cracked, sending spiderwebs through it and knocking the door off its sliding track.

Avery sat back on his heels, pressing his hand to his head. Paul looked from him to the splintered mirror, eyes widening.

"Oh my God, Avery. Are you all right?" He rushed over and knelt down in front of Avery, moved Avery's hand aside to look at the injury. "Did you crack that mirror with your *head*?"

Avery made a feeble attempt at a laugh. "Looks like."

"Jesus Christ, you're a menace. Get up. I want to get a better look at it under the light."

Paul led him into the bathroom, and Avery leaned against the counter as Paul probed the back of his head with gentle fingers.

He continued his exploration, running his fingertips through Avery's hair and soothing his temples with his thumbs.

"You're not cut. How does it feel? Do you need a doctor?"

Now that the shock and adrenaline of the accident had worn off, Avery realized his head was throbbing.

"It's nothing some paracetamol won't fix," Avery said. Paul looked confused, so Avery clarified. "We call it Tylenol over here."

"Ah. I have some ibuprofen in my bag. Will that work?"

Avery nodded, then winced. That had been dumb.

Paul had obviously noticed the wince, but he snapped his mouth shut like he'd wanted to say something and thought better of it.

He left Avery in the bathroom and came back a minute later with a bottle of water from the kitchenette and two tablets.

"Do you think you hit it hard enough to worry about a concussion?"

Avery hadn't had a concussion since Jimmy Peak had sidelined him during lacrosse practice in ninth grade. All he remembered about that was a blinding headache, some unfortunate vomiting in front of the team, and missing three games before the coach would let him play again.

He rubbed the back of his head. There wasn't even a goose egg. "I think most of the damage is to my pride. That wasn't my most graceful moment."

Paul laughed like Avery had hoped he would.

"I took you by surprise. It was my fault."

"You didn't make me fall. That was all me. I was expecting Kevin. He was supposed to be my roommate."

Paul made a face. "Bran checked me in this morning to save time. Now I'm thinking there was an ulterior motive."

Shit.

"I didn't—"

Paul cut Avery off before he could defend himself. "I know. If you'd orchestrated this, you'd have been waiting for me splayed out on the bed, not falling through a glass door. Your seduction game is much stronger than that."

Avery grinned. "So you think I have game?"

Paul gave him a flat look. "I *know* you have game, Avery. That's never been the problem."

He sighed and rubbed a hand over his face. He was still in his rumpled tuxedo.

"You should get ready for bed," Avery said.

Paul's mouth dropped open. "Avery, you have a head wound! We're not—"

Avery held his hands up. "I am not implying we should have sex. I'm saying we're both exhausted, you're still in your tux, and the sooner we turn that light out the better, because it's making my headache worse."

"Right," Paul said sheepishly. "Sorry. I just—you've been on my mind all day. And I don't know that I have it in me to fight it anymore. Not when every time I turn the corner, you're there."

Avery weighed his options. He could retreat and live to fight another day, or he could push things and try to gain some ground.

Patience had never been his strong suit.

"I won't apologize for that. I want a chance to get to know each other. Last night wasn't enough."

Paul looked exhausted and every bit as beaten down as he'd said he was, and Avery had a pang of conscience.

"If you want to talk to Kevin tomorrow and switch with him, I won't interfere. But there isn't anything we can do about it for tonight, so let's go to bed, okay?"

Paul sighed. "You're right. I'm going to change and we can get some sleep. If you're sure your head is okay."

Avery poked at the back of his head tentatively. Still no knot, but it was going to be one hell of a sore spot tomorrow.

"I'll see if there's some ice in the freezer," Paul offered. "We can wrap it in a towel and make you an ice pack."

Avery waved him off. "I can do that. You get ready for bed."

Avery ceded the bathroom to Paul and gingerly made his way past the broken mirror, carefully inspecting the carpet for glass. It all seemed to be contained. The mirror was safety glass or something. And thank God for that. It was going to be embarrassing enough to call the front desk tomorrow to tell them about the door. The last thing he wanted was housekeeping hating them because of broken glass in the carpet.

He hadn't been too hopeful, but there was ice in the freezer. Avery wrapped some up in a kitchen towel and held it to the back of his head. He grabbed another towel to protect his pillow and made his way to the bed, turned down the covers, and climbed in, propping himself up and using the headboard as a backrest. It felt amazing to be in bed, and he couldn't help but groan at how comfortable the mattress was. Though at this point he was so tired that even the vinyl monstrosity at the pod hotel from last night would have felt luxurious.

The bathroom door flew open, and Paul hurried out, toothbrush hanging out of his mouth.

"Are you okay? Did the pain get worse?"

Avery laughed, which *did* make the pain flare. Karma. "No, just my old bones happy to be lying down."

Paul looked visibly relieved to hear that. "I feel you on that," he said before returning to the bathroom.

He brought Avery's bottle of water out with him when he came back, putting it on the bedside table that separated their beds.

"I don't know what to do for head wounds," he said. "But water's good for headaches, so you should probably drink more."

"I think that's for hangovers and dehydration headaches."

"Can't hurt," Paul said, his expression serious as he studied Avery's face.

He sat on the edge of Avery's bed, hand hovering over Avery's hair until Avery nodded and leaned forward, letting Paul take the makeshift ice pack away and feel the back of his head again.

The towel insulated the ice a bit too much, but it was still cold enough to help take the edge off the soreness. Or maybe that had been the ibuprofen. Or Paul leaning over him with concerned affection. No matter what the reason, he was feeling better.

"It's fine."

Paul didn't look convinced. "What is it you're supposed to do with concussions? Wake the person up every hour?"

Avery glared at him. "I will literally kill you. The sleep deprivation is worse than the head injury. It has been *days* since I got any proper sleep, Paul. Please don't torture me."

Paul seemed to mull it over for a moment before replacing the ice pack and letting Avery take control of holding it.

"Compromise. You let me wake you up every couple hours and I won't insist we get in my car and go to the ER right now."

Avery wanted to sleep uninterrupted, but Paul was obviously concerned about him, and it was endearing. Besides, the bedside clock said it was nearly two, and they had to be up for brunch in seven hours. His plan to sleep for two days was already a wash.

"Okay," he said, smiling when Paul slumped a bit in relief. "Yes. Fine. You can wake me up every few hours and ask me who the president is. But don't ask me what day it is because I have no sodding clue anymore."

"No sodding clue?" Paul teased. "So British."

Avery was tempted to throw his towel-wrapped ice at him, but he restrained himself. Mostly because it was helping, and he didn't want to jeopardize that when he was so close to being able to sleep that he could practically taste it.

Paul stood up and turned off all the lights, leaving the room bathed in the dim glow of the moonlight.

"Those windows don't face east, so we won't get the brunt of the sunrise. Do you want me to shut the curtains anyway? Kind of creepy, I guess, that anyone could look in."

"I don't think anyone will," Avery said, scooting down and trying to find a position to sleep in where he could hold the ice pack but keep pressure off the sore spot.

Paul paused by the side of his bed, and Avery felt the mattress dip as he knelt on it.

"It would be easier to check on you if we shared a bed," Paul said after a moment. "And I could help you find a position where the ice pack stays put."

Avery's heart caught in his throat. "As much as I would love that," he said carefully, "you were pretty clear that last night was a one-night stand."

Paul hesitated, then lifted the covers and climbed in behind him. Avery turned onto his side, his head feeling much better without the weight of it resting on the ice pack. Paul moved it around until Avery sighed as he found a position that helped without making him uncomfortable.

"This isn't sex. Last night *was* a one-night stand, but this is simply being practical," Paul finally said. He spooned up behind Avery, curving around him and supporting the ice pack with his hand.

Avery didn't think there was much practical about it, but he also didn't want to turn down the chance to sleep next to Paul. It was what he'd wished for last night and hadn't gotten.

Paul scooted in closer, draping his free arm around Avery's waist. "Is this okay?"

Spooning under the pretext of it being easier to check on him was an even worse idea than the one-night stand had been, but Avery didn't have enough sense of self-preservation to turn Paul down. No matter how Paul meant it, and Avery was certain there was more to it than being easier, the result was the same. He and Paul got to share the bed for the night.

"Yes, of course."

Avery was going to do his damnedest this week to show Paul what they could have together, but he knew he had to be careful not to push too hard. If Paul realized what he was doing, he'd call everything off. Even if Avery wasn't successful in convincing him to date him when they got back to Chicago, at least they'd have this week of friendship, and Avery would know he'd done everything he could.

"Avery?" Paul whispered, his breath hot against Avery's ear.

"Yeah?"

"Who's the president?"

"Sod off," Avery groaned, grinning even as he drifted off to sleep.

THEY ALMOST slept through brunch.

True to his word, Paul had woken Avery up every two hours. But instead of quizzing him on current affairs, he'd gently shaken him awake and asked him something silly. The last question had been about beans on toast and why Brits thought they belonged on the breakfast table.

They woke to pounding on the door and the room phone ringing simultaneously. Avery sat bolt upright, groaning when his head throbbed in response. Paul was slower to respond, slinging his arm over his eyes to block out the light and grumbling.

"Rise and shine. There's only one golf cart left, and if you're not up and ready in five minutes, it's leaving without you and you'll have to walk up to the lodge," Marnie shouted through the door.

"Shit," Paul muttered, sitting up. He rubbed the sleep out of his eyes and ran a hand through his hair, making his bedhead even more pronounced.

Avery had forgotten that Paul wasn't a morning person. He'd often stayed up into the wee hours coding when they'd lived together, which hadn't been that weird for a college student. But grown adult Paul's reaction to mornings was exactly the same as college Paul's had been. It was adorable.

"Coming!" Avery yelled when Paul didn't answer her. "Five minutes, I swear!"

He rolled out of bed, and Paul flopped back down, shooting up dramatically when his head landed in the wet spot the melted ice had left on Avery's pillow.

"Goddamn. What?" Paul said, eyes finally opening.

"Ice pack," Avery said. "Don't worry. You didn't forget anything fun. Just a platonic night of bed sharing, remember? For practicality's sake."

Paul had the good grace to look chagrined at that, confirming Avery's hope that it had been a line Paul had tried to sell them both on to justify wanting to be close to Avery. That was very good news.

Marnie pounded on the door again, and that got Avery moving. His head still hurt, and he could feel a bump on the back of it when he probed, but it wasn't too bad. The mirror looked even worse than he remembered, and he made a mental note to warn the front desk about it before housekeeping came by and assumed someone had been kidnapped or murdered.

He was giving his teeth a cursory brush when Paul stepped into the bathroom, still bleary-eyed and looking adorably confused. He didn't say anything but made a beeline for Avery, holding his hand up and letting it hover behind Avery's head while he met his eyes in the mirror, silently asking for permission.

Avery leaned his head back so it hit Paul's hand, and Paul took it as the invitation it was to gently explore the bump. It didn't even hurt that much to the touch.

Avery broke away from Paul and bent over the sink to spit out the toothpaste and rinse his mouth. He stepped aside, letting Paul have the sink as he hurried out to find something to wear.

The jeans he'd traveled in were wadded up in one of the bags. He crossed the carpet, wary of any unseen shards of glass. There didn't seem to be any, but the last thing he needed was a glass splinter while Marnie was impatiently waiting outside.

He glanced at his watch, grimacing when he saw the time. Had Marnie gotten this late a start, or had she come back for them once she realized they were missing? Brunch started in ten minutes.

Avery had his jeans on by the time Paul appeared, still looking out of sorts but with less bedhead. His suitcase was still lying open on the other bed, and he dug around and came up with a long-sleeved T-shirt that he tossed to Avery.

Avery put it on without looking at it and focused on finding his shoes. He could wear the dress shoes from last night if he had to, but he'd rather not. Kevin had put his casual shoes in the closet with everything else he'd brought over the night before. Thank God it had been open when he fell into it and knocked it off track or his meager collection of clothes would have been locked behind it until maintenance could fix the door.

Marnie was waiting for them in the golf cart at the end of the sidewalk, despite it being several minutes past the five-minute warning she'd given them. She took off the moment they were both inside, and Avery had to grab on to Paul's shoulder to keep himself from flying off the bench seat.

"I forgot the flowers," Marnie said, giving the two of them a dirty look. "That's the only reason you're getting a ride. Bran noticed you were both missing and asked me to check on you when I came back to get them."

Well, that answered that question, Avery thought.

Water sloshed over the side of the bucket as Marnie took a tight corner. The lodge came into view as they rounded it, but unlike yesterday, there were dozens of people swarming over the manicured grounds surrounding the main building.

"Easter egg hunt," Marnie said, her distaste evident.

As they got closer, Avery realized most of the people darting around were children with baskets full of colorful eggs. When he looked around at their surroundings as they zipped by, he could see eggs tucked into the lower boughs of the trees and scattered around the ground.

"It looks like fun," he said, earning himself a scoff from Marnie.

"It looks like a bunch of little kids getting in my way when I'm in a hurry," she muttered.

The kids seemed to be smart enough to give the path a wide berth. Avery watched them scurrying around, exclaiming over eggs. He'd had no idea Easter was so soon. The last few weeks of a term were always stressful, and he'd been so preoccupied with packing for the transatlantic move that the holiday hadn't even registered.

His family used to have big dinners on all the holidays. They probably still did, he realized. He just hadn't been there to notice. Next Easter he'd have a nibling. Bran and Ellie would likely pop out a kid soon too. Everything was changing.

Avery missed whatever Paul had said to him and turned to him with a guilty expression. Paul's look morphed into concern.

"I asked if you had a headache," he repeated.

"Oh. No. Well, yes. I should have grabbed some more of your paracetamol. But I'll be fine."

"Ibuprofen," Paul corrected him. "And I grabbed the bottle. You can take some once we get you something to drink."

Paul was good at being an adult. Avery doubted *he* was surprised that it was almost Easter.

"You're a lifesaver, thanks."

"Too much to drink last night?" Marnie asked, grinning suggestively.

He looked at Paul, hesitant to answer. It's not like it was something that needed to be kept secret. He'd had an accident, and he was fine. But it felt private, like something to keep between them. Paul seemed to have no opinion, because he shrugged his shoulders, leaving Avery to answer.

He went with obfuscation. When in doubt, be vague.

"I didn't need that last shot," he said. She didn't need to know that he'd only had one, shared with his brother at Bran's insistence before he and Paul had gone off to decorate the honeymoon cabin.

He nearly slid off the seat again when Marnie screeched to a stop in the hotel's circle drive. Paul grabbed the bucket of flowers, and the three of them hurried inside to the restaurant. Marnie had already found vases for the table. Empty water pitchers from the looks of them, but they'd do. No one was seated yet, which was a good sign. Or maybe a bad sign, depending on whether Ellie and Bran had waited to start until they'd gotten there with the flowers.

"They're having mimosas in the garden," Marnie explained when Avery craned his neck to see if he could find them. "I told Ellie we'd come out and get them once the room was ready."

Marnie had already done most of the work to decorate the private dining room. Paper lanterns in the wedding colors hung from the ceiling, with a garland of felt pennants that spelled out Congratulations.

The table was already set for a family-style brunch for thirty-some people. It would only be family and the bridal party today, the last wedding hurrah before everyone else left and the ski vacation celebration with some of the bridal party would begin.

Avery didn't know the faintest thing about skiing. But the itinerary Paul had sent him weeks ago had a lot of other things, like golfing, hiking, and a craft-beer crawl. He planned to stay back while they were skiing to finish his marking for the term and get his grades submitted. Once that was done, he needed to get serious about his job search. Plenty to do that didn't involve strapping sticks to his feet and hurtling down a mountain.

"Why don't you go get everyone?" Paul said to him. "I'll go tell the servers we're ready to start the brunch."

Avery would rather stay here and figure out if Paul was acting weird because he regretted last night or because he wanted more nights like last night, but he followed instructions and stepped into the lobby. The sign said the gardens were out the back doors, so he took a moment to stop at the front desk and explain about his accident and ask to have the door replaced. The clerk fussed over him and fell over herself apologizing, which only made him feel guiltier. It hadn't been the hotel's fault—he'd been the idiot who'd fallen over when Paul walked in.

A fresh wave of mortification hit him as he dealt with the clerk's concern and then made his way outside. He'd been so caught up in making sure he wasn't bleeding and then getting into bed with Paul last night that he hadn't had a moment to think about what had happened. He'd fallen over when he'd seen Paul. That was like the opposite of having game.

Though it *had* gotten Paul into his bed, so maybe Avery's seduction skills weren't so bad after all.

Ellie broke away midconversation when she saw him and gleefully waved him over.

"So how was last night?" she asked, giving him a knowing smirk.

"Aren't I supposed to be asking you that, Mrs. Laniston? You're the newlywed, after all."

She blushed and took a sip of her mimosa. "We were exhausted when we got back to the cabin. Thank you for the cheese board, though. The reception flew by so quickly that I didn't have a chance to eat."

Avery gave himself a mental pat on the back for the gift and the change of subject.

"Paul sent me to tell you brunch is ready," he said before she could redirect the conversation to him and Paul.

The look she gave him told Avery she knew exactly what he'd done, but she seemed to let it go. For now, at least. He had no doubt she'd ask again later. Likely at an even more inopportune time. But that was a problem for future Avery.

Ellie helped him gather everyone and herd them back to the private dining space. He was glad Marnie'd had the foresight to book the room. The restaurant had been deserted when he'd first come in, but now it was teeming with families. The Easter egg hunt must have ended.

Avery was one of the last to come to the table, and he was pleased to see that the only open seat was between Paul and Avery's mother. They were talking about plants when Avery slid into the seat between them. His mother was an avid gardener, but he'd never known Paul to have a green thumb or any interest in cultivating one.

"I don't want to make the same mistake again this year," Paul said. "That late frost in May nearly killed my hibiscus. I'm not putting her out until June this summer."

"That may be a little overkill," his mom said. "And just because we had a late frost last year doesn't mean we will this year. May should be perfectly fine to put it back outside. It needs the sunshine or it won't bud out."

Paul cast a brief glance at Avery. "Weather follows patterns like everything else does. Burn me once, shame on you. But burn me twice, shame on me. I'm not going to risk it."

His mother sighed. "At least let me mix up a fertilizer blend for you. Your soil isn't acidic enough."

Leaving her garden had been the hardest thing about downsizing for his mother. He hadn't realized she'd started back-seat plant mothering other peoples' plants. Especially not Paul's.

Paul seemed used to it, so it must happen fairly often. "I'd appreciate it. The African violet in the kitchen needs some attention too. And I think it's time to repot the ficus in the entryway."

His mother beamed. "I'll call you to see when you have a free day, sweetheart."

His mom and Paul hung out? That hadn't been in any of Bran's updates. But then again, neither had Paul's horticulture hobby. There was a lot he was going to have to relearn about Paul.

Bran stood up and started thanking everyone for coming, and everyone quieted down and turned to watch him.

Paul reached into his breast pocket and pulled out two ibuprofen, which Avery tossed back with a swig of his orange juice. He'd tried to be discreet, but his mother leaned over, concern all over her face.

"Is something wrong?"

Avery had operated on a need-to-know basis with his parents since his teenage years, and this wasn't the time to stop. He did *not* want to explain his head injury to his mother, both because she'd almost certainly overreact and because he didn't want to admit how it happened.

"Just woke up with a bit of a headache this morning. Paul gave me some headache tablets."

His mother brought her hand up and rested it against his forehead, like she had when he was a kid.

"You aren't warm. Could you have picked up a bug on the plane?"

"It's probably jet lag and the late night yesterday. I'm fine, Mom."

She didn't look convinced, but Bran was still speaking, so she couldn't pursue it. She and his dad had a late-afternoon flight back to Chicago, so with any luck she'd either forget or run out of time to interrogate him before they had to leave.

The smell of bacon from the buffet the servers were setting up in the room made his stomach grumble, and Paul nudged him with his knee and grinned.

"Hoping they have beans on toast?" he mouthed.

Avery grinned. In truth, he hated beans on toast. And marmalade. And black pudding, grilled tomatoes, and mushrooms. Most of the components of a full English breakfast put him off the idea of breakfast altogether. But he wasn't going to let Paul know that. He seemed to enjoy teasing Avery about it, and Avery enjoyed being teased. He didn't want this easy camaraderie with Paul to stop, and he liked having an inside joke, even if it was at his expense. Hell, especially if it was. That meant Paul was thinking about him, and that meant he had a chance.

When Bran had finished talking and everyone filed through the buffet, Avery filled his plate with pancakes and a pile of crispy bacon. That was another thing the Brits did differently. They served fattier, floppy bacon that was wholly unappetizing to his American palate. He may have picked up some of the accent, but he hadn't picked up the traditional British taste in food. He found lamb gamey, hated popovers, and didn't like the textures of bangers and mash together.

"How do you not have scurvy?" Paul asked when he sat his plate down next to Avery's.

Avery pointed at him with a piece of bacon, inwardly rejoicing that it was crispy enough to stand up on its own. "How do you know I don't?"

"You have all your teeth, for one."

"That is a harmful British stereotype."

Paul rolled his eyes. "It's a symptom of scurvy."

Huh. Avery hadn't known that. Unsurprisingly, scurvy wasn't something that came up often in his life.

"I'm drinking orange juice," he offered, toasting Paul with the glass once he'd polished off the strip of bacon he'd been holding.

"So you still eat like a twelve-year-old boy, I see."

He didn't. If he was home, he'd be paying for this stack of pancakes with time in the gym or a long run. But he didn't want to admit to Paul that his metabolism had slowed, so he didn't answer. He cut himself a chunk of pancake instead and made a show of mopping up as much syrup as it could hold before popping it into his mouth.

"Gross," Paul said, wrinkling his nose. "Way too much sugar this early in the morning."

So Paul had become a health nut as well as a gardener. Interesting.

"Is there an appropriate time of day for that much sugar?" he asked, genuinely curious.

Paul thought about it for a moment. "Late afternoon. That's when I crave sweet stuff."

Avery filed that knowledge away for future reference. It could be useful to have a list of Paul's likes and dislikes in case he succeeded in his campaign to get Paul to date him.

"What are your plans for the rest of the day?" he asked, since the trip itinerary had left this afternoon blank so the newlyweds could have some unscheduled time to themselves before their group dinner tonight.

"I need to return the tuxes and get the centerpieces and other assorted crap shipped back to Chicago." Paul leaned over Avery to get his mom's attention. "Joan, is it still okay if I have those shipped to your condo? I can pick them up when I fly back. Bran's condo charges to keep boxes in the office, and having them sit on my porch until I'm home would probably go badly."

"Of course, sweetheart. But you don't need to stop by. I can drop them off at Bran's when I water the plants. I meant to ask if you wanted me to take care of yours while you're gone. Did you want me to go by? I could fertilize the hibiscus and take a look at the African violet while I'm there."

Paul smiled. "If you don't mind, that would be amazing. I watered everything before I left, but I have a flat of seedlings I'm starting inside for the garden, and they dry out so quickly that I'm afraid they'll die before I get back. I should have waited to start them, but I didn't even think about how long I'd be gone."

"Oh, I'll definitely go by, then. Those poor things won't last. And I haven't seen the raised beds in the back yet, either. I've been wanting to see what you did with them since you told me about them at Christmas."

"It'll be an interesting experiment. You said yours lengthened your growing season, so I wanted to try. Plus the soil in my backyard was all clay."

Avery felt like he was having an out-of-body experience listening to Paul and his mother banter back and forth about gardening. They talked a bit more about the raised beds—including his aunt Joyce chiming in that he should invest in some worms for them—how was that even a thing?—before his mom got pulled into a conversation about his sister's upcoming baby shower.

"I didn't know you were that into plants," Avery said when he had Paul's sole attention again. "Raised garden beds? Seedlings?"

Paul shrugged. "The house I bought had been pretty recently renovated, but the people had run out of money to do the landscaping. It was a mess. Mounds of dirt from the foundation repairs they did, more weeds than grass in the back, and the front was totally overgrown to the point I couldn't tell what was junk and what was worth saving. Your mom spent a ton of time helping me prune things and plant flowers out front, and she suggested I turn the back into garden space. I enjoy being outside, so it's a good project for me. I built a back deck last year, and then in the fall I put in the raised beds. I want to lay some stone and make a fire pit this summer."

Seeing Paul light up talking about his hobby made Avery want to learn even more about it. The thought of Paul building a deck or laying out a fire pit was incredibly sexy. Avery doubted the reality lived up to his mental image, but he'd love to find out.

Just knowing Paul, who was so cerebral and lived in his own head so much, was capable of manual labor was a huge turn-on.

"I like making something with my own hands," Paul said defensively, apparently mistaking Avery's silence for judgment.

"You're a software designer, Paul. You make things out of nothing with your hands for a living," Avery teased. "I think it's great. A much more productive hobby than diamond painting or stamp collecting."

Paul laughed. "You don't collect stamps."

"No, I do not. Nor do I diamond paint."

"I could see it, though," Paul said, his smile returning. "You bent over one of those canvases, bedazzling the hell out of it."

"I don't know what bedazzling is, and I think I'm happy to keep it that way."

"I've heard diamond painting is really relaxing. It's okay to admit you have a hobby, Avery."

Avery had actually tried it a few years ago during a particularly stressful term. One of his teaching assistants suggested it as a way to zone out and relax. He'd gotten too focused on finding the perfect technique for it to actually be fun. It had added to his stress rather than take any away. He'd never even finished the first project.

"I have been sorely lacking in hobbies. Being an associate professor doesn't leave a lot of free time, not if you want to be tenure track."

"Publish or perish—that's what it's called, right?"

Avery laughed. "In terms of tenure, yeah. It's a rat race, and I'm tired of running in it. My goal is to find a position where I can put down some roots. I'll have to keep up with the research and publishing at this pace until I can prove myself and get tenure, and after that I can slow down a bit and consider getting some hobbies."

"That sounds exhausting. I prefer programming. If you're good at your job, you have stability. No tenure-track race."

Paul *was* good at his job. Bran bragged about him all the time, including telling him about conferences Paul spoke at and big projects he headed up. They were both still working for the company they'd interned for in college. If this was academics, Paul would be a full professor. A grown-up, just like Avery wanted to be.

Bran clinked a spoon against his mimosa glass, stopping all the chatter at the table. Avery was surprised to see that quite a few people had already left. He'd been so caught up in his conversation with Paul that he hadn't noticed.

"Thank you all for having brunch with us this morning. It means so much to both of us that you could all be here for our wedding, and we can't express how much we appreciate you making the trip here to Lake Tahoe. I know it was a haul for most of you, but we are so happy that we were able to share one of our favorite places with you. Ellie and I are going to have some coffee in the gardens if you'd like to catch up some more, and if we don't see those of you who are leaving before you go, have a safe flight, and we love you."

The servers were all hovering along the wall, and Avery could see they were impatient to move the group along so they could clear the table. They'd been there for nearly two hours, which definitely pushed the bounds of dining etiquette.

"I'm going to see what Ellie wants to do with these flowers," Paul said. "Why don't you walk your parents out? I'm sure they want to have some time with you before they leave."

Avery couldn't tell if Paul was being thoughtful or if he was getting rid of Avery. Though the answer could be both. Either way, he was right. Avery needed to go out to the garden with Bran and Ellie so he could say his goodbyes to his parents and the rest of the family. He hadn't seen most of their extended family since he left for Europe, so there was little chance his mother would let him escape without making the rounds.

"Sounds good. I'll see you back at the cabin after?"

Please, he added silently. Paul hadn't promised more than taking care of him last night. He might decide to switch cabins with one of the other groomsmen now.

Paul hesitated but nodded. "Sure. I'll see you later."

It was hardly a resounding endorsement of rooming together, but it hadn't been a flat-out rejection of it, either. Avery decided to take the win. He'd just have to convince Paul that the two of them sharing the cabin was a good idea.

Chapter NINE

PAUL WOULD rather drink battery acid than have one more cup of coffee, but if he wasn't drinking coffee then he had no excuse to be lingering in the garden with Bran and Ellie and the few guests who were still chatting with them after the wedding brunch.

He'd hung back around the edges until he'd seen Avery disappear with Bob and Joan. Paul needed to get his head on straight before going back to their cabin. He didn't want to do anything he'd regret, but the problem was he didn't know which course of action that was.

Would he regret staying with Avery this week and inevitably ending up sleeping with him again? Paul had used the situation last night to indulge himself, not because he wanted to take advantage of Avery but because it had been a convenient excuse to skip past his own defenses. He'd also known when he'd climbed into bed with Avery that nothing sexual was going to happen. He wouldn't take advantage of him like that, and Avery had been in no shape for sex anyway.

But tonight? That would be a whole different story. Paul could lie to himself and say they'd stick to separate beds if they were rooming together, but he knew that wasn't true. He simply didn't have the willpower where Avery was concerned.

So that meant he had to decide what he'd regret more—having a no-strings-attached affair with Avery for the week or *not* having a no-strings-attached affair with Avery for the week.

It was a hard one, because he very much wanted to be in Avery's bed for real. But he wouldn't be able to separate himself emotionally from it. Paul knew that. If he was being honest with himself, which he usually was but didn't want to be right now, he'd admit that the one-night stand in Dallas had been a total failure because it had catapulted him off the deep end back into a pool of unresolved feelings for Avery. He hadn't been as successful at paving it over as he'd thought.

So really, his choices were heartbreak now or heartbreak later.

Usually Paul used spreadsheets to help him make difficult decisions, but this wasn't as cut and dried as a cost-benefit analysis of what house to buy.

He also couldn't talk it out with Bran the way he normally would. He could hardly ask Bran to be an impartial arbitrator for a situation that involved his brother, especially when he'd done everything he could to push the two of them together since they'd arrived.

Orchestrating the meet-up at the airport, the boutonniere, the dance, switching up the room assignments so they had to spend the night together—Bran and Ellie were not being subtle here.

Bran had been the one to help pick up the pieces after Avery left, so he knew exactly how hurt Paul had been, even though they'd never outright talked about the details. Bran was much better at things like this than Paul was. It was past time for Paul to stop leaning on him so much. Bran had Ellie now, and they didn't need Paul as an emotionally stunted third wheel.

If Bran thought Paul should give Avery another chance, it meant Avery had grown up, at least a little bit. Or maybe it meant he thought Paul had grown up enough to handle a casual relationship with Avery.

Paul was clueless as to how he'd weigh that in a spreadsheet.

He looked up as Ellie joined him, slipping next to him on the oversized hanging rattan chair he'd been dangling in for the past twenty minutes.

"You're going to have to face him eventually, you know," she said, patting him on the knee. "Especially because the tuxes have to be back at the rental shop by three, so you have to go get his."

Paul laughed. "My relationship drama isn't worth losing the deposit?"

"I don't think Greg would think so, no," she said, grinning. Greg had complained bitterly about the cost of the trip for months, so Paul didn't doubt that he'd blow a gasket to be charged a penny more than he'd agreed to.

It was a good catalyst to get him out of the chair. He had errands to run, which would keep him out of the cabin for another hour or two. He could punt this emotional crisis down the road a bit, which sounded like a fabulous idea to him.

"Before you dash off, you should know that Greg and Kevin's cabin had a water heater leak and they moved up to the lodge because it's going to take a couple days to fix it. So if you were planning to switch with one of them, it might be a hard sell. The resort comped their room, so they're not going to want to give that up."

Was Ellie scheming enough to have orchestrated a leaking water heater? Paul studied her for a moment but dismissed it as paranoid. She and Bran were opportunistic meddlers, but they wouldn't have wrecked hotel property to keep him and Avery together.

That left switching with Marnie or Jill, the only two bridesmaids who were staying for the week. Paul would rather have his heart broken four times than have that conversation with Marnie, so that made the decision for him. He'd be rooming with Avery.

Given how much Avery had pursued him over the last two days, it was a pretty sure bet he would be on board with keeping the living arrangements the way they were. He'd likely also be a wholehearted plus in the casual sex column. Paul had no hesitation about where he fell on that—if they were sharing a room, he hoped they'd also be sharing a bed.

But they'd need to have a conversation first. A real one, more in-depth than the one-night stand agreement he'd insisted on in Dallas.

"What is the outcome you're hoping for here?" he asked her. "Because you and Bran have pulled every string you could to get Avery and me together this week."

Ellie gave him a hard look. "You don't think I made the water heater break, do you? I mean, really? I don't even know how someone would go about doing that."

"No, but you *did* scheme to get Avery and me into the same cabin. I just want to know what your angle is."

She frowned. "I don't have an angle."

That was a riot. Ellie always had an angle. She had good intentions, but she was one of the nosiest busybodies he knew—and he had Chicago's premier gay matchmaker on his softball team, so that was saying a lot. Ellie was always in her friends' business. She did it with love, but she was not subtle.

"Then why did Avery show up in my cabin last night when I specifically made the reservation for me and Kevin?"

She had the good grace to shift her gaze away.

"And the flowers? And the dance? You could convince me that setting me up to have dinner with him at the airport was Bran's idea, but not any of the other shenanigans. He's not that sneaky."

Bran was an open book. He didn't have a conniving bone in his body. Opposites really did attract, apparently. Ellie was totally the sneaky yin to his honest yang.

"He agrees it's a good idea, though," she said defensively.

"He agrees *what* is a good idea? Because Avery and I are not together. We're two grown men who are attracted to each other and will probably spend the week screwing each other's brains out—"

"God!" She cut him off, throwing her hands up over her ears. "I don't want to hear that about you and my brother-in-law!"

Paul pried her hands away from her ears and held on to them, giving them a squeeze before he released her. "What did you expect? That Avery and I would discuss trickle-down economics over room service tea? You put us in a secluded cabin together, Ellie."

"I know that," she said. "But we hoped you two would hit it off and rekindle your romance now that Avery is moving back to the US. If you two are together, maybe he'll decide to stay in Chicago."

Paul sighed. This was what he'd feared would happen. He had to manage expectations here—Ellie and Bran's, his own, and Avery's.

"That's not going to happen, El," he said gently. "Avery isn't a settling down kind of guy. He won't stay in Chicago for me. Or you guys. I'm sorry, but he's always had itchy feet, and he's going to let them take him to whatever great teaching opportunity presents itself next."

"That's a really cynical view."

It was, but it was also an honest view. "Whatever happens between me and Avery this week is just that—between us. And it'll be no-strings-attached fun, okay? So don't get your hopes up, or Bran's."

"He wants to have you as a brother," she said, but from her tone he could tell his message had been received. There would be no more meddling from Bran and Ellie.

Paul gave her a hug. "He already does. I think of Bran as family, which means you're family too."

She hugged him back. "We only want you to be happy."

Fending off Ellie's expectations had helped him solidify what he wanted from the week. Paul was going to do something he rarely did—throw caution to the wind and do what felt good, regardless of what his spreadsheet tally told him was the best course of action.

"I am happy. I'll see you at dinner."

He left Ellie to explain the situation to Bran, which was for the best because Paul didn't want to talk to his best friend about how he was going to spend the week thoroughly enjoying Avery's sexy body and the ridiculous accent that had kind of grown on Paul. He wondered if Avery would stick around in the US long enough to lose it and adopt his old American accent again.

Avery was dozing in a chair by the window when Paul got back to the cabin, his laptop and a file of papers in his lap. He looked every bit the absentminded professor that he was, and it was strangely endearing.

Paul rescued the laptop and put it on the table, leaving the papers because there wasn't an easy way to gather them up without waking Avery. No doubt he was still sleeping off his jet lag, and Paul didn't want to disturb him. Especially because he had plans to keep Avery up all night tonight if their talk about expectations went well.

The closet door had already been fixed, to his surprise. He slid it open and retrieved Avery's tux, slipping back out of the room with both suit bags without waking Avery.

Marnie had Bran's, and she offered to ride into town with Paul and help him take the tuxes back and mail the boxes. He put her in charge of finding Greg and Kevin's room to get theirs while he retrieved the boxes from the hotel's storage room.

"What did you say to Ellie in the garden?" she asked once they were in the rental headed toward town. "She looked like you kicked her puppy."

"For starters, they don't have a puppy yet because I told them I wouldn't dog sit during their honeymoon, so they had to wait until they got back. And secondly, none of your business."

Marnie laughed. "I told her not to mess with you and Avery. That man has bad idea written all over him."

Paul bristled at that but shrugged in response. He felt defensive of Avery even though Marnie had read him right. Avery *was* a bad idea. He was Paul's bad idea, though, and Paul didn't like hearing anyone else highlight Avery's problems.

"That's not going to stop you, though, is it?" she asked, rolling her eyes when Paul glared at her. "Your funeral. He's pretty to look at, but he's the kind of guy you window-shop for, not buy. He's not relationship material."

Paul didn't know how much Marnie knew about his history with Avery, but Ellie and her sister were very close, so he bet she had the gist of it. And he couldn't argue with her. She wasn't wrong.

Maybe she could be his spreadsheet.

"No one's talking about a relationship," he said. "I told Ellie that Avery and I are two consenting adults, and if we want to have a vacation fling, then we will. It's a temporary thing. He's fun to flirt with, and the sex is great. He'll be gone by the end of the summer at the latest. I'm not pining for him or starting a wedding trousseau. It's only for this week, and it's just physical. No feelings involved."

Marnie turned in her seat to study him silently for a moment. "I think you believe that. I don't think it's true, but I think *you* think it's true. Go for it. As long as you're willing to risk getting your feelings hurt when he cuts and runs, then what's the harm?"

"Well, as long as we have your approval," Paul said sarcastically.

"You need an antiwingman," she said, ignoring his comment. "Someone to remind you of what you really want. I've been told I'm great at killing a vibe."

Paul's jaw dropped at her bluntness. She laughed. "We all are born with some innate skills, and cutting through bullshit is mine. Ellie loves you, and you're growing on me, so I don't want to see you hurt. So if you want an antiwingman, I'm your girl."

It was actually a great idea. "An antiwingman. All right."

She grinned. "I'm going to third wheel you so hard! Okay, drop me off at the FedEx here on the corner and I'll get the boxes mailed while you return the tuxes. That way we'll have time to hit up the wine shop down the street."

Marnie's take-no-prisoners approach to life was jarring and often unpleasant, but she got shit done, and that made her okay in his book. He was growing to like her.

"There's a chocolate shop around here too," he said, earning himself a high-five from her after she unclipped her seat belt. "This shouldn't take long. I'll park near the wine shop and walk back this way if I don't see you down there."

She shook her head. "I'm fine. It's not like I'll have the boxes to carry. You should pop into the little shop next door to the tux place. Ellie and I were in there to make a present for Bran before her bachelorette. If you're going to have a week of debauchery then you'll need supplies."

He threw on his hazards and helped her carry the boxes into the store, but thankfully she didn't continue the conversation. Paul could imagine what kind of store she was talking about. She wasn't wrong, though. He hadn't planned for this, so stopping for condoms and lube would be a good idea.

Of course, that assumed Avery was going to take him up on his offer of commitment-free sexcapades. The wine store was four blocks down from the tux place, so he parked near that and gathered up the tuxes to walk down to the shop. The little sex store next door to it was the most tasteful and inconspicuous one he'd ever seen. If Marnie hadn't told him what it was, he'd have assumed it was another tourist-trap boutique like the dozens that lined the main thoroughfare.

Once he'd rid himself of the tuxes—and secured a receipt for Greg because he was so paranoid about losing his deposit—Paul popped into the store next door. Outside it looked quaint and unassuming, but once he was inside the door, he did a double take. This wasn't just a sex shop, it was a boudoir photo studio. Paul's cheeks filled with heat as he realized why Ellie had likely been here.

He needed to stop that line of thought right now or he wouldn't need to buy condoms. Paul now had a better appreciation of why Ellie had been so disgusted when he talked about him and Avery having sex.

"Can I help you? Are you looking to book a session, or are you here to shop for someone special?"

Paul wasn't uptight about sex, but he wasn't sure how to respond to that question. The answer was neither.

"I need some condoms," he said, hoping she'd point him to them and leave him be.

No such luck. "Of course! Follow me. We have a pretty big selection, including our biggest seller here, Sustain."

He must have grimaced at that or something, because the clerk fell all over herself apologizing.

"I'm so sorry. I didn't mean—it's, like, named after sustainability? It wasn't a commentary on you needing help in that area. Tahoe has a big ecofriendly culture, and a lot of our customers prefer brands that are non-GMO, vegan, and fair-trade certified like Sustain is."

Paul had never once wondered if his condoms were non-GMO or had ethically sourced latex. He didn't intend to start now either.

"I just need some basic condoms and some lube," he said, pulling the first box that looked familiar off the shelf.

"I recommend this one," she said, handing him a green squeeze bottle. "It's water based and certified organic. It has aloe in it."

That sounded disgusting, but it would do the job.

"Is there anything else I can help you with? Do you need any toys?"

Paul saw Marnie walk by the front window, cringing inside as he prayed she wouldn't stop. The only thing that could make this more awkward or unfortunate would be her chiming in.

She continued on toward the wine store, to his relief.

"Just these," he said, waving them.

"I'll check you out up here, then." The clerk led him to the front and rang him up, and Paul left the shop with most of his dignity restored.

Marnie already had three bottles in her hands when he joined her in the wine shop.

"Mission accomplished?" she asked, nodding toward the bag he carried.

Paul stuck it under his arm, feeling like a sixteen-year-old getting caught in the condom aisle at the drugstore. Marnie shoved the bottles she'd been carrying into his arms and grabbed four more.

"Yes. Planning a party?"

There were only eight of them. That many bottles of wine seemed excessive.

"The shop ships for a fee. We did a wine tasting here for Ellie's bachelorette, and I liked this local label."

She put the four she was carrying into a box on the counter next to the cash register, and he followed suit.

"We can get a few more bottles for the cabins if you think everyone would enjoy them."

"I think if we're hanging out drinking, we'll be doing it in the lodge lounge or at a bar."

He had no desire to sit around drinking in the cabins, and he didn't think Bran and Ellie would either. They were here to go out and have fun, after all. If they wanted to spend their time staying in and drinking they could have done that in Chicago.

"Fair point."

She called over the clerk to pay, and Paul wandered around the shop while she took care of setting up the mailing. Like everything else he'd seen in Tahoe, it was tastefully decorated and quaint. Not his speed, but Tahoe wasn't the type of place he'd vacation on his own. Paul was more a beach or big city kind of guy.

He stepped outside, mindful to stay within sight of the shop's front windows so Marnie could see where he went. She followed him out a minute or two later, and he was relieved to see that she had decided against buying wine to share here. Selfishly, he wanted cabin time to be alone time. He had precious little time left with Avery as it was—late-night drinking sessions would waste even more of it.

"Did you want to stop in at that chocolate shop?"

He did. Paul had planned to buy some to send to his mom for her upcoming birthday, and if Avery still had the same sweet tooth he'd had when they'd been dating then having some to grease the way for the uncomfortable conversation they were going to have would help. Avery had bristled at the one-night stand idea in Dallas, and while Paul was confident he'd succeed in negotiating an extension of that, chocolate wouldn't hurt.

Marnie came back to the lodge with him afterward, but she had an appointment at the spa, so she didn't come back to the cabins with him. Her absence gave him too much time with his own thoughts. He was second-guessing what the right course was with Avery for the millionth time, and the indecisiveness was driving him crazy.

Paul was the type to stick to his decisions without waffling after he made them, but he was used to dealing in facts, not emotions. He could very well ruin the rest of the vacation if he propositioned Avery and Avery turned him down. That would make everything awkward, and Bran and Ellie would blame him for causing drama on their prehoneymoon.

He'd almost talked himself out of it by the time he parked the golf cart in the now-familiar lot and walked down the path to his cabin. His prepared greeting died on his lips when he opened the door to an empty room. Avery was nowhere to be seen.

Paul walked in, relieved to see that Avery's things were still in the room. So he hadn't *left*; he just wasn't there.

That answered one question at least. Paul had wondered if he truly liked Avery or if it was a proximity thing, but his panic at thinking he'd left was a good indicator that he actually did like him and wanted to spend time with him.

It was almost like having the spreadsheet. There was nothing like having a choice taken away from you to reveal which choice you wanted.

He tossed the bag from the sex shop and the box of chocolates he'd bought for Avery on the bed and walked to the window that faced out into the forest. Avery was outside in a hammock on the small porch, reading a book.

Paul backtracked through the cabin and joined Avery outside. "Did you get your grading done?"

Avery put his book down and tucked his hands under his head like a pillow. "Not by a long shot. But there are only so many essays about noncompetitive market structure one can read before they all blend together. Did you do everything you needed to do in town?"

Paul shifted a guilty gaze at the cabin, thinking about the condoms and lube on the bed. "Yeah. Tuxes are returned, and Marnie helped get the boxes sent back to Chicago."

"So your last official best-man duty is done, then?"

"I suppose so."

Avery rolled to his side, the hammock swaying precariously as he moved. He patted the space he'd made. "Then let the vacation begin. Come lie with me."

Paul nearly tipped both of them out more than once before they settled in the hammock. The only way for both of them to fit was to lie on their sides facing each other, which was an uncomfortably intimate position to be in with someone who might be about to turn down your offer of casual sex.

But there was no time like the present. Especially because they were due at the lodge to have dinner with the group in about an hour. Paul didn't want this hanging over his head.

He decided to dive right in.

"Sleeping together last night, that was nice," he said. "It's something I'd like to do the rest of the time we're here."

Avery lifted a single brow. "Sleeping together or *sleeping together*? Because last night I was possibly concussed and we were both exhausted, so nothing but sleep was going to happen. But if we share a bed now, I'm going to want more than sleep, Paul."

Paul appreciated the bluntness.

"I'm on board for sex. And I'd be lying if I said I didn't enjoy all the flirting. It's been fun. But that's all I'm looking for, Avery. A bit of fun."

Avery nodded. "So you're looking for a similar arrangement to the one we had in Dallas?"

"Yes. But I won't freak out and sneak off in the middle of the night this time," Paul said, and Avery chuckled. "But this thing between us has an expiration date, okay? I'm not expecting anything from you, and after this week we go our separate ways as friends. No obligations, no strings. What do you think?"

"I think the same thing I thought in Dallas. A one-night stand was a bad idea, and letting it turn into a week of meaningless sex that we can pretend we never had is a worse one. But I want you, and I understand your rules. I don't think keeping feelings out of it is possible for us, but I'm in."

That wasn't a ringing endorsement of the plan, but Avery was a grown-up, and he was in charge of his own feelings and actions. Paul could only speak for himself, and he intended to keep it light and casual. A fool's errand, maybe. But he'd deal with the emotional fallout from it if there was any. This was his chance to stop wondering what life with Avery would have been like if they'd stayed together. It was likely that sexual chemistry was all they'd have. Both of them had grown up since college, had different interests and responsibilities. They *were* virtual strangers, as adults at least. And Paul could have a vacation fling with a stranger without catching feelings. There was precedent for that. It was the reason he preferred beach vacations—easier to find casual sex.

"Okay. In that case, I have condoms and lube in the room."

Avery laughed and swatted at him. "We have dinner plans."

"I didn't mean right now," Paul said, ending their tussle by grabbing Avery's hands and rolling on top of him. The hammock swayed dangerously but didn't tip.

"On second thought, we might have time for a quickie," Avery said, wiggling under Paul's weight suggestively.

Paul tried to lift himself up but failed. The hammock had too much give, and all he accomplished was setting it swinging again.

"Definitely not a quickie," he answered, earning a groan of disappointment from Avery. "There's a lot I didn't get to do to you in Dallas, and I intend to rectify that tonight. But it all requires a bed and nudity, which we do not have time for right now."

He tried again to push into a sitting position but couldn't. "Though we may be stuck here until someone comes looking for us."

Avery snickered and held his hands out. "Push against me."

Paul lined his palms up with Avery's and pushed, disappointed the move worked. He could think of worse things than being stuck in a hammock with Avery for hours.

He put a leg down on the patio to steady the hammock before it dumped them both, and with more than a little effort, they both climbed out of their fabric trap. Paul made a mental note that hammock sex fell into the category of things that sounded more appealing than they were.

"I should grab a shower before dinner," Avery said. He stretched his arms over his head, revealing a tantalizing strip of belly as they walked inside. "Wanna join me?"

He did. But he'd meant it when he'd said he wanted to take his time with Avery and have him splayed out on the bed. The cabin's small shower wouldn't get it done, and Paul wanted more than a quick grope.

"No time," he reminded Avery.

"With you naked in the shower with me, I'd need ten minutes, tops," Avery joked.

Paul almost said no, but then he reconsidered. Ten minutes wasn't enough time to do the things he'd been fantasizing about doing to Avery for years, but it would be more than enough time for a shower quickie with a stranger.

He needed to reframe how he thought about Avery if he was going to survive this fling with his heart intact.

"I think we have enough time to make it twenty," he said, letting Avery pull him into the bathroom.

Chapter TEN

"No, THAT'S okay. I appreciate you taking my call. I'll talk to you soon."

Avery tossed his phone on the bed and scowled at it. He'd been reaching out to everyone he knew in economics departments around the country, and he'd yet to find an opening. Most schools already had a candidate in mind to fill open positions before they were even listed, so it was a game of who you knew and how good your network was. Unfortunately, his US network was a damn sight weaker than his European one. He'd done his undergraduate and masters at Northwestern, and most of the professors he'd had during his tenure there had retired. He knew plenty of professors from the lecture and publishing circuit, but they'd all been coming up dry on leads on positions that might open up.

It didn't help that the term was almost over. Universities in the US were in session later into the spring than their European counterparts, but professors who were retiring or moving on after the term would have already announced that months ago. Once again, his impulsiveness was biting him in the arse.

Paul walked in before Avery could get too deep into the self-loathing routine he'd settled into over the last two days.

"You look like you belong on the cover of a ski magazine," Avery said, taking a moment to admire the picture Paul made standing in the doorway in his ski suit, cheeks rosy not from the snow but from being overheated on the drive back. The weather was crazy here.

"It was gorgeous out there this morning. You should have come."

They'd fallen into an easy routine. This late in the season the snow was fickle, so most of the runs had already closed. Mount Rose was the best bet for good snow this time of year, since it was the highest elevation in Tahoe. It was also a good half-hour drive from their resort. Since Avery didn't ski, he stayed back while the rest of the group made the trek. Everyone seemed to prefer early morning skis before the sun heated the runs too much, which worked in his favor. Otherwise he'd have to choose between being alone all day in the cabin or renting equipment and learning to ski.

"The views from here are every bit as gorgeous, but they don't involve me falling on my ass," Avery said, leering at Paul as he peeled his form-fitting snowsuit off.

"We wouldn't want to risk the ass." Paul knelt on the bed where Avery was sitting and gave him a lazy, filthy kiss before standing back up to finish stripping out of his gear. "We're going to grab lunch in town before the brewery tour. Are you at a stopping point?"

Paul had been great about giving him space to finish his grading and work on his job search. Almost too great. No matter how Avery tried to connect, Paul remained distant. The sex was amazing and the flirting was fun, but Paul was careful to keep everything superficial. No discussions about their past or either of their futures, including keeping his distance when Avery talked with Bran about his job search.

It was frustrating, but Avery had known what he was signing up for. Paul's discipline in keeping things light would be admirable if it wasn't flying in the face of what Avery wanted to accomplish with their week together.

At least they'd confirmed that they were still sexually compatible. If anything, sex with Paul was better than it had been in college. They might not have the stamina to go at it all night like they used to, but orgasms now were more about quality than quantity, and they had the quality part down fine.

"Yeah, I've hit a wall, actually. Just talked to my last lead, and he hadn't heard of any prospective openings."

Paul made a sympathetic noise and wandered into the bathroom to turn the shower on. They'd learned it needed a few minutes to heat up after their first disastrous shower together had resulted in him stepping under a blast of icy water that had nearly derailed their first bout of shower sex.

"Grades all done?" he asked when he walked back in to dig through his suitcase for clean clothes.

Avery's suitcases had shown up yesterday, and he was a bit put out to not have an excuse to wear Paul's clothes any longer. They weren't a perfect fit, but he'd liked the symbolism of it.

"Done and dusted. Everything is submitted, and I'm officially done with my duties." He lay back on the bed and stared at the ceiling with his arms pillowed behind his head. "If a professor doesn't have a teaching position, is he still a professor?"

Paul snapped a clean shirt at him like a towel in a locker room, hitting him in the ribs. "You sound like a philosopher, not an economist."

Avery made a face.

"You'll find something. You always do," Paul said dismissively. "Do you want to shower with me?"

Avery didn't.

God help him, he'd rather lie here and sulk than get a blow job in the shower. He really was screwed.

"Go ahead. I'm going to lie here and have an existential crisis."

"Just be sure it's a short one. Marnie made reservations for lunch, so we can't be late."

Paul and Marnie becoming friends had been unexpected. They'd started the week barely able to tolerate each other, and now they were seeking out each other's company. She was still prickly as hell, but Avery had to admit she'd grown on him. She was Ellie's polar opposite, which was amusing. Their dynamic was a fun one to watch.

Every time Avery thought he was making headway with Paul, Marnie would swoop in and settle between them to talk to Paul about some ridiculous thing or suggest a new group activity. Avery had been suffering from the emotional equivalent of blue balls for days.

And it wasn't like they were having pillow-talk conversations either. Paul stopped any attempt at a heart-to-heart by either initiating sex or falling asleep.

He had three more days in Tahoe with Paul, and Avery had to make them count. It was hard to do when they were so overscheduled with group activities that they hardly had enough time for sex. Tonight they had plans for a sunset cruise after the brewery tour, and Avery suspected Marnie would insist on nightcaps and board games or something like that when they got back.

At least they didn't have plans to ski tomorrow. Marnie, Ellie, and Jill had a whole day at the spa booked, so the rest of them were going golfing and to some off-road adventure course that Paul hadn't stopped talking about for days.

Neither were ideal activities for deep conversation, but at least they wouldn't constantly be interrupted by Paul's new bestie.

Avery's phone pinged, and he made a mental note to prioritize getting a US number once he got back to Chicago. His cheap UK phone plan was expensive to use here in the US, which meant every rejection call was costing him literally as well as figuratively.

It was a text from a friend at Northwestern. He'd talked to him a month ago when he'd first decided he was coming back to the US for sure, but there hadn't been any openings in the department.

Are you in the US yet? Do you have availability to sub till the end of term for a prof who's out on leave?

Avery sat up.

Yes, I'm in California till late this week, then back in Chicago after that.

This wasn't what he'd hoped for, but it was better than nothing. Northwestern would be in session for another month, possibly two. Avery would have to check their academic calendar. It wasn't a long-term solution, but it was a foot in the door.

I can have a contract emailed over to you if you're in. Unplanned absence that is starting immediately. Freshman-level macro classes and a senior capstone. TAs can cover the intro classes this week, and seniors will be okay. Start Monday?

From the pit of despair to cloud nine in less than ten minutes. That was a new record.

Send it over. I can be on campus by Monday no problem.

No matter what the pay, Avery was in. This was the perfect excuse to stay in Chicago. Now all he had to do was convince Paul to extend their vacation fling into something more serious once they were back home.

Avery was bouncing with energy by the time Paul came out of the bathroom in a T-shirt and boxers, toweling his hair dry.

"Someone beat you with the happy stick," Paul said, eyeing him warily. "What's up?"

"There's a temporary opening at Northwestern. I'm going to take over some classes for someone who's out on leave for the rest of the semester."

Avery hadn't expected Paul to flinch at the news, and that hit him hard. But Paul recovered, pasting a smile on his face that almost looked genuine.

"See? I told you things always work out for you. Better buy a lottery ticket while we're in town."

"I've already won the lottery," Avery joked, putting a hand over his heart. "First you, then the job. Going for three would be greedy."

Paul rolled his eyes. "Eh, lottery winnings you get to keep. The job sounds temporary, kinda like me."

Ouch. Direct hit.

"With any luck, I'll get to keep the Northwestern job too. Though I don't have any details about who I'm filling in for or why they're going out on leave. Maybe I shouldn't hope for it to be permanent because it might mean something bad for that professor."

Paul shook his head. "You're such a dork. You can't manifest something by saying it."

Avery's rational brain knew that, but he also kind of believed that you could. Intention mattered, and he didn't want to put anything out into the universe that would cause harm to someone else. His good luck shouldn't mean someone else's misfortune.

"Well, I'm going to tell the universe that I hope the professor I'm filling in for recovers but also decides to retire or takes a position somewhere else so I can stay in Chicago."

Paul didn't respond to that, but his gaze lingered on Avery's face for a moment before he turned away to finish getting dressed.

"Manifest yourself out of your pajamas, because we're going to be late."

THEY DIDN'T get back from their dinner cruise until after midnight. Marnie had insisted the group stop by a pub that was hosting a *Family Feud*–inspired game night, and one drink had turned into enough that they'd ubered back to the lodge instead of taking the rental cars.

Avery's head was pounding when his alarm went off, and he cursed his brother for booking such an early tee time.

From the smell of coffee that filled the cabin, Paul must already be up. Bless him.

"I feel like we fell asleep minutes ago. How is it morning?" he groaned, pushing himself up by his elbows so he could use the headboard as a backrest.

Paul leaned in and gave him a quick kiss before putting a steaming cup of coffee in his hands.

"Someone had the bright idea to keep drinking after we got back to the cabin," he said.

"Because someone dared me to take a body shot." Avery took a sip of coffee and rested his head against the padded backboard, keeping his eyes closed.

"I didn't dare you to take a body shot. I told you it wasn't physically possible to take a body shot off someone's knee."

They'd lost the final round of *Family Feud* on that question. Apparently the most common places on the body to take a shot were neck, belly, lower back, and collarbone. Avery had answered knee.

"The *back* of someone's knee. And it would have worked if you weren't so ticklish."

It hadn't worked, but it had led to a giggle-fueled sex marathon, so Avery couldn't complain. Except now it was morning, he'd only had a few hours of sleep, and his entire body ached with his hangover. So maybe he could complain a little.

He flinched and squeezed his eyes shut even tighter when Paul yanked open the curtains, expecting the cabin to be flooded with bright sunlight like it had been every other morning. Avery cracked an eye open experimentally, then opened both when he realized the room was still pretty dim.

Rain spattered against the windows, the trees backlit by low-hanging gray clouds. Paul settled back on the bed next to him with his own coffee and tucked the blanket up around Avery's waist to ward off the early morning chill.

"I don't think we're getting in eighteen holes today," Paul mused, looking out the window.

Avery hated golf, so the rainy morning was a blessing.

"Let's go back to sleep," he muttered, putting his barely touched coffee on the nightstand and sinking back down in bed.

Paul's cell phone rang, and Avery pulled the covers over his head. "Tell him no golfing."

"Good morning, Bran," Paul said, laughing at something Avery's brother said in response.

"No, I haven't checked the forecast."

Avery peeked out from under the covers, enjoying the chance to watch Paul. He was shirtless, and his hair stuck up in every direction. The entire tableau was cozy and comfortable and oh so domestic. It might be Avery's favorite look on him.

Paul made a low, contemplative sound. "Do you think Marnie will agree to that?"

From the look on his face, Paul didn't think she'd be on board with whatever plan Bran was hatching. Avery took a moment and sent up a silent prayer that whatever it was didn't include them. He wanted a day alone with Paul without his shadow.

"I mean, yeah. That's fine with us if that works for everyone else. If it looks like it's going to rain all day then it doesn't make sense to plan around getting out on the course later."

Avery did a little fist pump under the blankets. Whatever the new plan was, it didn't involve golf.

"We'll see you later, then. I'll check in and see where you are, and we can figure out if we're all riding over together or meeting there. Yeah, the reservation is for eight, so that should be fine."

Were they really not seeing anyone until *dinner*? Avery's drowsiness melted away. If he had all day with Paul, he didn't want to waste any of it napping.

Paul lifted the blanket and climbed into the little tent Avery had made over his head.

"It's going to rain all day, so Bran is going to spend the day at the spa with Ellie and the others."

Avery cut him a look. "Greg is going to the spa?"

Paul made a face. "I don't know, I didn't ask. Bran knows I hate that kind of stuff, and he said you would rather spend the day with me than get a massage and a facial. So we're on our own unless you want to join them."

He could take or leave massages, but nothing sounded better than a day alone with Paul.

"I'd rather skip it. What should we do instead? I bet we could find some weird local museums if you want to get your geek on. Or—"

Paul climbed on top of him. "Or we could spend the day in bed."

That was a hard offer to turn down—literally. Avery's body responded before his mind even caught up to the fact that Paul was straddling him. But filling their day with more meaningless sex wouldn't help Avery break through Paul's shell. This was the opportunity he'd been waiting for, and he had to make it count.

"How about we spend the morning in bed, and then you let me surprise you with a date?"

Paul stopped nuzzling against Avery's neck and sat back on his heels. "A date?"

"What could it hurt? Spend the day with me, Paul. Let's have fun."

Paul wiggled his ass, grinding down into Avery's growing erection. "This is having fun."

Avery couldn't argue with that. He thrust up, satisfaction buzzing through him when Paul moaned softly in response.

"There are lots of ways to have fun, my friend. And we have all day to explore them."

He pulled Paul down into a kiss, rolling so they were both on their sides. He'd reacquainted himself with every inch of Paul's body over the last few days, and he'd enjoyed every minute.

Paul had thrown on a pair of loose sleep pants when he'd gotten up to make coffee, but Avery was still naked. It gave Paul the advantage, since he had full access to Avery's bare skin. Avery thrust his hips idly as Paul stroked him, more focused on his own exploration of Paul's body and working his hands down into Paul's pants.

Paul broke their kiss and pulled away before Avery reached his erection.

"I thought you wanted to have a different kind of fun," he teased.

Avery mock growled and reached out to grab Paul and pull him back. "I believe I said I could show you multiple ways to have fun. A compromise was struck."

Paul lifted his hips, pulling his sleep pants off with one graceful movement that made Avery's mouth go dry.

"Continue on with your plans, then," he said with an inviting grin.

DESPITE BEING the first one up, Paul had fallen asleep after their bout of morning sex. Avery didn't wake him because it served his purposes well. He snuck out of bed and grabbed his laptop to plan their day. By the time Paul stopped dozing half an hour later, Avery had reservations secured and a plan to woo the crap out of him.

They were in the rental car and headed north by ten, with Paul driving even though Avery refused to tell him where they were going.

"It wouldn't be a surprise date if you knew what we were doing," he said when Paul protested for the third time in ten minutes. "We're already halfway to the first stop anyway. Quit being a baby."

Paul made a triumphant noise. "So we're going somewhere in Truckee. The highway sign said that was the next town."

Avery hummed noncommittally.

"How many stops do we have? I'm dying of curiosity here."

Paul liked to be the planner, as evidenced by the way he'd taken charge of the itinerary for the Tahoe trip. Avery was enjoying seeing him off-kilter, not knowing what was coming. For all his complaints, Paul seemed to be enjoying it too. He'd been whining nonstop, but he was smiling and clearly excited.

"Two, but we'll have lunch after the first one, so I guess it's kind of three stops. Well, technically, you might want to add another stop before lunch, but I'm leaving that one up to you."

"This is incredibly frustrating," Paul said, cutting him a mock angry scowl.

"Think of it as foreplay."

"Not that kind of frustrating," Paul said flatly, but his lips curved up into a reluctant smile, so Avery counted it as a win. It was *totally* that kind of frustrating.

Paul looked confused when Avery directed him to turn at the sign that said Donner Memorial State Park.

"Is your surprise that you're making us go for a hike when it's raining and cold?"

"It is not," Avery said, feeling smug. "I told you I bet we could find a weird museum, and this is the weirdest one I could find."

Paul followed the road to the parking lot, brow furrowed as he tried to puzzle out what was happening. Once they parked in front of the visitor center, it seemed to dawn on him. He turned to Avery, his eyes lighting up like a kid in a candy store.

"No! Are you seriously telling me there's a museum about the Donner Party?"

"And other things, but yes. It's about the emigrant experience. We can drive across Donner Pass after this if you want, but it's in the opposite direction of where we're going next. I don't think it would add too much time, though."

Paul was practically skipping as they walked inside. "This is the weirdest date I've ever been on. Thank you."

Avery fought the urge to preen. "We don't know if the museum's any good. It could be a wagon wheel and a plaque for all we know."

Paul caught his hand and squeezed it. "Even if it is, it's still cool."

He didn't let go, and Avery didn't either. The visitor's center looked pretty nondescript, but the quality of the exhibits inside was impressive. It was a lot more than the Donner Party, though those were the exhibits they spent the most time at. But there were a surprising number of other exhibits about the area, and he learned a lot about how the railroads were built. They even sat through the thirty-minute movie detailing what went wrong for the Donner Party and the full scope of the tragedy. Avery had intended for it to be a quirky way to spend an hour, and it had delivered.

"Should we check out the gift shop?" he asked as they wandered toward the exit. "Though I wonder what kind of things they'd sell there. Hopefully not a cookbook."

Paul burst out laughing, drawing looks from a family who'd come in about ten minutes after them and a smattering of other tourists milling around.

"That was terrible."

"But funny."

"Yes, but funny. I don't know what you've got planned for the rest of the day," he said, raising an eyebrow at Avery, who shrugged, "but as awful as it sounds after that, I'm hungry and could really go for lunch. I'm assuming you're planning to feed me?"

"And you said *my* joke was bad," he said with a snicker. "Yes, that's what's up next. Unless you want to drive over Donner Pass."

Paul wrinkled his nose. "I'm good."

Chapter ELEVEN

THE LITTLE town near the museum where they stopped for lunch was quaint in a much less artificial way than Tahoe City. Paul was having a good time getting to see this playful side of Avery.

He'd forgotten they weren't on an actual date, and that was dangerous. Avery was creeping past his defenses, and Paul didn't know if he had it in him to fight it anymore. Maybe it was better to live in the moment and deal with the inevitable consequences of a broken heart later. If he was being honest, it was already too late. He was lying to himself with this play at just having fun.

"Ready to get back on the road?"

Paul let Avery slide a hand through his and pull him up from the table at the little diner they'd wandered into to eat. It had been nice to have a burger that didn't have aioli and fries that weren't dusted with truffle salt or something else highbrow. The food in Tahoe City was good, but sometimes he wanted something simple.

Avery slid into the passenger side of the rental. It would be a hell of a lot easier if he drove, since he still wouldn't tell Paul their destination, but Paul understood his reluctance. It would be an adjustment to drive in the US after being away for so long, and winding mountain roads in the rain were not the ideal place for his inaugural effort.

Paul pulled onto the main road, letting Avery guide him back to the highway.

"We'll be on this all the way there," Avery said, consulting the map on his phone. "It says about half an hour."

Paul did the mental math, calculating how far they'd come and how much time they'd need to leave themselves to make it back to Tahoe City to meet the others for dinner. It was nearly one now, and he didn't know how long whatever they were headed toward would keep them occupied. It was stressful not knowing what they were doing, but it was also kind of exhilarating.

"Are we going to another museum?"

Avery shook his head.

"Can I have a hint?"

"Your hint is you'll never guess it, and you should give up and focus on enjoying the drive. Do you want to listen to a podcast?"

Which was how Paul ended up engrossed in a podcast about polygamy and cults that he'd never have chosen on his own but would definitely be finishing later because it was fascinating.

Avery was full of hidden depths and interests. Paul was enjoying the chance to see this side of him. He wouldn't have pegged Avery as a podcast kind of guy, unless there was one on macroeconomics or the World Bank.

He was shocked when Avery told him to take the next exit. The time had flown by with the two of them sitting comfortably and not talking, just listening to the podcast. It wasn't the kind of thing Paul usually did—share quiet time with someone else. It was surprisingly relaxing.

"Lemon Canyon Road? Are we going to an orchard?"

"If life gives you lemons, make lemonade?" Avery joked. "No. We're only on this a little bit, and then we're looking for Campbell Hot Springs Road."

"Are we going to a hot spring?"

Paul hoped he said yes, because it was something he'd always wanted to do. He hadn't even considered the possibility that there might be natural hot springs in the area or he'd have suggested it himself.

"We are. I made reservations because they don't take walk-ins. The woman at the front desk took pity on me because she said they don't do same-day reservations, but it's a light guest load today, and I begged."

"I can't believe we're doing this. Did I ever tell you how much I've wanted to go to one?"

"You told me a long time ago that you wanted to visit Iceland for the hot springs and northern lights. I'd hoped it was still something you were interested in."

It had been on Paul's bucket list since high school, but now that he had the money to go, none of his single friends were interested in vacations like that, and he didn't want to go alone or be a third wheel for a couple. He couldn't believe Avery remembered.

"Still do. I haven't been to Iceland yet. Or any hot springs."

Avery perked up. "So I'm taking your hot-springs virginity?"

Paul made a face and turned in at a big sign that said Sierra Hot Springs. "Pretty sure they'd frown on that."

"They're public pools," Avery said. "But I'm really glad to share an experience with you that neither of us has done before."

Paul hadn't been to a museum memorializing a cannibalistic family before either, but he knew that wasn't what Avery meant. It was nice that he was so excited to have a new experience together. It was the kind of thing couples did.

The main building looked like the plantation houses Paul had toured on a trip to Savannah a few years ago, which was bizarre enough on its own. But Paul couldn't see any springs or pools anywhere either.

"Park here and I'll go in and get us checked in. The property is huge, so we'll drive over to whatever pool you want to start with."

"There's more than one?"

"There's a mix of indoor and outdoor pools. We can try them all if you like."

"Wait," Paul said, reaching out to grab Avery's hand before he could get out of the car. "I didn't bring a swimsuit."

"I've taken care of it."

Avery's grin was a tad too sharp, so Paul figured there was more to this than Avery sneaking the trunks he'd brought out of his suitcase.

"Relax and trust the process," Avery said with a wink before he disappeared out the door.

Trusting the process was how he'd landed himself here. First the no-strings-attached process, and now the come-what-may, consequences-be-damned process. In for a penny, in for a pound, he figured. What was one more leap of faith where Avery was concerned, when he'd already taken so many?

Avery wasn't gone long. He came back out of the large house with a shopping bag, which Paul hoped had swim trunks in it. He handed Paul a map when he climbed in.

"There's a really cool geodesic dome with a hot pool down here," he said, pointing on the map, "and there's an outdoor pool over there too. And at the far end of the property, there's supposed to be a nice meadow and another spring-fed hot pool. Somewhere in the middle there are some smaller private pools too, but those are first-come, first-serve, so we might be out of luck. We'll have to play it by ear."

The rain had slowed to a cold drizzle, and while it wouldn't be fun to hike or play golf in, it was probably great weather to be in a hot spring. In fact, this was optimal weather for it. Paul wished there was snow on the ground to give them the full experience, but he wasn't dressed for dashing through the snow into a steaming pool anyway.

"Let's ease into this and try the indoor one first," Paul decided. He followed the road until it wound around to a parking lot that opened onto a short trail leading to a huge dome.

Avery plucked his cell phone out of his pocket and held his hand out for Paul's. "There's a strict no-phone policy here. She said it was best to leave them in the car because they don't have secure lockers."

Paul wouldn't have wanted to risk dropping it in the hot spring anyway, but it would have been nice to get some photos of it. He handed it over and watched as Avery put them both in the car's glove box.

"I have towels, robes, and some flip-flops for us here. There should be a locker room area we can get undressed in once we're in there. I figured we might want them if we wanted to check out the private pools. They're close."

It had been thoughtful of Avery to grab those supplies, but there was an important element he hadn't mentioned. Paul quirked an eyebrow at him, and Avery smiled and mimed jazz hands.

"Avery," Paul said, drawing his name out, "is this a nudist colony?"

"Not a colony per se," Avery hedged. "But nudity is encouraged in the pools so you can get the maximum benefit from the springs."

The parking lot was far from full, but there were three other cars in it. There were also walking trails along the road for guests to travel around the hot springs on foot. Who knew how many people might be here?

"So we're going to do this? Just be naked. In a hot spring. With other people?"

"It's an adventure," Avery said. "Trust the process, remember?"

Paul had literally talked himself into trusting the process five minutes ago, but back then he hadn't realized the process involved public nudity.

"It's fine," Avery said, cutting him off before he could protest. "Seriously, Paul. No one is going to be concerned about anyone else there. All you need to do is relax and enjoy yourself."

Paul unbuckled his seat belt and got out of the car. "*No* sex."

Avery held his hands up innocently. "Definitely no sex."

"Don't even think about sex," Paul warned.

"One, you can't police my brain. And two, if you don't want me thinking about sex, then telling me not to think about sex is an awful way to do it, because now it's all I can think about."

"You're terrible."

"You've said. Remember? At the gift shop?"

From cannibal cookbook jokes to nudist hot springs. Avery sure knew how to plan a memorable date.

"I can't believe I'm doing this," Paul muttered as he followed Avery toward the dome.

"If you're uncomfortable we can go back. The gift shop might even have swim trunks. Or we can skip it altogether and find something else to do."

A week ago, Paul would have taken the opportunity to flee the uncomfortable situation. But he was all about pushing boundaries lately, so why not add public nudity to the list?

"No, I want to see the hot springs. I can deal with nudity. I think."

Avery beamed. "I'm glad, because I really, really want to go in. The photos were insane, and I bet it's even better in person."

Entering the dome felt like walking into a greenhouse in the middle of winter. Hot, moist air slapped them in the face, but instead of the sharp rotten-egg smell he'd been braced for, Paul was pleasantly surprised that it smelled only faintly sulphury and metallic.

The hot spring pool itself was smaller than he'd expected, though they'd passed a much larger one outside, so there was plenty of room to spread out if it became crowded. He and Avery left their clothes in a little cubby in the co-ed locker room and followed the instructions posted by the door telling them to take a shower before entering the pool. Avery held a robe out to him, but Paul waved it away. There wasn't any reason to feign modesty when he was about to walk out and get into a pool naked.

Besides, there weren't lounge chairs or anything to put it on anyway. The ceiling soared overhead, gorgeous wood planks that looked like knotty pine forming patterns on the faces of the dome. There were enough skylights cut into it to let in natural light, gray as it was today. The stone floor and flagstone walls gave the place an almost medieval look, complementing the round stone pool with wide steps leading into it.

The other couple left while they'd been undressing, and Paul was relieved not to have an audience as he made his way to the pool. He dipped his hand into one of the bathtub-sized elevated pools along the edge of the dome, recoiling when he realized they were cold.

"The website said there were cold plunges here. It's supposed to be healthy?"

Paul fought off a shiver and decided that was close enough to get the basic idea. "I think I'll pass."

"You might change your mind after you've been in the hot spring," a third voice said. Paul jumped and resisted the urge to cover himself. It felt illicit being naked out in public. He'd never wondered whether or not he was an exhibitionist, but this decisively answered that. He was not.

An older man with a handlebar mustache and more hair on his body than his head walked out of the changing room and hopped into one of the cold plunges, letting out a loud whoop when he submerged himself up to his neck. Paul took the opportunity to hurry toward the hot spring and climb in, hissing at the temperature of the water. He eased himself down the steps, his body unsure how to react to the hot water. It was hotter than the jacuzzi he used after his workouts at his gym. Then again, he didn't get in that one naked.

Avery joined him at a more leisurely pace, and they settled in along the rim of the pool while the older man climbed out of the tub and into the hot spring. The floor of the pool was sandy, and Paul liked the way it felt against his bare feet. The heat of the water seemed to make him hyperaware of everything. Or maybe it was his discomfort at being naked with a stranger. Either way, every sensation was heightened, and it was almost overwhelming.

"The cold plunge sounds good right about now," Avery muttered, his skin flushed and his upper lip dotted with sweat.

"First time?" the other man asked.

Paul worried he was going to wade over and offer to shake their hands, but he stayed on the far side of the small pool. Paul wished he knew what nudist bathing etiquette was. He didn't want to be rude, but he also didn't want to have a conversation while both of them were casually naked.

"We're just trying it out," Avery said, seemingly unbothered by how awkward this was. "We drove down from Tahoe and got a day pass."

"You should come back at night some time. Totally different place. There's nothing like floating in that big pool outside watching the stars."

"Sounds romantic," Avery said, voicing a thought Paul had had but wouldn't have said out loud to a stranger.

"Really helps seal the deal on a date," the older man said, "if you know what I mean. There are smaller pools farther down the trail that you can have some privacy in. People here are pretty good about leaving you be if you're in them. Might want to check them out before you go."

Paul ducked even lower into the water, the heat of it hiding his blush. He didn't want to be talking to this guy about the two of them having outdoor sex. He didn't want to be talking to him at all, and from the signs around the dome, they shouldn't be. They all proclaimed it a quiet space.

The man didn't seem inclined to talk more, thankfully, and after a few minutes in the skin-prickling heat, Paul had had enough. He nudged Avery with his foot, and Avery seemed as overheated and done as he was.

"It was nice to meet you," Avery told the man as they waded past him toward the steps.

"Enjoy your stay. Be sure to check out those private pools. They'll be pretty empty on a rainy day like today."

Paul wished he'd brought his robe out after all so he had something to cover with, but he hadn't, so he focused on not slipping on the stones as he walked to the locker room. It was blissfully empty.

Avery grabbed one of their towels and wrapped it around Paul like a burrito, collapsing against his chest with a case of the giggles.

Paul could see the humor in it, but it was still too fresh to laugh at for him.

"Let's walk down to the private pools," Avery said, handing him a robe.

Paul put it on and followed Avery out. "I'm not having sex in the pools, no matter what Foghorn Leghorn says."

"He did kind of sound like him, didn't he?" Avery mused. "I know. But I think it would be more relaxing to soak alone, and we didn't drive all the way up here to go back to Tahoe after ten minutes in the hot springs. We should at least go see."

That was true. The dome wasn't exactly what Paul had been expecting from a hot spring, aside from the steaming hot water and the sulfur smell.

They fell into step side by side, and Paul didn't pull away when Avery reached over and took his hand. The gravel path was a little unpleasant in their flip-flops, but the cool wet air felt great after the hot soak.

"It's gorgeous out here, isn't it?"

Paul looked around, appreciating the view. There were snow-capped mountains in the distance, and impossibly tall evergreens dotted the flat landscape around them, intermixed with rocky outcroppings that were as tall as he was and a lot of scrub. He tried to imagine it in the summer when the brown grasses were green and the scrub bushes flowered. It would be stunning.

"It is," he said after a moment. "Thanks for bringing me here. And for not telling me about the nudity thing before we got here. I probably wouldn't have come."

Avery snickered. "You definitely wouldn't have come."

They rounded a bend in the path, and the first of the private pools came into view. It was little more than a large puddle, but it was deep enough that the two people who were in it could stand and be submerged up to their chests. At least, Paul assumed they were standing. There wasn't any way they could be doing what they were doing if they were both floating.

Paul averted his eyes and they stayed on the trail, speeding up a bit to get out of earshot of the splashes and moans.

Avery let out an uncomfortable laugh when they were past them. "Guess he wasn't kidding about the sex."

"Makes me a little reluctant to get back in the water, to be honest," Paul joked.

"I'm sure it's fine," Avery said. "But I'd for sure hesitate to sit on any of the benches or chairs."

They both burst out laughing.

The next pool was bigger, and even better, it was empty. It was smaller than the one in the dome, but it didn't look man-made. Paul wasn't sure if it was natural or not, but he was happy to pretend it was even if it wasn't. This was more the experience he'd been hoping for. A stand of tall rocks with a slight overhang that would keep their towels and robes safe from the misty rain bordered one side of the pool. They left their flip-flops there too, padding over the dormant grass that felt spongy and odd beneath his feet.

The water here was still steaming but much cooler than the first pool they'd been in. It felt nice against his skin, which had gotten chilled the moment he'd shucked off his robe. It was a little surreal, his body submerged in hot water and his face left exposed to the chilly drizzle.

He looked over at Avery, who had embraced the sensation fully, his face upturned toward the sky, his eyes closed. He looked like a sacrifice in some sort of pagan ritual. Sudden gratitude flooded through Paul—thankfulness for being here, for sharing it with Avery. Paul didn't have these moments often, but right now he was overcome with the certainty that he was exactly where he was supposed to be in this moment.

The sulfur smell was stronger here, but not unbearably so. Still, Paul didn't know how people could ignore it and get into a sexy mood. He didn't find egg farts to be particularly mood-setting.

"This is more like it," Avery said, wading through the small pool. He ducked under the water and came up a second later, shaking water from his hair like a duck clearing its feathers.

He caught Paul staring at him, his expression turning serious. "What?"

Paul shook himself out of his reverie. "Nothing. I just like seeing you like this here."

"I like being here. With you."

Paul didn't want to ruin the afternoon by getting dragged into a conversation trying to define whatever they were doing, so he swam over and splashed Avery. After a few minutes of wrestling with each other, both of them were breathing hard from the exertion and the laughter.

"Uncle, uncle," Avery pleaded. "Let's just soak here for a bit."

Paul released him, and the two of them floated in silence. It was strange, being naked with Avery like this. It felt much more intimate than the sex they'd had. He kind of liked it.

Paul had no idea how long they'd been at the little pond—it could easily have been ten minutes or two hours. He'd lost track of time enjoying the moment. That wasn't like him, but he was beginning to notice that he was different when he was with Avery. The resentment, hurt, and anger had disappeared some time over the last week. Paul couldn't pinpoint when, but his feelings for Avery had changed. It was like he'd gone through all the stages of grief that he'd been stuck on for the last twelve years, and now he was finally at acceptance.

Except instead of walking away like a responsible person would, he was getting right back on the roller coaster.

"Penny for your thoughts," Avery said, nudging him with his foot as he floated by.

"Wouldn't it be a pence?" Paul asked, trying to distract him.

"Actually, no, it would still be a penny in dollars or pounds."

"How convenient."

Avery floated up next to him and stood on the bottom, making eye contact. "I know you want to keep things fun and you don't want to get serious, but I have serious feelings for you. I'm going to be in Chicago, Paul. I'd like to keep dating if you'll have me."

Decision time. No spreadsheet or decision matrix was going to help him with this one, so Paul embraced the new him and spoke his mind.

"I'd like that, but it scares me. I didn't like who I was after you left, Avery. I was in a bad place for a long time. I didn't start dating again for three years, and I don't want that again. I like my life, and I'd like to see if you can fit into it, but I can't let you wreck it again."

Avery surprised him by not jumping in with reasons why he wouldn't. That alone was the biggest reassurance he could have given Paul. The old Avery was all brash impulsiveness and thoughtlessness. This new one took more care, and that was why Paul was willing to take the chance, knowing that he'd very likely be bitten again. He didn't think this would end well, but it would at least end amicably.

"I can't make you any promises. My work is important to me, and I have to go where I can find a job. But I will be at Northwestern through May, so that at least gives us two months to see where this goes."

It was the most honest promise he could make, and Paul appreciated his candor.

"Okay, yeah. Let's give it a go."

Avery grabbed him and twirled him in the water. "Yeah?"

"Yeah. But we're still not having sex in the hot spring."

Chapter TWELVE

"I STILL can't believe my mom has a key to your house."

Paul looked up from the box of clothes he was packing and shrugged. "To be fair, your mom *used* to have a key to my house. Now *you* have her key to my house."

They'd been back from Tahoe for two weeks, and it had been a relief to find that Avery fit into Paul's life here in Chicago. After spending a week living in each other's pockets, he'd enjoyed having some time apart. Avery had spent the last two weeks at Bran and Ellie's house, commuting to Northwestern daily to teach and usually stopping at Paul's in the evening so they could make dinner together and hang out.

Bran and Ellie were due back from Bali in a few hours, which was why Paul was packing up the off-season clothes he kept in the guest-room closet to make room for Avery's stuff.

"And you're sure it's okay if I move in with you? That won't be rushing things?"

Avery had been trying hard to be mindful of the boundaries Paul had put up. They'd spent their last few days in Tahoe setting up ground rules for their relationship. Living together had definitely not been part of that, and Avery was afraid that moving too fast might spook Paul and send them back to where they'd started.

"It makes sense. I'm a much shorter commute to Northwestern than Bran's, and they're going to have that gross newlywed glow when they get back. They shouldn't have to share their space with a third wheel. Besides, it's not like you're moving in forever—this is just until the end of the semester when you figure out what your next step is."

Avery had still been reaching out to his network across the country looking for a permanent job, and Paul had accepted that. Or at least he'd said he did. Avery wanted to promise him the moon—that he'd stay here no matter what because Paul was more important than his career. But that wasn't true. Paul *could* be more important than his career—someday.

But Avery wasn't in a place where he could gamble his future on that. Especially with Paul still holding him at arm's length.

"And if I get a spot at Northwestern?"

It was possible. The professor Avery was filling in for had made some noises about not wanting to come back to teaching full-time after she recovered, but it wasn't like there was a guarantee that Avery would get the position even if she left. Academia was an old-boy's club. It was all about who you knew, and Avery didn't have a deep network here. The Northwestern job only fell into his lap because it was his alma mater and he still knew professors there.

"If you get the spot at Northwestern then you can get your own place. There are some gorgeous condos going in near campus."

Avery would cross that bridge if they came to it. "Okay. I just don't want to take advantage or push you into something you're not ready for."

"For God's sake, Avery. We're going to be roommates for a few months, tops. We're not adopting a goldendoodle and getting matching tattoos."

Avery laughed. "Fair enough. But I'm not sleeping in here, right? This was because you didn't want my mom to know how hot you are for my bod?"

His mom had brought his things over earlier that morning since his boxes had been delivered to her house. It was pretty jarring to see his entire life condensed into a few meager boxes he'd shipped from overseas. The boxes would remain unopened and stay in the guest room, along with Avery's clothes in the closet and Avery's toiletries in the guest bathroom. Paul had been very clear about that. Separate closets, separate bathrooms, separate lives.

Paul finished clearing the closet and picked up the box. "Pretty sure your mom knows we're going to be sharing my bed. I am not, however, willing to share my closet or my bathroom. Which is why you are keeping your stuff in here."

He wandered out of the guest room before Avery realized he didn't know if they were the ones who were supposed to go pick Bran and Ellie up.

"Hey, are we picking Boris and Natasha up from O'Hare?" he yelled, too lazy to go find Paul.

"No, your dad's going to go get them. I think Ellie wants to have brunch this weekend, though. After they've had some time to unpack and deal with the jet lag."

Yelling back and forth between different rooms of the house felt very domestic and adult. It amused Avery.

He wasn't sure how having Ellie and his brother back would affect the dynamic he had going with Paul. Ellie was certainly invested in the two of them being together. She'd had hearts in her eyes every time she looked at them after they'd come back from the hot springs and announced they were going to try casually dating.

Avery hadn't talked more than that about the twist their relationship had taken with Bran and Ellie, and he wasn't sure if Paul had. Either way, he didn't want to explain the agreement they'd come to. It sounded cold and practical, this "take it one day at a time" thing he and Paul had going. He didn't want to see their pity or have to justify why keeping himself a little detached was the best route. Not everyone was destined for the storybook happily ever after they had, but it was going to be impossible to convince Bran and Ellie of that, fresh off their picture-perfect wedding and honeymoon.

All that mattered was that it worked for him and Paul, and so far, it did. They were grown-ups, and this was how grown-ups navigated dating and relationships. At least, he assumed that was how grown-ups did it. Avery didn't have a lot of practical experience there. The last time he'd actually tried something domestic had been with Paul. Not a raging success, that one.

It hadn't escaped Avery's notice that Paul hadn't introduced him to his friends, nor had he invited him along when the softball team went out for drinks after their first practice this week. He hadn't visited Avery on campus or talked to him about what was going on at work. Paul was being very careful to keep things separate, and Avery knew it was because he expected Avery to bail. When this burned out, Paul didn't want to have empty spaces where Avery should have been in his life.

Avery popped up in his doorway after Paul had stashed the box of clothes in the master bedroom closet.

"In that case, do you want to make popcorn for dinner and binge watch something while I grade a mountain of freshman essays?"

Paul gave him a quick kiss and scooted past him. "Sounds perfect. Something from my queue, though. You were too into the podcast we were listening to last week, and you made me keep recapping it for you. Find something that I won't have to narrate for you after."

"At least I'm not falling asleep on you. Dad always complains that Mom picks a movie and then conks out ten minutes in."

"She's barely made it past the credits, the times I've been over for a movie," Paul said, and Avery looked away to hide the hurt that flashed over his face.

Paul wasn't trying to remind him he was closer to Avery's family than Avery was, but he saw evidence of it all the time. The key, the way his mom helped Paul with his yard. How close Paul and Bran were. That Ellie was close friends with Paul and she'd only met Avery a few weeks ago. It wasn't Paul's fault—it was Avery's. But he was tired of the consequences of his choice to spend the last decade in Europe slapping him in the face.

"You go make snacks and pick something to watch. I'm going to unpack and get settled in."

Avery needed a minute to regroup. He and Paul had turned a corner at the hot springs, but there was still very much a wall there that Avery hadn't been able to get past. Part of him was holding back because he understood why Paul was keeping a piece of himself distant. It hurt, but he wasn't wrong. Avery loved him—he'd never stopped—but this was different. Spending the last few weeks with Paul had shown him the life he could have had if he'd stayed in the US, and he wanted it. He wanted to be allowed to go to Paul's softball games and meet his coworkers and spend Sundays at the nursery picking out plants for the backyard. That was the partner Paul deserved, and Avery wanted to be that guy.

But he also wanted to teach and research and lecture at conferences, and if he turned his back on his career, he knew he'd end up resenting Paul for it. Not that Paul had asked him to—he'd been very clear that he knew Avery's priority was finding a tenure-track professorship.

He knew he couldn't have it both ways, but that hurt a bit too. Knowing that Paul wasn't going to fight for him, that he was closing part of himself off because he knew he'd always be second fiddle in Avery's life. But he wasn't wrong. Avery was a selfish guy. He knew it. He'd made his life around one thing: his career. It had taken precedence over family, over his love life, even over his own self-care.

Avery needed to change that, but he wasn't sure if he wanted to. He didn't want to wake up in ten years with regrets, but he was clueless about what choices to make now to prevent that.

He dug his laptop out of his satchel, took a leaf out of Paul's book, and make a list. It wouldn't be one of Paul's infamous spreadsheets, because Avery's brain couldn't wrap around putting a value on intangible things like happiness and fulfillment, but he could at least do a good old pro-and-con list.

The Northwestern job was a hypothetical, so he couldn't use that because it would throw everything off. That would be his number one option, the one that kept him in Chicago with Paul but didn't set him back in his career. His unicorn. Perfect, but unlikely.

Much more likely was a job in another state. He had a few nibbles on the West Coast and one on the East Coast at an Ivy League school that would be a stretch with his credentials, but nothing solid. Most of his leads were little more than rumors from former colleagues or classmates that there might be an opening coming up in their departments.

He titled that list Unknown University. The pros were easy. Access to world-class research, tenure-track position, job security, intellectual fulfillment, full-time teaching. The cons were harder to quantify. He couldn't be with Paul, but that didn't mean he'd never find someone. He wouldn't be close to his family. He'd miss seeing his niece grow up, along with any future niblings. His parents were aging, and he'd lose out on what time he had with them. He'd disappoint Bran. He'd break his own heart not being with Paul—again.

Avery started a new list. Stay in Chicago. The pros were all emotional. He'd get to have a real relationship with Paul. Be closer to his family so he could have relationships with his niece and future kids. Be there to help when his parents needed it. Get to have his siblings in his life. But the cons were huge. He could find a teaching job, but it might not be the kind he wanted. Illinois had a ton of community colleges, so even if the temporary position at Northwestern ended, he'd be able to find a spot. But was that what he wanted to do? Teach a steady stream of undergraduate intro courses at a community college? He was self-aware enough to know that it wouldn't be the academic environment he wanted for himself. It was snobby and pretentious of him, but it was true.

Avery lay facedown on the bed for a moment, suppressing the urge to scream.

It would be easier if he could talk to Paul about this, but that wasn't fair to him. Paul was doing an amazing job being supportive, but Avery suspected that would change if Avery forced these discussions.

What he needed to do was put on a smile and go downstairs to watch a movie with Paul. There was no point in wasting the time they had together. This could all evaporate in a month, and the only thing that was certain was they were together right now. Might as well make the most of it.

Avery closed the doc with his pro-and-con lists without saving it. He didn't need to see them written in black and white. He was already well aware of his choices, and right now they all sucked.

"Do you want butter on your popcorn?" Paul yelled up the stairs.

At least that was an easy question to answer. "Of course! Are you some kind of monster? Who doesn't put butter on their popcorn?"

He tucked his laptop under his arm and jogged down the stairs to join Paul in the kitchen, where he was popping popcorn on the stove in a heavy-bottomed pot. It seemed like such an adult thing—owning a pot like that, knowing how to use it to make popcorn from scratch instead of using a bag of the microwave stuff. It was sexy.

"*I* like butter on my popcorn," Paul said when Avery came through the doorway. "But I didn't want to assume you did. Tuesday I watched you put tuna on your baked potato. You've been assimilated into British food culture, so nothing is safe."

"Okay, listen, tuna in a jacket potato is a classic. You wouldn't even try it, so you have no idea what you're missing."

Paul wrinkled his nose. "You tossed it in mayo and then put it inside your potato. It was hardly haute cuisine."

"To do it right, you need to put it back in the oven after you stuff it. But I'm too impatient for that step."

"Hot mayo?" Paul mimed gagging. "You've made it worse."

"I mean, is it that different from a tuna casserole? You're just substituting the starch and having it in a potato instead of over noodles."

Paul made a face. "I hate tuna casserole too."

"See? It isn't that it's British, it's that you're biased against tuna."

"You dip cookies in your tea. You added Marmite to the shopping list. You're more British than American now."

"I dipped my pizza in ranch sauce last night. If that's not American, I don't know what is."

Paul laughed. "Okay, but that is also disgusting."

"But disgustingly *American*," Avery crowed, triumphant. He put his laptop on the table and got a bowl down for Paul to pour the popcorn into.

They'd been cooking dinner on the nights they didn't go out, and Avery liked the way they moved around the kitchen together. It felt homey. He'd never been much of a cook, so it had been fun learning from Paul.

"Do you want to grab us some beers from the garage fridge? I need to melt some butter, and then we're set."

Having a refrigerator in the garage for drinks was about as American as you could get. Avery had gotten by with a refrigerator smaller than the one he'd had in his freshman dorm room when he lived in London. Things were different here for sure.

He was still grading two beers in and halfway through the movie Paul had picked out. The professor he was filling in for had a sadistic essay schedule for her intro to economics classes, and since he was going off her syllabus, that meant *he* had a sadistic essay schedule to keep up with. Luckily Paul didn't seem to mind nights in like this one.

It was pretty close to Avery's ideal, though if he had his choice, he would be cuddled up watching the movie with Paul instead of sprawled out next to him grading with half an ear on the dialog. This was nice too, though. It didn't make him love grading, but it was much nicer than sitting alone at his kitchen table like he usually did when he plowed through essays.

That table had been sold, along with the rest of his furniture and the tiny ancient Renault that had been his biggest indulgence in London. It was stupid to keep a car in a city where he rarely needed to drive, but buying it had been an American reflex. And he'd loved getting away for the weekend and driving for driving's sake. The concept of a true road trip, one where the point is the journey, not the destination, had been foreign to his British colleagues. He'd never been able to put into words why he insisted on having a car and driving it around when petrol was expensive and public transportation was top-notch.

He needed to get a car here, but that should wait until he knew where he'd be settling. Avery would need a new kitchen table to grade at as well, but that was also on hold until the gaping question mark that was his future resolved itself.

"I wonder if the parks department will do outdoor movies in the park this year," Paul said out of the blue. "Last year they did some classics mixed in with newer movies. Bran, Ellie, and I went to a bunch of them."

Avery wasn't sure if Paul was thinking out loud or if there was a question in there for him, so he looked up from his grading and waited to see if Paul would continue.

"Is that something you'd want to do? I don't even know if you like movies. Or being outside."

"I love movies, especially ones from the eighties and nineties. And I'm allergic to grass, but as long as we're on a blanket, then being outside is great."

"You're allergic to *grass*? Is that actually a thing, or is that a way of saying you're too citified for picnics?"

"For starters, picnics are mostly a city thing, I think. People who live with easy access to nature don't cart half their house out into it to eat. And yes, it's a real allergy. I get hives if I sit on it, and I sneeze whenever I leave the windows open when someone is cutting grass."

It had been handy growing up. Bran had been the one who had to do all the lawn work.

"So I should strike the fantasy of us being in a barn and rolling around in literal hay?"

"Unless that fantasy included uncontrollable sneezing, watery eyes, and my sexy body covered in welts, then yeah, that's best tabled."

"Got it. But a lumberjack fantasy, that would be okay, right? You're not allergic to tree pollen?"

Avery closed his laptop and put it on the coffee table. "I'm happy to climb you like a tree whenever you want."

Paul cast a glance at his laptop. "Can you take a break?"

"For you? Always."

"You mean for *sex*, always," Paul teased.

Avery knew the flippant jokes and deflections were a self-defense mechanism, and he tried not to be offended by them, but this one slipped through. He didn't let it show, though. The one thing Paul was completely open to with him was sex, and he craved that intimate connection.

"That too. How about we go for a walk and get ice cream?"

Paul gave him an incredulous look. "It's April in Chicago, Avery."

That was true. The wind off the lake was still brutal this time of year. "Okay, so we can go for a walk *or* get ice cream. Or go grab dessert at a sit-down restaurant. I just want to spend some time with you."

"We've spent all day together," Paul said.

They had physically been in the same place all day, but that didn't mean they'd been together. He was learning it was possible to not be alone but still be lonely.

"And now I want to spend the evening together too. Walk? Dessert?"

Paul's brow was still furrowed in confusion, but he turned the television off and stood up. "Okay, let's take a walk and grab dessert. There's a diner that has great pie a couple blocks away."

"I haven't had pie in ages. That sounds lovely."

"Ages," Paul snorted, rolling his eyes. "Do they not have pie in the UK?"

"Not this again," Avery said, sighing in mock exasperation. "When will you stop coming for my accent? And I'll have you know Brits love pies. Sweet, savory, they will make anything into a pie. I eat a lot of sandwiches and ready-made meals because I'm lazy, but if I was a real Brit, I'd be pie mad."

Paul's teasing smile fell. "Ready meals? What am I going to do with you, Peter Pan? You've got to grow up sometime or you'll end up with scurvy."

"I am growing up. I made pot roast last night. No scurvy."

He'd chopped up the vegetables and watched Paul make pot roast last night. But it was close enough.

"Right, teaching you to cook is going to move up to top priority. I can't in good conscience release you into the world without some basic skills."

"Hey, I have basic skills. I kept myself alive this long," Avery protested.

They grabbed their parkas and headed out the door. Bickering as they walked down the sidewalk wasn't what he'd had in mind when he said he wanted to spend time together, but at least he had Paul's full attention.

"You need a pet. Or a house plant. Something to come home to at night and take care of," Paul said.

"You're allergic to dogs, and you hate cats," Avery pointed out.

"Which is why I went the plant route," Paul said. "Maybe getting a pet would be cheaper. They won't multiply and take over your entire house and then your yard."

He'd tagged along when Paul and his mom went to the nursery and planned what they were going to plant in the spring. Between that and all the mulch and landscape timbers, whatever those were, Paul had ordered, a pet *had* to be cheaper.

"I'll be a stepdad to your plants."

"That's not a thing."

"I'm making it a thing. I'll give them love and affection and words of validation if they need it, but I'm not in charge of watering them or fertilizing them or setting their curfew."

"So only the fun parts?" Paul snorted.

Avery was freezing by the time they arrived at the diner. It leaned heavily into fifties kitsch, with bright red vinyl booths and a black-and-white tiled floor. There was a jukebox in the corner lit with neon lights, and memorabilia covered the walls.

"It's a bit goofy, but you can't beat their pie. Or the patty melt."

Paul unwound the scarf he'd been smart enough to wear and piled it with his coat next to him in the booth the waitress sullenly showed them to without a word. She was wearing a poodle skirt and a pair of Mary Janes, so he forgave her the attitude. He'd probably feel about the same in her position.

Avery slid into the seat across from Paul grudgingly. He'd rather be cozied up next to him, but the literal wall of Paul's outerwear was a pretty solid sign he didn't want that. Always at an arm's distance, Avery thought uncharitably.

What a ridiculous thing to be upset about, he scolded himself. Like being resentful of Paul's scarf because it was a sign he was right—Avery *wasn't* a functional adult. If he was, he'd have grabbed a scarf and gloves himself before setting out on a cold, windy evening walk. He hated that Paul was right about him.

A different waitress approached the table. This one had the same uniform on but didn't seem to hate it, and her smile seemed genuine. More genuine than the name badge that said Madge.

"Good evening, fellas. I'll be taking care of you tonight. What can I get you?"

Avery leaned in conspiratorially. "I hope it isn't rude to ask, but is your name actually Madge, or is that part of the diner ambiance?"

She looked both ways before covering her mouth with her order pad and whispering. "My name is Katlyn, but the management has a box of badges with popular names from the fifties, and we grab one every day. You're the first person who's ever asked."

She winked at Avery and put her pad back down. "Now what can I get started for you?"

Paul looked a bit mortified, but Katlyn was clearly amused. "I'll have a coffee, please."

"Same for me," Paul said, still shooting Avery a dirty look. "And can we have the pie menu? We're here for dessert."

"Sure thing," she said, putting her pad away. "I'll grab that and your coffees for you, hon."

"I can't believe you asked her that," Paul sighed after she left.

"I was curious," Avery said, a bit baffled by how embarrassed Paul was. "It seemed like an affectation, like the way she speaks. Did you notice she was totally normal when she was answering my question? And then back to fellas and hon. It's all part of the costume."

"Costume?"

Had Paul really not noticed the poodle skirts?

"The uniforms. I bet they get a list of things to call customers and slang to use when they're hired."

"Do *not* ask her that."

"Why not? I'm not annoying her. She didn't seem to care."

"Because you can't just say everything that comes into your mind."

"It's not like I said something offensive. I asked a question related to her work. Why are you so bothered by this? Don't you get curious about things and ask questions?"

"Not in public, no. The poor woman just wants to take our order so she can get back to her other tables, and you're chatting with her. It's not like she could say no. She's literally paid to be here and interact with us. It's rude to monopolize her time or put her in an awkward position since she can't walk away."

Avery suspected this was about a lot more than him chatting up a waitress, but this didn't seem like the time to explore that. Paul protesting about awkward situations made him think this was an extension of the argument they'd been having for days about Avery wanting things to be more serious between them. So even though he had more questions, he took the coffee and the menu Katlyn offered him when she came back and didn't say anything other than thank you.

"Satisfied?" he asked after she'd walked away again to give them a moment to look over the pies.

"No, because we could be in bed, but we're here getting pie because you wanted to spend more time together even though *that* would also be spending time together," Paul muttered.

Yeah, he was definitely annoyed about more than Avery asking about the name tag. Avery didn't respond, because no matter what Paul thought, he *was* an adult, and he knew how to avoid being baited into an argument.

"How big are the slices?" he asked instead. "Are we sharing a piece or each having our own?"

Paul's gaze didn't leave his menu. "I'm sexually frustrated and annoyed and eating my feelings, so I'm having my own piece."

Avery wasn't sure if that was a joke or not, so he bit back his laugh. If he wanted to salvage this night, he was going to have to meet Paul halfway.

"In that case, why don't we order a few pieces of pie to go, share them at home, and call it foreplay?"

Chapter THIRTEEN

PAUL'S MIND was a million miles away while he packed up his stuff after softball practice, which is why he nearly fell over when his teammate caught him in a tackle hug as he turned to grab his bat from the dugout.

"I hope your trivia skills aren't as rusty as your shortstop game, 'cause I don't want to lose twice tonight."

The scrimmage hadn't gone well for his team, but Paul blamed that more on the beers half his team had slammed down before practice than the missed grounder he'd had in the third. Their first game of the season was in three weeks, and if they played like they had tonight then he may as well cancel the time off he'd requested for the national finals in Miami at the end of the summer. Their team usually made it, but if tonight's showing was any indication, that streak was at an end.

"Bad news, I'm not going to be able to carry you through trivia night. I've got to get home."

Finch punched him in the arm. "This is the third practice in a row that you've ditched out on drinks afterward."

Paul loved hanging out with the team, but he didn't want to miss out on time with Avery.

"Can't. I have plans," he said. He danced out of range when Finch took another swing.

Finch wrinkled his nose and made kissy faces. "This is more serious than I thought. What's his name?"

"Who says there's a guy? Maybe I'm hanging out with other friends."

Paul had never been in this position before. He hadn't been serious enough with any of the guys he'd dated to miss out on standing plans like trivia night or softball practice. The guys on the team knew he wasn't a monk, but they also knew his dating life never interfered with the rest of his social life.

"Bran's coming for trivia night, and you don't have any other friends," Finch said matter-of-factly. "Spill or I'll just ask him."

That was patently false. Paul had other friends. No one that he'd miss trivia night for, though.

"I'm seeing someone," he admitted. "And that's all you're getting out of me."

"Hey, someone check the temperature in hell," Finch yelled. "Paulie's got a boyfriend!"

Paul closed his eyes and sighed, all hope of slipping out of practice quietly dashed. Damn Finch and his big, nosy mouth.

Half the team crowded around them.

"Why haven't we met him?"

"Is he ugly? Is that why? You know we don't judge."

"We absolutely judge. Is he young? Is that why?"

"Does he hate sports? Are you dating an anti-jock?"

Finch broke in, yelling over the cacophony, "Is he dumb? Is that why you didn't invite him to trivia?"

Practices usually ended with most of the team meeting across the street at the sports pub for drinks, and on Tuesdays everyone invited their partners and various friends too, since it was trivia night. Bran had been coming for years, and even Ellie joined them occasionally.

Paul groaned. "He doesn't hate sports. I just didn't want to introduce him to you guys because it's casual."

Jake snorted. "If you're passing on trivia night for him, it's not *casual*."

"Remember that time Paul's parents were in town and he skipped dinner with them on their last night because it was a Tuesday?"

Frank pulled out his phone. "I'm texting Ellie."

Shit.

"Don't!"

Frank paused, phone in hand. The entire team was silent, waiting for Paul to speak.

Paul blew out a breath. He'd wanted to avoid a scene with the team when he and Avery inevitably broke up, but now not telling them about him was stacking up to cause an even bigger one.

"His name is Avery."

Finch shot him a withering look. "And?"

His teammates gossiped like old women. Paul had no hope of coming out of this without telling them more about Avery.

"And he's an old friend who came back to town and we reconnected."

"An old friend or an *old friend*?" Jake asked, wiggling his eyebrows. The team laughed and catcalled.

"An old friend," Paul said flatly. "And he doesn't hate sports. I just haven't invited him to come to practice because he's busy grading in the evenings."

"A teacher, then," Ruben said, stroking his chin thoughtfully. "What grade? Are we talking early elementary, all chipper? High school jaded? I can't see you with either, to be honest."

So. Damn. Nosy.

"College. He's an economics professor."

"You're dating a professor and you didn't invite him to trivia night? We'd have it in the bag!"

Everyone started talking at once again, until Frank made a triumphant noise.

"Ellie says he's not busy tonight if we want to invite him."

Paul froze. They'd planned to order dinner and watch a movie tonight, so he knew Avery was free. And he also knew Avery would jump at the chance to meet his friends. He'd probably wipe the floor with everyone at trivia too.

It would be fun to see him like that. But it meant opening one of the last barriers Paul had put up to keep Avery partitioned from the rest of his life.

"Where does he live?"

That was definitely not a conversation Paul wanted to have, considering Avery was currently living with him.

"Close enough to make it before it starts," he conceded. "I'll ask him if he wants to meet us over there. But take it easy on him, okay?"

Everyone cheered and scattered back to gathering their things, and Paul stepped away to find a quiet spot to text Avery. This felt bigger than it probably should, and Paul was freaking out a little.

The guys want to meet you. Up for pub trivia?

Avery hadn't pushed, but Paul knew his feelings had been hurt last week when he'd offered to come watch softball practice and Paul had quickly shot him down. He'd seen the disappointment that flashed across Avery's face, and that had been a blow. It was ironic, since keeping Avery away from the rest of his life had started as a way to limit how much Avery could hurt him.

Absolutely. But are you sure?

Ouch.

Avery had been open about his feelings about wanting a real relationship, and Paul had deflected and danced around the discussion every time it came up. Eventually Avery had just stopped trying to talk about the future, and they'd settled into a slightly uncomfortable détente where Avery stopped asking questions and Paul pretended to be satisfied with their arrangement being temporary.

He wasn't sure, though. But the fact that Avery was worried about that meant this was probably the right time.

Yeah. Bar's across from the park. I'll wait outside for you.

It was close enough to walk from the house, which made it even worse that Paul had forbidden Avery from coming to watch practice. God. He was an ass.

Paul zipped his bag around his bat and backtracked to the dugout to look for anything the team left behind. They teased him about being the team dad, but someone had to be the responsible one. He was usually the one who acted as the de facto manager, signing the team up with the league and scheduling games. He booked the bus when the team got invited to tournaments and negotiated rates with the hotels so everyone could get rooms in a block.

Most of the guys on the team were younger than him, and Paul was protective of them like an older brother would be. He didn't like feeling vulnerable around them, which was why tonight was going to be so uncomfortable. They'd all be sizing Avery up, and Paul knew he'd pass with flying colors. He was gorgeous, smart, funny, and charming. The accent alone would win over most of the team. On paper he and Avery were the perfect match. Career-driven, educated, ambitious. They shared a morbid sense of humor and were interested in a lot of the same things. Part of Paul hoped the team didn't like Avery. Anything to help Paul put the brakes on this runaway relationship that was gathering steam faster than he could put up the roadblocks. There was no real chance of that, though. They'd love him, just like Paul did.

He was in so far over his head.

Paul lagged behind the stragglers, following them toward the bar. Bran would already be there, holding down tables for them since trivia night was popular. Paul would bet the first round that Ellie was there too. Even if she hadn't been planning to come before Frank's text, there was zero chance she'd pass up the opportunity to see Avery meet the team.

They'd just seen Bran and Ellie a few days ago. Avery had joined their weekly Sunday brunch. He fit so perfectly in all parts of Paul's life. It was maddening. The four of them had met Avery and Bran's mom at the nursery afterward to pick out plants for the garden. Paul bought several tomato plants, even though he hated them. Avery loved them, though. Paul hadn't given it a second thought until they'd unloaded them at home and he'd realized that it was unlikely Avery would be there to harvest them. He'd probably be picking them alone.

It was dark enough that the streetlights were on, and Paul was blown away by how striking Avery was with his features shadowed as he moved through patches of yellow light while making his way over to the bar.

He must have changed after work, because he was wearing a pair of frayed jeans and a light sweater that was thin enough Paul could tell he wasn't wearing an undershirt. The team was going to eat him up.

Avery's face lit up when he saw Paul, and he broke into a jog. It made Paul's breath catch like he was in some sort of stupid romantic comedy. He hated himself a little for being so sappy.

"Hey," Avery said when he reached him. He leaned in and gave Paul a quick kiss. "Thanks for inviting me."

Paul wanted to brush him off and say he hadn't had a choice, but that wasn't true. He could have told the team no. The truth was he was tired of working so hard to keep Avery out, and it was time to open the door.

"Don't thank me until you've seen how sloppy they get after a few rounds," Paul said dismissively, but he took Avery's hand and didn't let go as he led him inside.

Chapter FOURTEEN

"YOU'LL DO just fine on the exam if you keep this pace up with studying," Avery told the student who'd lingered after the exam prep session that had just finished.

He normally didn't mind his office hours running over, but he'd gotten a text from a former colleague who was the assistant dean of economics at a university in California. It had taken all of his willpower not to check the text immediately when it had dinged on his Apple watch, but he'd always vowed to give his full attention to his students, and he wasn't going to break that promise now.

In two minutes when office hours were officially over, though, was another story. If he had to push this kid bodily out of the office, he would.

"Just stick to the study guide and prepare for the essay. That part is open notes, so as long as you're putting in the time on the exam guide, it will be a breeze."

He moved toward the door, and the student followed. Avery breathed a sigh of relief when she crossed the threshold into the corridor.

The minute the door shut behind her he pulled out his phone. Harvey had texted, *You around for a call?* forty minutes ago.

Had to finish up an exam prep session. I'm free now, he texted back.

His phone rang about ten seconds after he'd sent it, and Avery nearly dropped it in his haste to answer it.

"Harvey, hey."

"There's a flight to SFO that leaves in less than two hours. Can you be on it? There's a university fundraising gala tonight, and I can get you face time with the dean afterward. We have an opening, and you're perfect for it, but we're under a lot of pressure to get it filled as soon as possible. The listing was posted today."

No pleasantries and no bullshit—that was Harvey in a nutshell.

"Yes," Avery answered without hesitating. "I'll book the ticket right now."

"Good man," Harvey answered. "I can have a car pick you up from the airport and bring you straight to the gala. You're having drinks with the dean in the hotel bar afterward. He'll be in a tux, but you don't need to worry about being black tie since you won't get here in time for the event."

He was still wearing his usual teaching uniform—jeans and a blazer. He'd ditched the coat at the beginning of the study session, but his shirt hadn't gotten too rumpled from rolling up his sleeves. He'd be fine in this. Which was good, because he didn't have time to fuss over it.

"Plan to stay a few days if you can. I've got a spare room, and there's a departmental event on Saturday. The dean and the hiring committee have already seen your CV and love you, so as long as you don't muck it up tonight, you're well placed to get an interview. They're doing those virtually for those who aren't local, so you'll be fine to fly back to finish up at Northwestern."

"I can do that. Thank you, Harvey. Seriously. I owe you."

This was exactly the type of opportunity Avery had been waiting for. Harvey was one of his closest ex-colleagues, and Avery had no doubt he'd been a big part of the committee's favorable impression of him. Personal recommendations went a long way in their field. Someone could look great on paper but be a real dud in the classroom, which was why schools relied so much on recommendations and networking to narrow their candidate pool for openings.

He was good at what he did, including the politics of dealing with administration and intradepartmental meetings. Once he was in front of the dean, Avery was confident he could convince him he was the right choice.

"Text me your flight information from the airport," Harvey said before hanging up.

Avery spared a moment for a victorious fist pump. He stuffed his laptop into his bag and hurried out the door, almost forgetting to lock it behind him. He took a breath and tried to calm down. He needed to be focused if he was going to make that flight.

First and foremost, he needed to book it. He stood there for a moment, paralyzed by indecision. He could call an Uber and book it while he waited, but the bus ran right through campus, so that would be faster than walking off campus to call a ride. Walking and surfing on his phone on a crowded college campus wouldn't be a good look or very safe.

The more time he wasted here dithering over what to do, the less he had to pack.

Bran. He'd call Bran as he ran to the bus. Avery dialed and started walking as soon as it began to ring.

"Can you do me an enormous favor?" he asked when Bran picked up.

"I live to serve," Bran answered.

"I need you to book me a flight to San Francisco. There's supposed to be one that leaves around five."

"Like, for today?"

"Yes, for today. I have a meeting tonight for a job. Remember that friend on the West Coast I told you about? The one who thought he might have something for me? He just called, but I need to meet with the dean today because they're fast-tracking the applications. I'd be coming back Sunday."

Bran let out a low whistle. "Who knew academia moved so quickly?"

"It normally doesn't. I don't know why they're in a rush, but I'm not going to look a gift horse in the mouth."

Avery could see the bus two blocks down, so he broke into a run. This was one of those days where everything was going his way. Paul liked to tease him that "everything was coming up Avery" when things like this happened.

Shit. Paul.

"I want to tell Paul myself, so don't say anything, okay?"

He'd stopped telling Paul about job leads weeks ago because Paul always changed the subject when Avery tried. But that meant he had no idea Avery even had prospects on the West Coast.

"He's in and out of meetings all afternoon today, but you should be able to catch him before your flight. I'm booking you on a nonstop that leaves at 5:05 p.m. and gets you into San Francisco a little before eight."

That should work. The dean wouldn't be out of the gala until nearly ten, if it was like the ones Avery had been forced to sit through.

"You're a lifesaver. Hold on just a sec."

Avery pulled up his transit app and scanned his phone as he got on the bus, not bothering to sit since he wouldn't be on that long.

"Okay, I'm headed to the house to pack. Forward me the receipt and I'll Venmo you."

"We'll worry about it later," Bran said. "I'm light on meetings this afternoon, so I'll pick you up. I'll leave now."

Avery knew he didn't deserve his family. They supported him without question, even when he asked them to book him a cross-country flight at the last minute.

"That would be amazing," Avery told him. "I need twenty minutes to get stuff together, tops."

"The sooner I get you there, the sooner you can call Paul," Bran said "Maybe he can fly out and join you Friday. He loves the Bay Area."

Avery's heart stuttered. He hadn't thought much past finding a flight. There was a difference between knowing he was interviewing for a job across the country and *knowing* he was interviewing for a job across the country. He'd be thousands of miles from Paul and his family. And while it wasn't insurmountable in terms of seeing his family for holidays and vacations, it was a significant obstacle for a relationship.

Bran hung up with the promise that he'd see Avery soon, and Avery spent the rest of the short bus ride with his thoughts buzzing in his head. His stomach was a swirl of excitement over the job and anxiety over telling Paul.

It took three tries to get his key in the lock, which didn't help his nerves. Avery took a minute standing in Paul's sunny entryway to gather himself. Focus on the task at hand, he told himself. He needed to grab toiletries and clothes and get to the airport—he'd think about Paul once he was there.

Paul kept his luggage in the guest-room closet, and Avery helped himself to a carry-on. It would be easier than checking one of his larger suitcases.

His clothes were still in the guest room, so it was easy enough to grab what he'd need. Harvey hadn't said what kind of event the department was having, so Avery hedged his bets and packed both jeans and something nicer. His blazer would work with either. He taught in trainers, but those seemed too casual to meet with the dean in. Traveling in brogues was uncomfortable, though, so he compromised and tossed a pair in the case to change into there.

His toiletries had all migrated to Paul's bathroom, and he lost momentum when he hurried in to get them and saw the unmade bed. Paul was a neat freak, but this morning Avery had distracted him with a quickie as Paul was leaving for work, and Avery hadn't thought to make the bed himself after.

He spared a minute to fix the covers now. Paul was going to be mad enough about him flying out to San Francisco. Avery didn't need to give him any more ammunition.

That wasn't fair. Paul had been amazing. Avery was messy by nature, and Paul hadn't complained. He'd picked up Avery's stray mugs of tea everywhere and dealt with his errant socks in the couch cushions, and to be honest, that had encouraged Avery to make more messes.

He wanted Paul to get mad about the messes. It would be better than him just ignoring them and treating Avery like a houseguest who would be leaving any minute.

Avery grabbed the covers and rumpled them, feeling vaguely satisfied by the petty action. That way, in case Paul *didn't* get mad about him leaving, at least he'd be annoyed over the bed.

That was the real problem, Avery realized. What if Paul didn't care? He was putting off telling him not because he thought he'd be mad, but because he thought he'd be indifferent. He wanted Paul to give him a reason to stay, and Paul wasn't going to. He wouldn't even talk about job prospects with Avery. He'd taken himself out of the equation entirely, so it was impossible to balance the columns.

Avery hurried into the bathroom and grabbed his toothbrush and the travel toothpaste from his kit. He'd been using Paul's weird cinnamon stuff since he moved in. Mint would taste weird after that.

His shampoo was in the shower, but it was too big to fly with anyway. He'd just have to pick some up at the airport. His hair gel was small, though. And the little tin of beard balm Paul had gotten him when Avery had decided to go on strike from shaving.

He was downstairs and ready by the time Bran texted that he was out front. Avery paused with his hand on the doorknob, knowing he might not be welcome back here if he left. He didn't look back as he opened it because that felt too much like the final goodbye he'd given a sleeping Paul last time he'd left him.

This wasn't permanent, though. There was a good chance he wouldn't get the job and all this trouble would be for nothing.

One thing was for sure, however. If he got on that plane, he was choosing his career over Paul. So far he'd been keeping his options open because he didn't know what Paul wanted, but leaving for San Francisco would make the decision for him.

He closed the door behind him and hurried to Bran's car.

Avery had expected the Spanish Inquisition from his brother the minute he got in, but Bran surprised him by staying quiet. He probably knew better than Avery did that going meant things were over with Paul.

Excitement and anxiety were at war in his stomach, and anxiety was winning.

"Do you know what he wants?"

Bran didn't have to ask him to clarify who he meant. Paul's absence hung heavy in the car.

"I don't," Bran said, his tone apologetic. "He seems happy. But we haven't talked about it. I figured you two were."

Bran and Paul talked about everything. It wasn't good news that Paul wasn't confiding in him. It probably meant he thought there was nothing to say.

Avery sighed. "He doesn't want to talk to me about my job hunt. Changes the subject whenever I try. He doesn't even know I was looking in San Francisco."

Bran made a soft noise, and Avery couldn't tell if it was meant to be comforting or censorious.

"What do *you* want?"

Avery looked out the window. Rush hour started early in Chicago, and they were already crawling, even though it wasn't quite four. Maybe he'd miss his flight, and then he wouldn't have to make a decision. The thought both cheered and depressed him.

"I want him," he said honestly. "But I also want my career. This is a tenure-track position, and Harvey has as much as said it's mine for the taking."

This time there was no mistaking the disappointment in Bran's hum.

"I want whatever you want," he said slowly, like he was choosing his words carefully. "But if you're making major life decisions without consulting him, that's not a relationship. It's an arrangement."

An arrangement. That sounded exactly like something Paul would say, which made Avery wonder if he and Bran *had* talked and Bran was keeping quiet out of loyalty to him. Not that Avery would blame him if he was. Paul deserved his loyalty more than Avery did.

They sat in silence until Bran pulled up to drop Avery off at departures.

"You should have your ticket in your email," Bran said. He put the car in park and leaned over to give Avery a one-armed hug. "Good luck."

Avery wasn't sure if he meant with the job or with Paul.

"I'll let you know how it goes tonight," Avery said. "It'll be late. I'll text."

He felt heavy as he made his way into the terminal, and this time he did look back. Bran was still sitting in his car at the curb, watching him go in. He gave him a little wave, and Avery returned it halfheartedly.

Even though the airport was busy, he had no trouble getting through security and finding his gate well before boarding. Hard to believe less than two hours ago he'd been in his office running test prep with worried freshmen.

Avery found a pillar to slouch against and took out his phone. There was plenty of time to text Paul to tell him what was going on and assure him he'd be back Sunday. Maybe he should be casual in his text, like it was picking up a thread of a conversation they'd already had.

He composed it ten different ways in his head before he thumbed open a text to actually write something. His throat caught when he noticed the last text Paul had sent. Yesterday he'd asked Avery to stop and get Pop-Tarts at the corner mini-mart because Avery had planned to get creamer there anyway.

He hadn't said what kind, but Avery hadn't needed him to. Paul only ate unfrosted strawberry Pop-Tarts, which Avery thought were gross and teased him endlessly about. Going without frosting didn't make them healthy, it only made them sad, he told Paul just about every morning while the two of them ate a hurried breakfast standing in the kitchen before dashing their separate ways.

Avery had walked to the mini-mart after work and gotten Paul's Pop-Tarts and the coffee creamer. He hadn't thought anything of it, but now it seemed unbearably domestic.

He'd told Bran that he and Paul didn't talk about the future, but that wasn't exactly true. They talked about the things Paul would make with the veggies they picked out together to grow in the raised beds Paul had made, and Paul had promised him he'd take him to a Cuban restaurant the team loved if they made it to the tournament in Miami again this year.

What if Paul didn't want to talk about Avery's job hunt because he didn't want to talk about Avery leaving?

The thought took Avery's breath away. He'd been too caught up in his hurt over Paul not wanting to be involved in his life that he hadn't looked at it from Paul's perspective. Paul had been clear from the beginning that their time together had an expiration date, but the deciding factor had always been Avery's career.

The gate agent called his flight's number, and Avery was surprised to realize he'd been woolgathering for forty-five minutes. They were already halfway boarded.

Shit.

Avery pulled up his texts with Harvey and didn't hesitate.

Sorry, mate. Can't make it tonight. Hope the search works out quickly for you!

If he hurried he could get back to the house before Paul got home from work. They needed to properly talk, and this time he wasn't going to take no for an answer.

Chapter FIFTEEN

"I'M SAYING there are better choices for this project. Choices that don't involve me flying to Florida." Paul rubbed his temples and prayed for strength. There had to be a patron saint of corporate drudgery, right? There seemed to be one for everything else.

He leaned back in his chair and listened as the CTO outlined his plans for a proposal that could land a huge client for the company. Paul was behind that a hundred percent. He was happy to take point on the programming side of things, but he wasn't a sales guy. Paul was the guy who made everything the project managers promised to the client work after the fact. Usually with a little cursing and a lot of overtime.

"Charlie, come on. You know that's not my skill set."

"I know, and I wouldn't normally put you out front like this. But the client specifically requested the technical lead be at the presentation so they could ask questions about specs in real time. I need you to go to Florida with the team."

Paul wanted to throw the phone, but instead he took a deep breath and agreed to go. He could hardly tell his boss's boss he didn't want to take a business trip because he'd miss his boyfriend, could he?

He wasn't sure what was worse—that he had to go be part of a client pitch meeting or that the part he dreaded most wasn't being put on the spot in front of clients but rather having to spend two days away from Avery.

They were nearing the end of their trial run, as Paul had taken to thinking of it, and things were going shockingly well. Avery was thriving after over a month teaching on campus, and the semester was ending in a week.

Once Avery had moved in, it had been impossible to segregate Avery from the rest of his life. His presence bled over into everything else, starting with his standing brunch date with Bran and their other friends, then the softball team, and now work.

Not that anyone at work knew about Avery. This was Paul's last stronghold. It was going to be hard enough managing the pity from his friends and teammates once Avery jetted off like he always did. He didn't want to have Janet from sales baking him her infamous breakup cupcakes.

But being with Avery was affecting the decisions he made at work, and that was bad enough. He'd become the whiny guy who didn't want to work late or take a business trip because he'd miss movie night with his boyfriend.

Ugh.

He had a ticket on an afternoon flight tomorrow. Paul packed up his laptop and grabbed a few other things he'd need since he wouldn't stop at the office tomorrow. He could finish up a few things at home before heading to the airport. Which also meant he could convince Avery to go have breakfast at the diner with him because his Thursday class wasn't until noon, so he'd be home.

Avery only had a week left on his temporary contract with Northwestern, and he still didn't know what he would do next. It was nerve-wracking for both of them. Avery was so ambition driven that not knowing where his career was going next was eating him up inside. And having him here for so long was making it impossible to stick to the rules Paul had made for himself. He'd shot past every boundary almost as soon as he'd put them up. The one-night stand in Dallas that turned into the week of fun in Tahoe, which bled into a month and a half of casual sex here in Chicago. Though no part of having Avery live with him was casual, no matter how hard Paul tried to convince himself it was.

And once that seal had been broken, there wasn't much point in pretending his heart wasn't going full steam ahead. He loved Avery. He'd loved Avery for all of his adult life, even when he'd hated him. And he couldn't be mad at Avery about it because Paul was the one breaking his own heart here. He knew exactly who Avery was, and he'd let him past every barrier anyway.

It would be easier if Avery was a selfish ass, but he wasn't. Not really. He loved Paul, and he loved his family. But his priority was his career, and Paul couldn't fault him for that. Not this time. Avery had been honest about not knowing where his career was taking him, so Paul couldn't even say he'd been misled.

Or maybe he had, by himself. Paul had lied to himself from day one about what Avery meant to him and what he could handle.

His last-ditch effort at protecting himself had been making Avery keep all his things in the guest bedroom. Having Avery in his home was one thing, but making space for him in his bedroom—closet space, drawer space—had different implications. Implications Paul wasn't willing to deal with. Avery leaving was inevitable, and Paul would rather not have to look at empty shelves in his closet when he did.

That was his last stronghold. The bathroom thing had died before it even really started. It had been ridiculous to expect Avery to keep all his toiletries in the hallway bathroom when Paul's en suite was right there. Things had slowly migrated over the first week Avery had lived with him. Now he knocked over hair gel, shaving cream, and all of Avery's other potions and vials every time he took his contacts out.

He'd looked at double sinks last time he'd been in the home improvement store. It wasn't what he'd gone in to do, but he'd walked past them and stopped absentmindedly, checking dimensions and prices and wondering if he could do it himself or if he'd have to hire a handyman like he did when he had the back patio built.

It had felt natural and normal, and it wasn't until he'd been debating with himself over cabinet finish that he realized that renovating his bathroom was unnecessary. Sure, there wasn't enough counter space now, but double sinks would be overkill if Avery moved on. Once the idea had taken seed, he'd been unable to stop thinking about it, though. It could be his summer home improvement project, now that the yard was mostly built out. If Avery ended up with a job in Chicago, of course. The uncertainty of it was killing him.

Paul stuck his head in Bran's office to tell him he was heading home for the day, but Bran's light was already off. He texted him instead.

Gone for the day? I stopped by to tell you Charlie's making me go to Florida with the sales team.

Paul's phone pinged almost immediately.

Avery needed a ride, so I decided I'd finish up at home. You flying out tomorrow? Want to come over for dinner?

Why would Avery have needed a ride? He'd been taking the bus to campus most days.

Thanks, but Avery and I will probably eat in.

Paul watched as dots appeared as Bran was typing, then disappeared, then appeared again. He was already in his car by the time Bran finally responded.

If you haven't left work yet, come meet me at my house. You don't have to stay for dinner if you don't want to.

Paul checked his watch. Avery's office hours should have ended hours ago, so he'd already be home. But Bran only lived ten minutes from the office; Paul could spare a few minutes.

Bran's car was parked in front of the building when he pulled up, so Paul opened the door and walked in without knocking since he was expected.

"I'm on the balcony," Bran called as soon as Paul closed the door.

The condo association didn't allow grills or firepits, so Bran and Ellie had put a faux electric fireplace on the balcony to keep them warm and let them use the space in the late fall and early spring when Chicago weather was too cool to sit outside without a heat source. Bran was out there now, sprawled on a rattan sofa that Ellie had dragged them all the way to the far west suburbs to buy off craigslist a few years ago.

Bran already had a beer, which was unusual for the middle of a workday. Another sat on the end table, already opened.

"What's up? Everything okay with Ellie?"

Bran frowned. "Yeah, she's going over to Jess's tonight to finish planning for the baby shower this weekend."

"Aren't those supposed to be surprises?"

"Do you think it's a good idea to surprise a pregnant woman? Especially when that pregnant woman is Jess? From what Ellie says, she has an entire Pinterest vision board for Ellie and Cara Sue to follow for it."

He had a point. Ellie and Jess's best friend Cara Sue were the official hosts, but it wouldn't be like Jess to step back and let anyone else take the wheel.

"Avery said everything on her registry was a specific shade of pink."

Paul had never been to a baby shower before. He'd always thought they were only for women, but Jess and her husband, Ethan, were having a couples shower. He wasn't looking forward to it, but Avery was weirdly hyped for it. He'd even volunteered to help set up.

Bran cleared his throat and took a sip of beer. "Have you talked to Avery today?"

They never talked during the day. Avery had classes and office hours, and Paul never checked his phone while he was at work. Half the time he forgot it in the car.

"No."

Bran cleared his throat again. "He heard about an opening. Tenure-track economics position. They want him to interview with the dean and the chair. It's in San Francisco."

That was great. Well, not great for Paul. But great for Avery.

Bran was studying his beer bottle like there'd be a test on the ingredients later, avoiding eye contact. Paul's chest tightened with anxiety.

"When is the interview?"

Bran looked up. "Tomorrow. I took him to the airport after his last class today. He got a call from an old friend who got him an interview. I didn't know he hadn't told you. I'm sorry, Paul. He's an ass."

The other shoe had dropped, then. Paul braced himself to feel a wave of betrayal and hurt, but instead, he felt... nothing. Just an emptiness where emotion should be. Maybe he'd prepared himself for this after all.

"How does the saying go? The definition of insanity is doing the same thing and expecting different results?"

He sat on the edge of the couch and picked up his beer, taking a long drink to swallow past the dryness in his throat.

"Paul—"

"No, I don't.... Don't try to explain or excuse him. I don't need it. He's Avery. This is what he does."

"He should have called. It was a last-minute thing, but he still should have told you. You deserve better than that, Paul."

He knew he did. It was why he'd set up all these rules for himself. Avery was never going to be a permanent fixture in his life. His rational brain knew that, even if his subconscious was starting to remodel the bathroom. He thought Avery had matured enough to communicate with him this time. He'd been pushing Paul to talk to him for weeks. Wheedling his way into places Paul didn't want him. Being part of things that Paul never wanted him to be part of because he didn't want to share those things with someone who was going to walk out of his life almost as quickly as he walked in.

Dammit.

He should be angry. He should be pissed, like he was last time. But the emptiness inside his chest wasn't getting the memo. It was hovering there, numb.

"Do you know when he's coming back?"

Bran was observing him carefully, and Paul hated that. He didn't want Bran to think he was responsible for cleaning up after Avery again. He'd done that once, put Paul's shattered pieces back together, and it wasn't fair to expect him to do it again. Paul *wouldn't* expect him to do it again.

"Avery said he'd be back Sunday morning. They were looking to move pretty quickly with filling the position, and it sounds like they were very interested in him."

Well, that was good for Avery. He'd be able to finish out the semester at Northwestern and slide right into something else.

Paul took another sip of beer and put the half-full bottle back on the table. If he started pounding drinks back now, he wouldn't stop, and that would make tomorrow hell.

"I need to get home and pack. There are a few loose ends I want to tie up before the presentation too. They wanted a technical guy on site to question, so I'm assuming someone there knows what they're doing."

"Paul—"

Paul shook his head. "I don't want your pity, Bran. I'll see you Saturday."

He probably wouldn't. Going to Jess's shower as a plus one for someone who wasn't going sounded like an etiquette faux pas. It was the kind of thing Avery would Google out of curiosity. Paul didn't. Instead, he let himself out and sat in his car for a few minutes before driving home.

Avery's stuff was still scattered all over the place. Discarded socks in the couch cushions, which Paul could never understand. Paul didn't check the guest room, but he imagined everything was still in there. Boxes stacked against the wall, clothes likely strewn on the bed and floor from a hasty packing job for the trip to San Francisco.

The bathroom counter was clear, though. Avery had taken all the small toiletries that had been scattered there.

Paul knew the void of feelings inside wouldn't last forever, but he wasn't inclined to look a gift horse in the mouth. He could fall apart after he got back from his business trip. It wasn't like it would do any good to get angry now. How could he, when things were going exactly like he'd known they would?

Last time he'd blown Avery's phone up, not that it had done any good. At least he'd learned that lesson. This was an improvement. Fixed the bugs from the beta test, he thought with a small laugh. Dumped Version 2.0 running smoothly.

Get through the rest of the week, he told himself as he moved through the motions of getting packed. *Pencil in a breakdown to fall apart on the weekend.*

Paul didn't want to be in the empty house alone, so he switched his ticket to fly out early. The client was in Orlando, and flights there were easy to come by. The hotel had room to add a night, and Charlie didn't object when he called to clear it, so it all worked out.

Usually Paul worked during flights, since they were billing the travel time to the client anyway. But he didn't this time. He didn't read or watch a movie either. He sat there, thinking. He hadn't worked up to anger yet, and the curious detachment he felt let him view the last two months like they'd happened to someone else. It wasn't healthy, but it was easier to deal with than actually processing Avery leaving would be.

The three-hour flight passed in a blink. Text notifications streamed across his phone screen rapid-fire like a stock ticker when he turned it back on after landing, and he didn't even check who they were from before clearing the notifications and putting his phone back in airplane mode. He didn't want to hear any of Avery's excuses, and he didn't want to repeat the same humiliating mistakes he'd made twelve years ago when he'd left tearful, pleading messages on Avery's voicemail.

The whole point of coming a day early was to be out of pocket for a bit, and that meant being unreachable. He'd turn his phone back on in the morning, but for tonight he just wanted his own company.

The corporate office always booked him into Marriotts, and depending on the location, that could mean anything from a three-star Courtyard hotel to a five-star boutique one. This was one of the nicer ones, which was handy. Paul could drown his sorrows in scotch and Wagyu in the on-site steakhouse or swim them off in the rooftop pool if he wanted to. It was a lot easier to wallow in self-pity in a fancy hotel.

Paul needed to shift into work mode and figure out what his role was for Friday's pitch. He was comfortable traveling and working with clients, since as a technical lead he went out to job sites quite a bit. But it was usually after the software was already deployed, to help train the client on it and troubleshoot any bugs.

Speaking to groups wasn't a strong suit. He'd proved that at Bran's wedding.

Paul wanted to blame how anxious he was on the sales part, but he knew that wasn't true. Business trips were formulaic, and this one was different from most not because of what he'd be doing.

This was still the first time he'd come on a trip while in a relationship. Even though he and Avery were over, he was still counting it.

Paul's usual angle was to hang out at the bar and see if he could find anyone to hook up with, but that wasn't an option tonight. He'd been freshly dumped, and he wasn't in the mood for a vengeful rebound.

Instead, he made his way through the shockingly garish bloodred lobby and retreated to his room. So much for the hope that this place would have a relaxing, spalike atmosphere.

He risked taking his phone out of airplane mode long enough to research food at the hotel, but no more texts came through.

There was a fancy restaurant downstairs, but he wasn't sure he was in the headspace to eat alone in a place that looked like it had been ripped from the set of *The Best Little Whorehouse in Texas*, no matter how good the reviews said its ribeye was. The photos showed literal red fringe curtains between the tables. It would be comical if he was in a better mood, but tonight was not that night.

He wasn't in the mood for any sort of human interaction, he decided. So room service it was. He settled on a local IPA and a bacon burger that was so fancy he couldn't even pronounce the cheese on it. Eating your feelings should always involve cheese.

When the room phone rang twenty minutes later, Paul picked it up, expecting it to be room service.

"Good, you're alive," Bran's voice snarled when he answered it.

He wasn't sure how to respond to that. "Yes?"

"No, he's fine, El," Bran said, his voice muffled like he'd covered the microphone. "He's at the hotel in Florida."

"Hello to you too," Paul said, annoyed. "Did you need something, other than to confirm I'm not dead?"

"Avery was frantic trying to find you, and Ellie somehow worked herself into a state and was convinced you'd been in an accident and were dead in a ditch somewhere," Bran snapped. "Why aren't you answering your damn texts?"

He hadn't considered that they might not all be from Avery. Oops.

"My phone's off. I didn't want to deal with Avery's explanations or apologies, or worse, waiting around to see if he even *would* try to explain or apologize. Tell Ellie I'm sorry."

He could hear Bran say, "He says he's sorry. No you will *not*," emphatically before coming back to the phone. "Ellie wants to fly out and kick your ass, but lucky for you, she's out of PTO after the wedding and the honeymoon."

He could imagine Ellie sticking her tongue out at Bran, and she probably threw in a few choice words as well, because he heard Bran chuckle softly.

"This was some diva-ass shit, Paul," he said. "Disappearing like that? I had to call Charlie at home to confirm you'd decided to go out early. We thought you'd been hurt or kidnapped or something. Your car is still at the house."

He'd taken an Uber to the airport like he always did for trips. Driving to O'Hare was the worst.

"You're at my house?"

Bran made a frustrated noise. "Yes, because someone had to come talk Avery down from filing a missing person's report."

"*Avery* is at my house?" He should have been in San Francisco by now.

"You'd know that if you'd read your texts. You know, you two deserve each other. Neither one of you is a functional adult, I swear to God."

That was uncalled for. All Paul had done was leave for a business trip early. It was hardly a capital crime.

Bran's words seemed to uncork the anger Paul had been expecting. The empty void in his chest was quickly filling with bitterness and rage.

"What I deserve is someone who respects me enough to tell me himself when he's taking a job across the country instead of ghosting me like a coward."

Yeah, there was the reaction he'd been waiting for. Paul was honestly relieved at the wave of emotions. He'd worried he'd be numb forever.

"It was an interview, and he didn't go. Which is why you should talk to him."

Paul didn't want to talk to Avery. He didn't want to forgive him for putting him through this again simply because he changed his mind at the last minute. Avery did what Avery always did—leave. Maybe it was for a few hours instead of years, but the result was the same. How could Paul trust him if his instinct was still to ghost him when his career came calling?

The worst part was Paul had tried his damnedest to be understanding. He knew Avery's job hunt took priority. If Avery had respected him enough to shoot him a text to tell him he was hopping a flight to California for an interview, Paul would have been fine with it.

Well, not fine. Upset that Avery wasn't staying. But not mad enough to play stupid games like turning his phone off and hiding from everyone like he was a middle-school girl whose crush asked someone else to the dance.

Bran was right; this had been some diva-ass shit. And Paul wasn't willing to be the bigger person just yet.

"I don't need to talk to him."

"He didn't *go*, Paul."

"This time. He didn't go this time. But if he's capable of dashing off without talking to the guy he's living with, then he's not serious about our relationship."

Bran argued with someone in angry, whispered bursts, and Paul's stomach dropped. If Avery was there, Bran might hand him the phone. And whether or not it was the mature thing to do, and he knew it wasn't, Paul didn't want to talk to Avery.

He wanted to be angry because it reminded him of why this entire thing had been a terrible idea. They'd been on a crash course with this trajectory from that first night in Dallas, and Paul knew it. He'd gotten complacent, and now he'd been burned. He didn't want to talk to Avery and let him explain. The only thing Paul needed to understand was that this was always going to be the outcome. He was the problem, not Avery. He'd let himself get drawn in, and now he was paying for it.

"Would you just—"

"No," Paul said, cutting him off. "I don't want to talk to Avery. I want to eat my dinner when it comes, watch some crappy television, and go to bed. I'll be back Saturday, and if Avery's still around we can talk then. But I have zero interest in litigating this over the phone."

"For fuck's sake, Paul, there isn't anything to *litigate*. He did something stupid, realized it was stupid, and came back to fix the stupid knee-jerk thing he did."

"I'm hanging up now," Paul said. "You've confirmed I'm alive. I'll talk to you Saturday."

He considered leaving the phone off the hook so Bran couldn't call back, but he wasn't willing to chance his burger on it. He might still need the phone in case room service needed to call him. He doubted Bran would, anyway. He'd always been good at giving Paul space when he asked for it.

Arguing with Bran had left him starving, so he hoped his food came soon. He really did want to curl up and watch something mindless and then go to sleep. Paul was more than ready for today to be over.

He was tired, hungry, cranky, and hurt. His grandmother used to tell him that everything looked better after a meal and a good night's sleep, and usually that was true. Paul didn't see how it would change the math on this one, but it was worth a shot.

Avery had come back, but there was always going to be another job. Another opportunity. And he didn't begrudge him that. But the fact that Avery's gut instinct had been to drop everything and go without talking to him first? That said more about his intentions than him calling off the trip did.

He jumped when a loud knock sounded on the door. A small part of him hoped it was Avery, even though that was both ridiculous and impossible. He got up and let the porter wheel in his dinner. Time to drown his sorrows in food.

PAUL'S ANGER had cooled considerably by the time he and the team finished their pitch on Friday morning. He had a plane ticket home that afternoon, but even though he wasn't steaming mad anymore, he also wasn't sure he was ready to have things out with Avery yet.

He was worried about his resolve. Avery was his soft spot, and he needed to sort his head out before he gave Avery another chance to mess with it.

Paul had a high school friend in Key West and a former softball teammate who had moved to Clearwater, but other than that he didn't know anyone who lived in Florida. Going home wasn't something he wanted to do, but staying here alone wasn't appealing either.

Wait.

Marnie lived in Tampa. Would that be weird? They'd hung out a lot in Tahoe, and they'd texted each other on and off afterward.

He shot off a message to her asking if she was free for the weekend before he could second-guess himself. She was a nurse practitioner at a hospital in Tampa, so she might be working. Or have plans with her actual friends, which he assumed she had but didn't know for sure because most of their conversations had been her playing agony aunt and being his antiwingman.

Still hiding from your runaway boytoy in Orlando?

He shouldn't be surprised she knew about the drama. Frankly, he was more shocked that Marnie hadn't immediately texted him to yell at him about it. She'd either shown amazing restraint or she'd texted Ellie when he messaged her and only just found out about it.

Thinking about extending my stay through the weekend, but I don't want to stay in Orlando.

He'd spent most of Thursday lounging at the pool and waiting on the rest of the team to arrive and then worked on the presentation with them late into the evening. The hotel was nice, but he didn't want another mindless day at the pool. And greater Orlando was a horror show of tourist traps, theme parks, and urban firing ranges. Not his idea of fun.

Reschedule your flight. Give me twenty minutes to figure out the details.

He'd missed Marnie's no-nonsense bluntness. He wanted to escape this mess and turn off his brain for a bit, and he had no doubt Marnie could make that happen.

Paul rescheduled his flight in the app while he waited for her to make a plan. He didn't know if she'd want the whole weekend or not, but he booked himself on an early flight on Monday. He shot an email to his boss telling her he was taking a personal day Monday and then texted Bran that he was spending the weekend in Florida. Odds were good he already knew, because Ellie and Marnie texted like fiends and told each other everything. Bran would probably know where he was going before he did.

He hesitated over his text thread with Avery, but decided to be an adult and opened it. He'd avoided it until now, but he couldn't help but read all the missed messages.

Hey, are you going to be late tonight?

Did you have softball practice today? I thought those were on Mondays only.

Paul, call me.

I talked to Bran, and you have every right to be mad, but call me. I'm worried.

I didn't go, Paul.

I fucked up and I'm sorry. Call me to let me know where you are.

You can't run away when things get hard. Will you please at least text me back?

Ellie says I need to let you have space. So I'm giving you space. I love you. I'll see you Saturday.

The last one had been sent Thursday night.

Paul swallowed past the lump in his throat. The texts were a lot like the voicemails he'd left for Avery after he'd ghosted Paul and moved to Europe. Part of him wanted to rebook the flight for today and go back, but his rational brain told him he needed more time. He needed to figure out what he actually wanted from a future with Avery, and he needed to give himself permission to ask for it.

It didn't mean it would happen. But Paul had been so focused on surviving the short-term arrangement with Avery that he'd closed himself off to the possibility that he could have more with him. He needed to figure out if he wanted that, and what he wanted it to look like. He'd spent so much time dogging on Avery for not growing up that he hadn't realized he needed to as well.

Marnie texted him before he could figure out what to say to Avery.

Text me your hotel address. I can be in Orlando to pick you up in a couple hours. Borrowing a place from a friend for the weekend for us to stay.

Paul let out a breath. It was a relief to have her take control. He'd spend the weekend figuring out his shit, and Marnie would take care of all the details.

I do need space. Flying back Monday, he texted Avery. *I love you too.*

Chapter SIXTEEN

"I KNOW he overreacted, but don't you think *you* overreacting is going to make things worse?"

Avery moved around Bran and put the box he'd been carrying on the kitchen counter. He'd been lucky to stumble into a fully furnished sublet. He'd found it on a board in the student union on Saturday morning when he'd stopped by campus to clean out his borrowed office on the way to Jess's baby shower, and by dinnertime he'd signed a lease for the summer.

"This is not overreacting. I'm not punishing him by moving out. This was what we'd always agreed would happen. I was only staying with him while I was teaching at Northwestern."

He didn't expect Bran to understand. Avery knew it looked backward if you were outside looking in, but moving into his own place was the biggest romantic gesture he could think of. It meant he was committing to staying in Chicago even though he didn't have a job here yet.

"But how are you going to convince him you're choosing him over a job if you're moving out? Isn't the point for you two to be together?"

"If I told him I was staying, he wouldn't believe me."

Avery didn't blame him. Even *he* was barely convinced, and he'd been the one to make the decision. He wasn't going to abandon his career, but he also wasn't going to abandon Paul.

Coming back to find Paul's house empty had been a relief at first. Avery had taken his time putting his things away, and he'd even remade the bed and picked up all his socks. He'd panicked when Paul hadn't come home and hadn't answered any of his texts. When he'd called Bran and found out that Paul knew about San Francisco, it had been the worst of both worlds—he hadn't been able to go after the job, but he had managed to hurt Paul and confirm his worst fears about their relationship. And it had been 100 percent his fault.

He didn't blame Paul for staying in Florida for the weekend, but he couldn't say the same for Bran. He'd taken Paul's disappearing act harder than Avery had.

Bran would *not* let it go.

"Do you really want to be with someone who doesn't take you at your word?"

"Why are you so willing to forgive me for what I did but not willing to forgive him for his reasonable response to it?"

"You didn't do anything!" Bran said, exploding into motion and pacing the small space.

"I did, Bran. I was going to. Then I came to my senses, but the damage was already done."

"Maybe you should take that job. I wanted the two of you to be together because you've both pined over each other since your breakup, but if this is what the two of you look like together then it's not healthy."

Avery wanted to tell him to butt out of their business because he had no idea what their relationship was actually like. But that wouldn't help his case. Most of all, he didn't want Bran to blame Paul. Avery had pulled the rug out from under Paul's feet, and Paul needed his best friend there to support him through the fallout. Even if that best friend was Avery's brother, who wanted to be angry at Paul because it was easier to be mad at him than be mad at Avery.

"We weren't in a healthy relationship," Avery admitted. "Not because of Paul, but because of me. I wanted to be with him, and I also wanted the freedom to not limit my job search because of it, and all I ended up doing was fucking everything up. Be mad at me if you want to blame someone for this. I'm the one who caused it."

"I've never seen this side of him, and I don't like it. He had everyone worried about him, and then instead of apologizing he doubled down and made things worse."

The hours Paul had been missing had been one of the worst afternoons of Avery's life. He'd imagined a dozen different horrible scenarios, so by the time Bran found him in Florida, it had been a relief just to know he was alive. And as much as that sucked, it had to be a shadow of the way Paul must have felt when he woke up in their shared apartment and found all of Avery's stuff gone. He'd moved across the Atlantic—at least Paul had only gone to Florida.

Avery picked up a box of books and moved them to the coffee table to get it off the floor. He'd have to buy bookcases if he stayed here long. What kind of student flat didn't have bookcases?

Ellie was out buying him sheets because she didn't trust the ones that came with the place. It was a good move, but he chafed a bit at the idea that she didn't trust him to take care of details like that on his own. Everyone treated him like a child, and he was fed up with it. Paul seemed to be the only one willing to hold Avery accountable for his fuckups, and that had to stop if he was going to stay here.

"I'm the one who owes him an apology. And you, for dragging you into this. I shouldn't have pursued a relationship with him until I knew I could commit to it. That's entirely on me. I put him in a bad situation because I wanted to be with him before all the details were ironed out. It was selfish of me. We both know that Paul deserves more than that."

That took some of the wind out of Bran's sails. Enough to stop the pacing, at least. Progress.

"I love you both, and I want both of you to be happy."

"I want that too. But Paul's not wrong about me, Bran. I've been a dick. The way I left him before? There's no excuse."

"You were young and stupid. That's different."

"I was twenty-three. I wasn't a child then, and I'm not one now. I am responsible for my actions, even when they're shitty. Paul didn't talk to me for over ten years after I left him. I've spent the last month breaking down those walls, and all it took was one idiotic thing to send them right back up."

"That's not all on you. He has commitment issues. He never gets serious with the guys he dates. It's why I was so happy to see you two move in together."

Avery snorted. "He has commitment issues because of *me*."

Bran took a second to process that, his face dropping. "Oh my God."

"Yeah. You've never put that together? His first love moves out and leaves the country without telling him, and you wonder why he has issues?"

Bran grimaced. "I didn't. He doesn't talk to me about you. I mean, at first he did, but we didn't want to let you leaving come between us, so we kind of put it away. And after a while I forgot how awful it was after you left."

"He said you gave him updates every time you talked to me."

"Because I always thought you two were perfect for each other and I wanted to keep you in his mind. So basically I tortured my best friend. Awesome."

"I tortured him. You just provided reminders I was thriving in the career I left him for."

Bran squeezed his eyes shut and rubbed his face. "So when I mentioned that you'd gone to San Francisco, not knowing you hadn't told him, I totally dropkicked his heart."

Avery didn't want to root for heartbreak, but he hoped so in this instance. Because Paul's strong reaction to him leaving had to mean that he saw a future with Avery. He wouldn't be so upset if he hadn't.

"So ease up on him, okay? I don't need you to fight my battles. If you want to be mad at him for leaving early or missing Jess's shower, that's kind of crappy, but okay. But don't be mad at him on my account, because he needs you as a friend more than I need you as my defender, all right?"

He was glad he hadn't come between Paul and Bran in college, and he didn't want to now. Bran was one of the most important people in Paul's life, and even if he and Paul didn't work out, he didn't want Paul's friendship with his brother to be a casualty.

"Did you tell him you got a place? He's not going to come back to his house tomorrow and be shocked to find all your stuff missing, right?"

"I texted him. He has the address and an open invitation to come over when he's back."

Paul sent him a photo Friday night of a bioluminescent bay where he and Marnie were doing a late-night kayak tour. It had been as close to an apology as Avery was likely to get, and he was happy with it. Paul didn't need to apologize for his reaction, but it was good to know that he wasn't cutting Avery out of his life. He'd asked for space, and Avery had given it to him, and he had to hope things would work out in the end.

"And you're fine waiting? You're not going to interview for the job in San Francisco?"

It was tenure-track and a gorgeous campus, but it didn't have Paul. Avery still didn't know for sure if the professor he'd filled in for was coming back or not, but he had enough savings to be comfortable for a few months and cover the lease on this studio through the summer.

If Paul was willing to have him back in his life, Avery wasn't going to make any big decisions without discussing them with him.

"I'm going to stay here for now. We'll see where things take us. I've been pressuring Paul into moving us along faster than I should have. We need to get to know each other. Date."

"You already know each other."

"We don't, though. I had no idea Paul was into plants and gardening, or that he liked fantasy but hates science fiction. He can't stand cooked tuna. He's prissy about being naked in public. I need to get to know the real Paul and let go of the Paul I've idealized in my head for the last twelve years of pining over him. And he needs to get to know the real me."

Bran made a face. "How do you know he's prissy about being naked in public? Why would that have come up?"

Avery made a vague gesture, finding himself strangely unwilling to share their crazy day date in Tahoe with him. It was nice to have some secrets that were theirs. Maybe someday Paul would loosen up enough that the nudity could be an inside joke.

"Okay, never mind," Bran conceded. "I don't want to think about you and Paul naked, in public or private."

"Yet you're so invested in our love life," Avery teased.

Bran held his hands up. "Truce. I'm going to do what you told me and butt out. You and Paul will work things out or you won't, but I'm done meddling."

That was good, but Bran didn't wear the primary meddling pants in their relationship.

"And Ellie?"

"I can't make any promises. But I'm sure she'll be too busy pulling all the details from this weekend out of Marnie tonight to poke her nose in here."

Paul had texted from the airport with his flight info. Avery had offered to pick him up, but since he'd have to borrow Paul's car to do it, it was a pretty empty gesture. Paul had told him he'd get home on his own but had left the possibility of dinner with Avery tonight on the table.

"The last thing we need is Ellie trying to play matchmaker. You should take her out to a movie or something tonight. Keep her occupied."

Bran grinned and wiggled his eyebrows suggestively, and suddenly Avery could appreciate why Bran had retracted his question about Paul and nudity.

"Nope, nope! I do *not* want to know."

They didn't stay too long after Ellie got back with the sheets and towels she'd bought. Bran had hustled her out the door before she could ask too many questions, and Avery appreciated his brother's help.

Avery puttered around, rearranging furniture to be more to his liking and unpacking. He'd left the majority of his things with friends and charity shops in the UK, figuring it was cheaper to replace them here than to ship them. If he stayed in Chicago, he'd have to find a bigger place. The studio wasn't much smaller than the flat he'd rented in London, but it felt more constrictive here.

He hadn't spent much time at home when he lived in London. He had a full schedule of teaching and enough friends that he never had to have dinner or drinks alone. That wasn't the case here. All he had were his family and Paul. Getting some new hobbies was at the top of his list. If he didn't find something to fill his time soon, he'd end up climbing the walls or giving diamond painting another go.

Paul's flight had gotten in a few hours ago, and he'd texted Avery to let him know he'd gotten home safely and would try to stop by for dinner. He hadn't given Avery any clue about where they stood, though, so while he was glad Paul was back, Avery's anxiety was still very much running full steam.

It was getting late, and Avery wasn't sure if he should keep waiting for Paul or give in and accept that he wasn't coming. The kitchen had a small stove he would likely never use and a microwave. Maybe he'd go out tomorrow and get a toaster. Really step up the adulting.

He settled on Thai and ordered enough to feed a family of eight thanks to his indecisiveness over what Paul might like. If Paul came over, they'd have plenty, and if he didn't, Avery could eat this for a week. It wouldn't go to waste either way.

When his doorbell rang just after nine, Avery assumed it was the delivery guy. His heart was in his throat when he opened it and saw Paul on his doorstep instead, laden down with bags hanging off both arms and a large plant balanced on top of a box of pizza.

"It's a pothos. Very hard to kill. One of its nicknames is actually Devil's Ivy because it's so resilient and can bounce back from so much neglect," Paul said, tipping the pizza box so the ceramic pot slid into Avery's hands. "It's a peace offering. A bad one, since I'm implying you're going to neglect it. I'm just realizing the flaw in that now."

Avery was rarely speechless, given that his job was to talk for hours, but he had no idea what to say. He'd had a whole thing planned where he begged for forgiveness and made promises about how things would change, but he hadn't expected Paul to turn up with a plant.

"I'm sorry, Avery. I have you cast in a role in my mind, and it's unfair. I shouldn't have jumped to conclusions when you left." He held up the pizza box. "I brought a pizza, but there was a delivery guy outside the door when I got here. He gave me your order."

"Thai," Avery managed. He stared at Paul for another beat before he realized he hadn't let him in. "Sorry. Here, you can put the food down on the counter. There's not room for a kitchen table, but there are stools, so we can sit there."

Paul crossed the room and put the pizza and the bags down. Avery watched him, still standing dumbly by the door holding his plant.

"Don't put it in the windowsill," Paul said, nodding to it. "It likes indirect light."

Right. The plant.

Avery didn't have a lot of flat surfaces to put a plant on, so he settled for plopping it down on the bedside table. It was tucked into a little alcove off the living room, and by the time he came back into the kitchen Paul had found plates and was taking food out of the bags.

"You didn't have to move out, you know. But I understand if me leaving for Florida like that made you want to," Paul said, not looking up from his task.

Not facing each other or maintaining eye contact made it a little easier to talk freely, so Avery crossed to the cabinet to get them drinks.

"That wasn't why I did it. Well, it was," he said, catching himself. "But that wasn't why it was a good idea. We were rushing things, and I don't want to do that."

"I didn't think of it as rushing because this had an expiration date," Paul said, nodding when Avery held up a bottle of beer. "So it wasn't like we were really living together."

The logic in that was so very Paul.

"But we were," Avery said. "And I don't want this to have an expiration date."

He brought two beer bottles and a bottle opener to the table but stood there and didn't put them down until Paul finally looked at him. This part he wanted eye contact for so Paul knew he was serious.

"I love you, Paul. And I want to see where being in a real relationship gets us. That's the reason I took this flat. We did things all backward. I want us to have space so we can date and get to know each other."

"I don't know what to say to that."

That was better than a flat-out refusal.

"That's okay. We can take things slow. I have the lease on this through the summer, and I've talked to a few of the community colleges around here. I'm going to teach the summer session at two of them."

It would give him a chance to see if a job like that would be fulfilling enough, though he suspected it wouldn't. But he owed it to Paul and to himself to at least make an attempt at seeing what a life here in Chicago would be like. Maybe he and Paul wouldn't get back together. Maybe he'd decide he hated the city. Maybe he'd decide he hated *Paul*. The point was he didn't know, and he didn't want this to be another regret that haunted him like the first time he walked away.

"I don't want you to throw your career away for me," Paul said earnestly, and it eased an ache in Avery's chest. Paul still cared about him and his future and still wanted him to do what was best for himself even if it wasn't here. That was a good sign.

"I'm not. I'm still looking, and there's a possibility the position at Northwestern could become permanent. I'm not banking on it, but I'll be honest, that's what I'm hoping comes through. Because I don't know that teaching nights at community colleges is enough for me."

Paul dished up food on both their plates. It felt cozy and homey and Avery liked it. But knowing that Paul would be going home and he'd be staying here made it sweeter somehow. Paul was here because he chose to be here. Not living together meant they would have to purposefully make time for each other, and that made the time they spent together more meaningful.

"I don't know how to be in a relationship with you," Paul admitted. "I don't know how to get past being nervous that you're going to leave."

"I might," Avery said. He'd been honest with Paul about not knowing what the future held past August. "But it won't be like last time. I can't promise you I'll end up here, but I can promise you that whatever happens, I'll be discussing it with you every step of the way."

"I don't think I could do a long-distance relationship," Paul said after a pause.

"I don't either. But I'd rather risk getting my heart broken at the end of the summer than not taking this chance. And maybe I'll get an offer somewhere and you'll come with me."

Paul looked a bit floored at that suggestion. He laughed and shook his head ruefully. "I actually never thought about that. I guess it's unfair to ask you to stay if I'm not willing to go with you."

"I'm not worried about what's fair or not," Avery said. "And Chicago is my number one choice, both because you're here and because of my family. But do you think you might consider it? If I get a position somewhere else?"

Paul took a drink of his beer, and for a moment Avery was afraid he wouldn't answer.

"Yeah," he said softly. He blew out a heavy sigh and nodded.

"Yeah," he said again, sounding more sure this time. "I want to see if there's anything between us. I think there could be, but I can't handle investing myself if I'm not sure we could have a future. So, yeah. I want to date you. And if we need to relocate, I'm willing to do that."

Avery hadn't known it was possible to smile so hard your face hurt. "Really?"

Paul beamed back at him. "Really."

"No more expiration date?"

"No more expiration date," Paul confirmed, and held out his beer to toast.

Avery clinked his bottle with Paul's, then put it aside without drinking it and grabbed Paul's hand.

"What about the food?" Paul asked as Avery pulled him off the stool and toward the bed.

"It'll keep."

Epilogue

Ten months later

"MARNIE SAID she took care of all the reservations, but I can't get her to send me the confirmation codes or tell me how much we owe her," Paul said, pushing his phone aside in frustration.

She'd been cagier than usual ever since she'd texted him to tell him she wanted to surprise Ellie and Bran with a long weekend in Tahoe for their first anniversary. They'd gone in together and given it to them as a group Christmas present. Bran and Ellie had been thrilled, and even more so when Avery and Marnie decided later that the three of them would join them for part of it. He and Avery were flying out today, and Marnie would meet them there.

"I took care of it," Avery yelled from the laundry room.

He'd moved back in six months ago, after he'd signed a contract for a tenure-track position at Northwestern. The professor he'd filled in for had decided to retire early, and Avery had been their first choice for a replacement. It could hardly have worked out better for them. The bread always landed butter side up for Avery, and now instead of resenting it, Paul was grateful for it every day.

"What do you mean, you took care of it?"

Avery walked into the bedroom with a basket of clean laundry.

"I mean I took care of it. Marnie and I were already coordinating the flights, so I had her send me the info and I took care of booking our room. Everything's done."

He loved Avery, but planning wasn't one of his strong suits. Plus Avery was still a little scared of Marnie. She'd come to see Ellie over the summer and had given Avery a *hurt Paul and I hurt you* talk, which had him out of sorts the rest of her visit. Paul was looking forward to seeing her, but he wasn't looking forward to mediating between the two of them. But if Marnie and Avery were getting along enough to plan this then maybe things would be fine.

"Pack swim trunks," Avery said, tossing him a pair from the laundry basket.

The memory of their trip to the hot springs made Paul shift uncomfortably, just like it did any time Avery brought it up. He still couldn't believe he'd actually gone swimming naked, in public. It wasn't something he was anxious to do again.

"We're not going to Sierra Hot Springs, right?"

Avery laughed. "We're not going to Sierra Hot Springs."

That was a relief.

He added the trunks to his carry-on bag. They were only going for the weekend because Avery had classes, and Paul figured since it was such a short trip, he'd skip checking a bag. He'd decided against bringing his skis because he wanted to spend time with Avery, so it wasn't like he'd need much.

He could hear Avery opening and closing drawers in the bathroom. "Do we have sunscreen?"

"I don't think so. What would we need sunscreen for? It's March."

Avery poked his head out of the door. "Never mind, we can get some there."

This was the first trip he and Avery had taken together as a couple, so Paul didn't know if this flurry of frenetic energy that had him darting around the house was normal or not. It was amusing, that was for sure.

"The Uber will be here in ten minutes," Avery said, zipping his bag closed. "You ready?"

When they got into the car, Avery pulled two printed tickets out of his bag.

"We're connecting through Dallas again," he said, handing one of them to Paul.

It didn't have the flight to Reno on it, which seemed weird.

"It was cheaper to fly to Dallas on Delta and book the flight to Reno separately," Avery said quickly.

"One-way tickets were cheaper than booking roundtrip? Did you check—"

"Do you trust me?" Avery asked, cutting him off.

He did. They'd been through so much together, and it had taken a lot of work on both of their parts, but Paul did trust Avery. They were a unit now, a team. Avery had promised him they'd discuss everything major before making life-altering decisions, and they had. The job at

Northwestern, Avery moving back in. Even the Prius Avery had settled on to commute to school with. The fact that they hadn't talked about any of the details for this trip was unusual. It had been strange to have Avery booking rooms and flights without talking it over with him first, but he'd chalked that up to the fact that Marnie was the one planning things.

Now he wasn't so sure. Avery was acting shifty. But at the end of the day, he did trust him. Avery had grown up a lot, and together they'd grown up even more over the last year.

"Of course," Paul answered.

"Then trust that this was the way it needed to be, okay? We're flying into Dallas."

There was something Avery wasn't telling him, but Paul let it go.

True to Avery form, he'd underestimated Friday rush-hour traffic, and they barely made it to O'Hare in time to clear security for their flight. It was frustrating for Paul, who always liked to be early, but plans with Avery very rarely turned out perfectly. It was one of the things he'd grown to grudgingly accept about him. If he was keeping a spreadsheet about their relationship, which he wasn't, the pros would still far outweigh cons like this one.

They were both slightly sweaty and out of breath by the time they boarded their flight to Dallas. Paul could have let it bother him, but he chose not to. Ellie said Avery mellowed him out, but Paul thought it was more that Avery showed him what was important. In the grand scheme of things, almost missing their flight didn't matter. He was there with Avery, and even now, after almost a year together, that felt kind of like a miracle.

"Hey, I brought entertainment," Avery said after they'd taken off and the flight attendants had been around with drinks.

He pulled a thin box out of his bag and put it on Paul's tray table. It was a beginner's diamond painting kit. Paul picked it up, laughing when he saw the picture on the box. It was a pothos plant.

"This has hundreds of tiny crystals. I don't think it's a good plane activity," he said, putting it back down.

"They give you extras. It'll be fine," Avery said, reaching over to open the box. "I got it because it said it took less than two hours to do, so we can finish it on the flight."

Paul's objection had been more about the mess, not worrying that they'd run out of gems if they dropped some. The cleaning crew would hate them.

"You told me you could see me doing this once, remember?" Avery said. "I've kind of been curious ever since."

Paul gave in and opened the box. He always gave in on the little things where Avery was concerned. The one-night stand that had spiraled out of control had only been the start. He'd even started dipping cookies in tea.

He was sure they annoyed the hell out of their poor seatmate, giggling like schoolboys as they bent over the canvas, bedazzling it with tiny gems. The box estimate was either wildly off or they were exceptionally terrible at it, because they worked diligently on it the entire flight and were still only half done when the flight attendant made them roll it up and put it away for landing.

"We can finish it at the cabin," Paul said after Avery tucked it back in his bag.

"About that," Avery said, looking nervous. "We're not going to the cabin. We're flying to Colorado to go to a definitely *not* nudist hot springs resort."

"So we're not going to Tahoe?"

Avery grinned. "Nope. We have a flight early tomorrow morning to Durango. I swear you'll like these hot springs. The resort is fancy, and everyone in the promotional photos is wearing clothes. No weird naked old men or hippies having sex, I promise."

Their seatmate shifted farther away from them, and Paul had to stifle a laugh.

"What about Marnie?"

"Marnie was a red herring. She helped me find this resort, actually. She said I owed you a nice hot-springs experience to make up for the last one," he said. "I wanted to surprise you for our anniversary."

Paul had been so caught up in this being Bran and Ellie's first wedding anniversary, it hadn't really sunk in that this was sort of their first anniversary too. He'd been counting from the day they'd sat in Avery's kitchen and committed to a real relationship, but technically they'd been together since that one-night stand in Dallas.

"Wait, did you say we fly out tomorrow morning?"

Avery winked. "We have a reservation for a lovely sleep pod in Terminal A. Would you believe Annie still works there? She was *so* excited to hear we're together."

Paul couldn't believe Avery was surprising him with an anniversary trip—or that he'd booked a pod. It was incredibly romantic, and also kind of terrible. They weren't going to be getting any sleep tonight, and not in a fun way. Well, maybe kind of in a fun way. But his back was going to be in knots tomorrow from the tiny vinyl sofa.

"I don't know what to say. This is incredibly sweet."

Avery grabbed his hand and squeezed it. Paul twined their fingers together and held his hand until it was time to get off the plane. Their seatmate had the aisle, and he stood the moment the plane stopped. Paul would do the same in his place—they were giving off crazy vibes. Diamond painting on the plane, giggling, talking about nudist colonies and naked old men.

His life with Avery was an adventure, that was for sure.

Annie wasn't on duty when they arrived at the sleep-pod hotel, but the clerk's face lit up when Avery gave his name.

"Mr. Laniston, Annie gave me all your instructions, and everything is ready for you," she said.

Instead of handing over the key, she motioned for them to follow her. She led them down the dark corridor to the exact pod they'd stayed in last time.

"I hope you enjoy your stay with us."

She opened it with a flourish and stepped back. Paul's jaw dropped open.

Battery-operated tea lights lit the room, and there were rose petals in the shape of a heart on the vinyl sofa. Still no sheets—special occasion or no, this was still the pod hotel—but it was clear someone had gone to a lot of trouble to make the room nice for them. There was a vase of real flowers on the desk and a bottle of the riesling Ellie turned him on to with two plastic cups.

She was gone by the time Paul stopped looking around and turned to Avery, who was holding the key and a tiny velvet box.

Paul stepped into the room, not wanting this private moment to play out in the corridor. Avery followed him, letting the door shut behind him, and immediately knelt. Paul couldn't help but laugh—the room was so small that it barely fit him and a kneeling Avery. Avery's foot was flush with the doorjamb.

"Paul Gladwell, a year ago you asked me to have a one-night stand with you, and I spent the whole night kicking myself for agreeing. Not because it was bad, but because it was so much less than you deserved, and so much less than what I wanted to give you. One night in Dallas turned into one year. And more than anything else in this world, I want it to turn into a lifetime. Now we're here again, and even though we know we don't have an expiration date, I'm asking you to make it official so everyone else knows too. Will you marry me?"

Paul wanted to kneel to face him, but there wasn't room. Instead, he reached down and grabbed Avery by the wrist to pull him up.

Avery's face fell, but he stood up, holding himself stiffly. Paul shook his head.

"I'm not saying no," he said quickly. "I just wanted to be able to do this."

He took Avery's face in his hands and cupped his jaw as he kissed him. Avery's stiffness dissolved as he melted against Paul, wrapping his arms around him as he deepened the kiss.

Paul pulled back after a moment. "I would love to marry you," he said.

Avery blew out a breath and opened the ring box to reveal a simple gold band. "Good. Because Marnie is in Chicago right now putting together a surprise engagement party for us at Ellie and Bran's, and it would be super awkward if you said no."

Paul let Avery put the band on his finger, shivering a bit when Avery's thumb caressed his palm after he slid the ring into place. It was one of the most intimate things Paul had ever experienced, and the weight of the emotions formed a knot in his throat.

"Marnie's party is the only reason you're glad I said yes, eh?" he joked, needing to break the seriousness of the moment.

Avery chuckled. "Yup. It's definitely not because I can't imagine spending my life without you."

Paul kissed him again. "I love you."

"I love you too."

Paul stared into Avery's eyes, savoring the moment. Then Avery leaned forward and nuzzled against his ear.

"Hey," he whispered. "Wanna have a not-one-night stand with me in Dallas?"

Keep Reading for an Excerpt from
Downward Facing Dreamboat
by Bru Baker

Chapter One: Namaste

"YOU CAN'T say savasana without the shhh! Please enter and leave the studio quietly."

Kincaid stared at the sign taped to the door. There was a ridiculous cartoon of a llama doing yoga on it, one hoof held up to its lips to signal for quiet.

This was a terrible idea.

He could count everything he knew about yoga on one hand, and that knowledge didn't include how the hell the *shhh* sound was in the word *savasana*.

The entire yoga studio was glass fronted, but the bank of heavy red drapes had been drawn, making it impossible for him to see through. The inside of the door was covered by a beaded curtain, and he could see through them just enough to confirm no one was seated at the tiny desk inside the small foyer.

He'd never been inside the studio, but that didn't mean he wasn't intimately acquainted with the layout. For starters, it was hard to hide anything behind floor-to-ceiling windows. When the curtains were open, he could see the length of the place, from the glossy wood floors to the mirrors that fully covered the back wall. The desk up front was big enough to hold a tablet and a plant stand, and next to it sat a water cooler with a cartoon of a dog doing a yoga pose above the words After You Sink, Drink!

It was a bizarre place. The only parts he couldn't easily see from the street were a couple of spaces hidden by more of the beaded curtains. He assumed there was an office or something back there. And maybe changing rooms or storage. He didn't know what you needed for yoga.

Kincaid liked to think of himself as open-minded, but yoga wasn't really on his radar as a viable form of exercise. The real reason he knew the interior layout of the place was because he peeked in every morning, hoping for a look at the dreamboat of an instructor who was more flexible than any man Kincaid had ever seen.

The drapes were always closed during classes, but when the instructor was alone, they were usually open. And if Kincaid had started going in to work thirty minutes early because he'd discovered that was when the guy warmed up before his 7:30 a.m. class, well, who was the wiser?

Kincaid backed up, taking a few steps away from the door. There was obviously a class in session, and he didn't want to interrupt. The note from his orthopedist crumpled slightly as he shoved it back into his pocket. He could stop by tomorrow or maybe call from the office. Another day wouldn't hurt, would it?

Kincaid gritted his teeth as his first step put weight on his ankle, and he tried not to limp as he made his way down the sidewalk. He'd always been able to power through pain when he was running. It worked for blisters and sore muscles, but not so much for stress fractures. To be fair, Kincaid hadn't realized that's what the shooting pain in his ankle was. He'd figured it was a mild sprain from coming down on it wrong on one of his long marathon training runs.

He'd forced himself to run despite the pain even when it worsened, but it didn't get better like his injuries usually did if he pushed through. It got worse. A lot worse. If he'd listened to his body a few weeks ago and eased off on his training, he probably wouldn't be suffering through a severe stress fracture that threatened to derail his running future permanently.

"Hey, did you need something?"

Kincaid started and spun toward the voice, wincing when it tweaked his ankle. Pain lanced up his leg, the sharp waves making his stomach lurch. The walking boot could only help so much. Mostly it was a physical reminder that Kincaid needed to take it easy. Not that it had been working very well for him. He wasn't used to having to take things slow, and it was killing him.

Kincaid started again when he realized the man who'd spoken to him was the yoga instructor. His dreamboat. Kincaid tried to smile, but the look of concern on the man's face told him he hadn't quite succeeded.

The man took a step forward, his arms out like he was ready to catch Kincaid if he fell. It was enough to tempt Kincaid to swoon on purpose.

"Are you all right?"

Kincaid cleared his throat and hobbled back to the studio's door. He'd fantasized about meeting his dreamboat plenty of times, but none of them started with him accessorizing his outfit with a clunky walking boot or nearly falling over from embarrassment when the guy greeted him.

He could rally.

"I'm fine. I didn't mean to interrupt your class. I was just looking at you. I mean, not *looking at* you. Looking for you. Or someone who could give information about getting registered."

So much for rallying and making a good second impression. Kincaid wondered if he should cut his losses and hobble away. He could find a new route to work. Maybe take the bus that was closer to his apartment. Sure, it would add an extra hour to his trip, but that would be better than suffering through this.

The guy laughed. "Well, you found me. Or rather, I found *you.* Class let out about ten minutes ago. I just hadn't opened the drapes yet. Why don't you come in, and we can chat? I'm guessing you are looking to start your practice?"

Kincaid tried to evenly distribute his weight as he walked in, but the yoga instructor watched him warily and motioned him over to one of the beaded curtains. Kincaid parted them cautiously and stepped through into a small office.

"It's that obvious that I'm not a pro?"

The guy's cheeks dimpled when he smiled. "Sorry, yeah."

Kincaid laughed as he lowered himself into the chair in front of the desk. "Guilty as charged. I'm here because my doctor suggested it."

"Let me guess," the man said, sizing Kincaid up with a thoughtful look. "Pickup basketball league, torn ligament in your ankle, and your doctor gave you the choice between mandatory PT and yoga."

"Marathon runner, lower tibia stress fracture, ordered into physical therapy, and strongly encouraged to take up yoga as well. You came pretty highly recommended by my ortho."

The man let out a laugh. "You must have really jacked yourself up for that. Training or race?"

Kincaid wrinkled his nose. "I noticed the pain about three weeks before the race, but I pushed through it. I was able to finish, but my time was shit. My ortho says I'm lucky I didn't complete the fracture running on it like that. It's pretty severe."

The instructor dropped into a low crouch and held his hand out to the ankle Kincaid had been favoring. His fingers hovered over Kincaid's ankle. "May I?"

Kincaid nodded and hiked his pant leg up at the knee.

"I'm Owen, by the way. I always think it's best to introduce myself before I start feeling a student up," he said with a bright grin. "First things first—let's see what we're up against."

Owen's touch was gentle as he unfastened the boot and put it to the side. He probed at Kincaid's sock-covered ankle, wincing in sympathy when Kincaid sucked in a pained breath as Owen's fingers found the right spot.

"Sorry. I'm guessing this is the fracture site?" He looked up, and Kincaid nodded, surprised that Owen had zeroed in on it. Owen smiled. "It's a high stress point in runners."

"So you've seen stress fractures like this before?"

Owen nodded. "It's a pretty common injury. I'm sure we can put together a practice that will help you as you heal."

Kincaid was skeptical of how much yoga could help him, but Dr. Chester assured him that it would be beneficial, especially if he went to someone who had a background in working with injured athletes. Kincaid wasn't a professional runner, but he wasn't a weekend warrior, either. He was dedicated to staying fit, and he liked the way running let him tune out. He didn't want to lose that release because of an injury that healed wrong.

"I won't actually schedule you until I get the okay from your physical therapist, but this gives me a better idea of your limitations." Owen made a face. "Sorry, I don't think I got your name."

Kincaid fought the urge to cringe when he realized he'd forgotten to introduce himself. This entire encounter had been one embarrassment after another. "Kincaid."

Owen smiled and tugged Kincaid's pant leg back down before he stood up. "Well, Kincaid, I'm glad you came in today. Even if I did have to chase you down."

Kincaid laughed and rubbed a hand over the back of his neck. "Sorry about that. Dr. Chester's nurse mentioned this place specifically when he recommended yoga. I pass it every day on my way to work, so I figured I'd stop in, but then I thought it might be creepy to come in during a class."

"It's not creepy. It's good for you to get a feel for the studio since I hope you'll continue on with yoga after your physical therapy." He winked at Kincaid. "You runners are notorious for falling into the 'too much, too soon' trap."

Kincaid knew that was true. He hadn't been for a run in three weeks, and restlessness buzzed in his muscles more every day. He'd known something was wrong with his ankle, but he hadn't wanted to throw away months of training because of a little pain. That little pain had been excruciating by the end of the 26.2 miles, but it hadn't muted the joy he'd felt at crossing the finish line. He'd probably be out there now, fighting through the pain, if not for the fact that Dr. Chester made it clear that if he didn't let the stress fracture heal properly that marathon would probably be his last.

"I've been on full rest for three weeks, but I've been procrastinating on setting this up," Kincaid admitted.

Owen's laugh was rich and full. Kincaid had seen him laughing through the window before, and he'd always been curious about what it would sound like. It definitely met expectations.

"Most people do," he said. He plucked a card off the messy desk. "I always do a get-to-know-you visit before we start when I'm working with someone who has an injury. That way we can be sure yoga is a good fit for you, and we can talk about what you need to get out of the program."

"I work a pretty set schedule, so as long as you have evening or late afternoon hours, it should work out."

"Do you have other evening commitments we need to plan around?"

Sadly, he didn't.

"I spend most of my free time training for races, so since I can't run I don't have a lot going on. I have a group of friends I travel around the country with for marathons, and we usually run together after work and on weekends. I'm hoping I can get over this injury and back into running shape without having to sacrifice the Maui marathon we do every other year."

Kincaid hadn't realized how much of his life revolved around running until he couldn't do it. He'd watched more Netflix in the past three weeks than he had in three *years* before that.

"Ooh, I can see why you wouldn't want to miss that," Owen said. "I'm here Monday and Wednesday evenings. I'd like to plan to do a few private lessons before we transition you to a class. That way I can help you modify poses that would put too much stress on your ankle. You can stop in or call when your PT gives you the okay to get started. If I'm not here, tell them I told them to give you my first available evening, okay? I'd rather not enable your procrastination."

Kincaid laughed. "I promise."

Owen's grin lit up his face. He had laugh lines around his eyes, and they crinkled up endearingly when he smiled. "Great. I'm looking forward to it."

Kincaid stood cautiously, but luckily the throbbing pain in his ankle had subsided.

Owen nodded approvingly.

"We'll be taking things slow, which I know will be frustrating for you. You need to focus on your actual physical therapy more at first because you need to address the issues the stress fracture has caused before we can start preventing future damage with the yoga."

"Yoga will help make sure this doesn't happen again?"

Owen nodded. "It's not a guarantee, but it will definitely help. Do you cross-train?"

Not as much as he should. Kincaid swam and lifted weights when it was too cold or wet to run outside, since he didn't like treadmills. But mostly he ran.

"Not really, no."

"Well, yoga will help strengthen your core and get you to stretch out those quads and hamstrings. Loosening up your legs will help your form, which can help avoid repetitive stress injuries like this one."

He tapped the card in Kincaid's hand.

"Be sure to call once you're given the okay. I can tell you're anxious to get back out there, and I swear this will help."

"I see Dr. Chester again today for another X-ray. He told me if this one looks good, he'll release me to physical therapy."

"Even then, no running. Your PT will probably have you hold off on weight-bearing cardio for another week or two. Sometimes bones heal in that month off, sometimes they take longer. We won't know till he sees your X-rays. Swimming, biking, and some faster walking will probably be the PT's recommendation. And I'll do my part to get your heart rate up, I promise."

Kincaid swallowed at Owen's unintentionally suggestive words. That wouldn't be a problem. He'd recovered from his initial nerves, but even now Kincaid's heart was racing from being so close to Owen. How was he going to survive having Owen guide him into yoga positions without embarrassing himself?

Owen seemed to read Kincaid's discomfort, and he tilted his head to the side for a moment, his cheeks coloring lightly. "Ah. I didn't mean it like that." He looked flustered, which was adorable. "It's just that most athletic guys figure yoga is a walk in the park, but it's actually as easy or as difficult as you make it. If you put effort into your practice, you'll find that it's very satisfying."

Kincaid's lips twitched at Owen's choice of words, which caused Owen to close his eyes and chuckle. "I mean, you'll find it's a satisfying workout. Wow. I apologize. My mind must be somewhere else today."

"I'm looking forward to you getting my heart rate up." Flirting openly wasn't something Kincaid usually did, but he couldn't help himself. Maybe he did have some game after all.

Owen coughed and looked away, but Kincaid was almost positive it was to hide a smile.

"Okay, getting us back on track. You're obviously an avid runner. How about other sports? Any yoga before, Kincaid?"

Kincaid grinned. Owen was changing the subject, and he definitely had a faint blush to his cheeks. Kincaid was usually horrible at gauging interest from other people, but he would bet good money that Owen was enjoying their banter. He hoped there would be time to explore that later.

"Once. My sister is into it, and she dragged me to a class a few years ago. All I remember is it being ridiculously hot and not understanding most of what the instructor said for the whole hour and a half."

"Sounds like Bikram. They heat the room to about 105 degrees Fahrenheit to help practitioners sweat out their toxins and loosen their muscles."

"I felt like I was trying to sweat out my spleen."

"So no Bikram yoga for you. Got it. Do you remember any of the positions? Were there any you particularly liked?"

"The only pose I remember was Natalie doing something on her belly with her feet arched up to almost touch her head. I didn't even try that one. It seemed like there was a high risk of accidental castration."

Owen barked out a laugh. "Probably purna salabhasana."

"Bless you?"

"So you're funny as well as handsome and athletic?" Owen teased, and Kincaid preened internally at the compliments. "In English it's called full locust pose, but I always find the Sanskrit words more fun to say."

Before Kincaid could respond, Owen held his hand up and shook his head. "Don't worry. I don't break out into Sanskrit until at least the fifth class."

Kincaid was sure he still looked horrified, if the way Owen laughed was any indication. "Kidding. I always call out poses in English, and I'm right there modeling the pose for the class. Obviously while we're doing the one-on-one sessions I'll be there guiding you into position. Don't worry. I won't get you in over your head."

"What do I need to wear? Do I need, uh…?" Kincaid flushed, thinking about the close-fitting shorts Owen usually wore at the studio. They weren't quite bike shorts, but they weren't basketball shorts either. Kincaid had spent an inordinate amount of time thinking about them, and he hoped that didn't show on his face.

Owen followed Kincaid's gaze down to his own close-fitting shorts. He threw back his head and laughed.

"Whatever you run in will be fine. The big thing is to make sure that things fit closer to the body. We won't be doing many inversions, but it can be pretty annoying to have your shirt fall over your face in crow or even downward dog."

Kincaid's face was on fire. "Good to know."

Owen laid a warm hand on his shoulder and squeezed it. "You'll never be forced to wear something or do a pose that makes you uncomfortable. Yoga is supposed to be challenging but relaxing. Every class ends with a rest pose and a short meditation."

Owen bent his elbows and brought his hands together in front of his heart. It was something that the students in the class Kincaid had taken had done at the end, and he tucked the papers under his arm and mimicked it. He felt silly, but the approving look on Owen's face made it worth it.

"The divine light in me recognizes the divine light in you. Namaste." Owen bowed his head until his fingertips touched his forehead, then released his hands and straightened. "It's a blessing we exchange before we end our practice. This is where you bow and say namaste."

Owen's joking demeanor was gone, replaced by a solemnity that was intriguing. Kincaid wouldn't have thought it possible for the man who'd been so fidgety and boisterous a minute ago to be so still and serious, but he was. Kincaid fought a smile and returned the bow. "Namaste."

An instant later, Owen was grinning again. He slapped Kincaid on the back. "There you go—your first painless yoga pose."

Kincaid heard quiet voices out in the studio and the sound of mats unrolling. Owen glanced up at a clock hanging on the wall and cursed softly.

"I have an ashtanga vinyasa class that starts in ten minutes. I'd invite you to stay and watch, but it's an advanced class and I'm afraid it would scare you away."

Kincaid didn't doubt it. "It's probably best that I don't."

BRU BAKER got her first taste of life as a writer at the tender age of four, when she started publishing a weekly newspaper for her family. What they called nosiness she called a nose for news, and no one was surprised when she ended up with degrees in journalism and political science and started a career in journalism.

Bru spent more than a decade writing for newspapers before making the jump to fiction. Whether it's creating her own characters or getting caught up in someone else's, there's no denying that Bru is happiest when she's engrossed in a story. She and her husband have two children, which means a lot of her books get written from the sidelines of various sports practices.

Website: www.bru-baker.com
Blog: www.bru-baker.blogspot.com
Twitter: @bru_baker
Facebook: www.facebook.com/bru.baker79
Goodreads: www.goodreads.com/author/show/6608093.Bru_Baker
Email: bru@bru-baker.com

Downward Facing Dreamboat

BRU BAKER

*Yoga isn't the only thing
that can tie a man into knots....*

Love is trying to catch up to two lonely men. Can they stop long enough to let it?

Running defines Kincaid's life. It's not until he loses it that he realizes how isolated he's become. But even if an injury hadn't forced him to slow down, the hottie in the yoga studio would have given him pause. In fact, admiring the man each morning is the only thing keeping the spring in his step when it feels like he's lost everything.

Owen's busy life as a yoga instructor doesn't leave him much time to meet guys, let alone date. He's convinced his passion for helping people is worth the sacrifice, but he's willing to spare a few moments for the cutie who walks past the studio every morning.

When their lives intersect and romance is set in motion, they stumble off the starting block. But no matter the obstacles in their path, this race won't be over until they reach the finish… together.

www.dreamspinnerpress.com

DREAMSPUN
BEYOND

STEALING HIS
HEART

Bru Baker

Connoll Pack

Love sneaks up like a thief in the night.

A Connoll Pack Novel

Love sneaks in like a thief in the night.

Danny's parents raised him to believe his wolf was a curse. He's part of the wealthy and powerful Connoll Pack, but only nominally. He abandoned that world to volunteer with supernatural kids, and he isn't looking for a mate....

Max is a shifter who is also a detective. He's working a case that could make or break his career. Danny's caught up in the case he's on, and he's also irresistible. They're a bad match—Max, an Alpha having trouble with his new powers and Danny, who trusts Alphas as far as he could throw one. But they can't get enough of each other, and they might bond before they even see it coming.

They could be amazing together, but they have to get past a few obstacles—especially since someone close to Danny might be involved in the thefts Max is investigating.

CAMP
H.O.W.L.

Bru Baker

Moonmates exist, but getting together
is going to be a beast.

A Camp H.O.W.L. Novel

Moonmates exist, but getting together is going to be a beast....

When Adrian Rothschild skipped his "werewolf puberty," he assumed he was, somehow, human. But he was wrong, and he's about to go through his Turn with a country between him and his Pack—scared, alone, and eight years late.

Dr. Tate Lewis's werewolf supremacist father made his Turn miserable, and now Tate works for Camp H.O.W.L. to ease the transition for young werewolves. He isn't expecting to offer guidance to a grown man—or find his moonmate in Adrian. Tate doesn't even believe in the legendary bond; after all, his polygamist father claimed five. But it's clear Adrian needs him, and if Tate can let his guard down, he might discover he needs Adrian too.

A moonmate is a wolf's missing piece, and Tate is missing a lot of pieces. But is Adrian up to the challenge?

www.dreamspinnerpress.com

"Promising low-
conflict romance."
-Publishers Weekly

UNDER A
BLUE MOON

CAMP H.O.W.L.

Bru Baker

Once in a blue moon, opposites
find they're a perfect match.

A Camp H.O.W.L. Novel

Once in a blue moon, opposites find they're a perfect match.

Nick Perry is tired of helping people with their marriages, so when a spot opens up to work with teens at Camp H.O.W.L., he jumps at it. He doesn't expect to fall in lust with the dreamy new camp doctor, Drew Welch. But Drew is human, and Nick has seen secrets ruin too many relationships to think that a human/werewolf romance can go anywhere.

Happy-go-lucky Drew may not sprout claws, but he's been part of the Were community all his life. He has no trouble fitting in at the camp—except for Nick's stubborn refusal to acknowledge the growing attraction between them and his ridiculous stance on dating humans. Fate intervenes when one of his private practice patients threatens Drew's life. Will the close call help Nick to see a connection like theirs isn't something to let go of?

www.dreamspinnerpress.com

HIDING IN PLAIN SIGHT

CAMP H.O.W.L.

Bru Baker

Happily ever after is right under their noses.

A Camp H.O.W.L. Novel

Happily ever after is right under their noses.

Harris has been keeping a big secret for years—his unrequited mate bond with his best friend, Jackson. He's convinced himself that having Jackson in his life is enough. That, and his work at Camp H.O.W.L., keeps him going.

Things get complicated when Jackson applies for a high-ranking Tribunal job in New York City—far from Camp H.O.W.L. The position requires he relinquish all Pack bonds… and that's when his wolf decides to choose a mate. Suddenly Jackson sees his best friend in a sizzling new light.

Their chemistry is through the roof, but they're setting themselves up for broken hearts—and broken bonds—if Jackson can't figure out a way to balance his career and the love that's just been waiting for him to take notice.

www.dreamspinnerpress.com